CONTENTS

FOREWORD

Jamaica Kincaid

This book is about a slave (a man named Babouk), slavery itself, and the world of a people (Europe and its inhabitants) who profited from it. The slavery business, the institution of slavery, has been around for so long that it is clear that no piece of literature, no matter how great, has been able to put a stop to it. It would seem that the thing we call civilization can't be achieved without uprooting whole groups of people from everything they have ever known—who and what they know their individual and collective selves to be; the place they have always lived; their mothers, their fathers, their children—and forcibly made subject to the will of others.

Why this is so is not a mystery to me. I look at it this way: Suppose I am living in a nice village situated in a nice forest, or, say, my nice village is surrounded by some beautiful mountains, their tops changing color with the changing position of the sun. I go fishing every day, and every day I catch some fish—just the right number to satisfy me. I cultivate a small plot of land and I always have as much food from this land as I need, so that I never have to have a larder. To keep myself company, I make up some tales about how I got here and where I will go when I am not here anymore. This is a nice little set-up I have here, my definition of contentment; and the thought of going off somewhere to pile brick upon brick in the hot desert sun to make monuments commemorating vicious people and their vicious deeds, or working in someone else's fields, or doing any of the horrible things that a civilization requires in order to be a civilization—none of this appeals to me at all.

Now, then, I try to imagine this: I am living somewhere that's not in the least nice—the weather is terrible (England); the people in other countries like your country better than they like their own because something more than the weather is terrible about where they live; I am surrounded by plenty but still I feel very greedy; I want more than I have; I have heard about all sorts of things somewhere else on the other side of the world and I would like to have them and I would like to have them for nothing. I have ideas about a lot of things. I feel I know how the world ought to look, the language most people ought to speak (my own), the sort of god they should believe in (my own again), and so on and on. Unfortunately, none of the things I want for myself or the things I want to do, none of my desires, can be realized where I am, so how terrific, how nearly perfect to find a defenseless people somewhere to be mere instruments of my will, some people over whom I have complete dominion. Who can resist this? No one has ever done so.

Different people require different things from life. Let me explain what I mean: Here is the opening paragraph of a book called *Africa Explored: Europeans in the Dark Continent, 1769–1889*, a collection of biographies of some of the restless parasites who came to Africa from all over Europe, hoping that the experience would rescue them from the meaninglessness common to every human life:

> Near the end of Pall Mall there once stood a fashionable tavern known as the St. Alban's. Early one summer evening in 1788 nine rich and distinguished members of a small dining club met here to enjoy one of the excellent meals provided by the establishment. During the course of the evening the conversation turned to Africa, that mysterious continent of which so little was then known; and before the club members parted they had decided to form "an Association for promoting the Discovery of the Interior parts of Africa," in the belief that "so long as men continued ignorant of so large a portion of the globe, that ignorance must be considered as a degree of reproach on the present age."

I would think that some people sitting in a nice warm club, eating some good food (even if it is English food), drinking a good claret, would be reasonably contented—I mean, taking all the things I know about life into consideration. But obviously I am wrong. For there was poor Africa, sitting contentedly in all its innocence and beauty, attracting the gaze of the powerful and miserable.

Here is another paragraph, this from the autobiography of a slave named Gustavus Vassa. He is describing the place he comes from and the people who lived there:

Our land is uncommonly rich and fruitful, and produces all kinds of vegetables in great abundance. We have plenty of Indian corn, and vast quantities of cotton and tobacco. Pineapples grow without culture; they are about the size of the largest sugar loaf, and finely flavored. We have also spices of different kinds, particularly pepper; and a variety of delicious fruits which I have never seen in Europe; together with gums of various kinds, and honey in abundance. All our industry is exerted to improve these blessings of nature. Agriculture is our chief employment; and everyone, even to children and women, is employed in it. Thus we are habituated to labor from our earliest years. Everyone contributes something to the common stock: and as we are unacquainted with idleness, we have no beggars. The benefits of such a mode of living are obvious . . . Those benefits are felt by us in the general healthiness of the people, and in their vigor and activity . . . Our women, too, were, in my eyes at least, uncommonly graceful, alert, and modest to a degree of bashfulness; nor do I remember to have ever heard of an instance of promiscuity amongst them before marriage. They are also remarkably cheerful. Indeed, cheerfulness and affability are two of the leading characteristics of our nation.

And so to *Babouk*, this work of fiction, the life of a free man living in reasonable contentment in Africa, of his capture by other Africans (a point not dwelt on long enough, in my opinion), who sold him to European slave-traders, his journey to a world of hells, his life as a slave, the rebellion he led to free himself and his fellow slaves, and his death in its defeat. From the point of view of "great literature," this is not a great book, but to people caught up in a catastrophe that was not of their own making, a catastrophe that five hundred years after it commenced shows no sign of abatement, great literature is nice but essentially useless. At a certain point in life it is better to read this book than *Remembrance of Things Past*, just to name one example of great literature. In fact, after you read *Babouk*, you may wish that the author of *Remembrance of Things Past* were still alive so that you could point out to him a number of things he seems to have missed, such as the source of the money that allowed his characters to live such lives of moral worthlessness.

Here are some other reasons to read this book instead of one of the titans of our times: you will be reminded that twelve years after Christopher Columbus landed in this part of the world, over a million of the people he found living here were dead. In addition, so many Africans were thrown overboard on voyages from Africa to this part of the world that it would not be an overstatement to say that the Atlantic Ocean is the Auschwitz of Africa. It is hard to turn a page of *Babouk* without finding reports—drawn from actual history—of beatings, murders, people nailed to posts by their ears, all because they tried to escape the brutality that had fallen on them; or of women with child stretched out on the ground so that they can be severely beaten for some task not properly carried out, the ground hollowed out to accomodate their protruding stomachs. Who is the savage here, and who is the uncivilized? This superior Western civilization, did it pass over the heads of some of these Western-civilization people.

On Christopher Columbus' tomb, someone wrote: "For him the known world was not enough, he added a new one to the old, and gave to heaven countless souls." Indeed! I found this quote in *Babouk*. The author, Guy Endore, placed it at the head of a chapter, and it made me feel that if I had met him I would have liked him. He was a white man and he wrote a work of fiction, a passionate human account of the life of an African slave. He also wrote screenplays in Hollywood, and at some point in his life he was publicly censured and humiliated for the views he held about American society. I am glad the author of this book was a white person. I think that every white writer should write a book about black slavery, as I think every writer who is not a Jew should write a book about the Holocaust. Perhaps some day someone will produce a work of such overwhelming literary merit that it brings the machinery of slavery and holocaust to a complete halt.

BABOUK

All you to whom I owe debts of gratitude, read your names here! This book is dedicated to you: kind friends who have responded to my too frequent importunities, and writers, living and dead, from whom I borrowed material all too freely.

1

King Louis XIII was greatly grieved by the law that
enslaved the Negroes of our colonies; but when his
counselors succeeded in persuading him that they
would thus be sure of conversion to Christianity,
he consented.

—*Montesquieu*

Slavery is God's first visit to the Blacks.
—*Opinion expressed in the eighteenth century*

The man with the broken nose, a nose squashed flat against his face,
was a genius. His fame had passed far beyond the French slave-
trading establishment at Goree, and echoed all along the coast of
West Africa. And, preserved in books, it has crossed nearly two
centuries of time and come down to us to admire.

For such genius is rare. But who shall measure the profitable
talents of man?

This one was a nigger-taster. He sat on a high stool in the center of
the compound and the prodded Negroes passed before him one by
one.

It was the latest caravan to arrive from the interior of Africa, a
starved, bedraggled, filthy lot gathered by various traders. The
captives had come a distance of several hundred miles, walking
single file, attached to each other by wooden forks and, in addition,
required to carry each a stone weighing forty or fifty pounds.

These stones had no value either as mineral or as building material, but their weight, borne by tired arms, mile after mile, subdued
the spirit of revolt and prevented the exhausted body from thinking
of anything but sleep at night.

With the butt of a little cane the Negro-taster caught each black
face, roughly but accurately, under the jawbone and brought it into
position.

He leaned forward.

And out came his tongue, his marvelously trained tongue, and licked each Negro under the chin. There was a brief, critical gathering of saliva, then he spat the contents of his mouth into the Negro's face.

And he pronounced judgment.

On all the black faces, except upon those which personal tragedy had made stolid, there were signs of surprise, of bewilderment, of fear, a fear so great that few dared to wipe off the nigger-taster's saliva.

Among them was one, by name Babouk, who, seeing that there were none of his own village about, dared raise his voice in the declamatory style of a poet:

"We have been tasted!" he exclaimed. "The red man has tasted us and now knows which one of us will make good meat."

Those who understood his Mandingo dialect groaned aloud at the thought that they were to be eaten and that their souls should suffer dismemberment along with their bodies and their qualities go to enrich the souls of others.

"Your ghosts," cried Babouk, "will whistle in the wind, at night, seeking the scattered soul. . . ."

Despite their weariness, the captives complained out loud, all talking together, some translating for the benefit of others, and making a great confusion of voices.

They had been imposed upon! Had it not been promised them, repeatedly, during the hardships of their long journey, that they were not to be eaten? Would they not have chosen rather to die at the hands of their captors than to go into slavery had they known that they were to be eaten?

They had been deceived! . . .

"Gmara!" cried one of the white men.

The interpreter, Gmara, a man of an ugly brown complexion, clad, despite the heat, in a heavily embroidered uniform, came running up. He shouted out in several languages his oft-told story:

"Quiet! You are going across the water in a great dugout. You are not to be eaten. The white man does not eat human flesh. You will wear bright golden clothes like these I have on. And you will work in the white man's fields."

This prospect was indeed delightful, and many accepted it and grinned with pleasure. But others, morose, suspicious, questioned the interpreter about the red man who had tasted them.

"He is a white man, too," Gmara informed them. "Why, that is to tell your age. His tongue feels the bristles on your chin."

Again his answer was satisfactory to some. They rubbed their chins, and the chins of their neighbors, and even licked each other's chins. But others, for there is always, in every crowd, an annoying remnant who want to know everything—inquisitive minds who hold up important business for trifling questions—others wanted to know what possibly sinister purpose the white man had in mind that he required to know their ages.

And Babouk had an objection all his own:

"He tasted the women, too."

Only for a moment was Gmara stumped by Babouk's observation. Then he answered witheringly. "You talk too much," he warned. "The white man will not want you for his fields. You will not wear such clothes as these. Talking never yet grew rice or brought home a duck from a hunt."

Babouk suffered under Gmara's scolding. At home, too, he was often reprimanded for his tendency to talk too much. Worse still was the fact that the crowd was on Gmara's side. The Negroes around him were laughing at him.

And yet he persisted, urged on by a mind that would not be satisfied by an answer that did not fully cover the question in dispute.

"He tasted the women, too," he repeated. "Women have no bristles on their chins."

"All the better," Gmara retorted. "They are all the more pleasant to taste."

This excellent retort aroused laughter among the blacks. Of course it was more pleasant to taste a woman. Relieved of their fears, and brought back to the everlastingly absorbing topic of women, they ceased to make objections and turned instead upon Babouk, showering him with ridicule.

Gmara, the ugly brown of his face pearled with sweat, returned, self-satisfied, to the shade of a tree.

Babouk sat, quiet, and let the scorn of his fellow captives fall about him.

"Babouk does not know that women are pleasant."

"Babouk is a child. He has never tasted a woman."

"Babouk is a sorcerer: he can grow rice with his talk."

"Babouk! Hunt us some meat with your tongue!"

But Babouk was puzzling over Gmara's words: The white man tasted the men to discover their ages. And the women he tasted, too. Because they are all the more pleasant. He repeated this train of thought until his mind was tired. And still he was not satisfied. Something was missing. But what?

And so he squatted, with his chains resting upon his thighs, and retired within himself. He was ashamed of his public discomfiture. The news of it might travel back to his village. They would have another laugh there at Babouk's pretensions.

Though Babouk was incapable of comprehending the purpose of the nigger-taster, nothing was really more simple. Since good wines are worth more than bad wines, and good tea more than bad tea, there are wine-tasters and tea-tasters to protect the buyer of merchandise.

And here is a man who can taste Negroes. With a certainty that compels admiration, he can pick out, from these groups of starving wretches, those who after a week or two of rest and good food will be plump and healthy, and separate them from those who will never recover.

The Negro-taster's tongue feels bristles, and more than that. It tastes the sweat. Now, a man may look in perfect health, but his sweat will give him away. Contrariwise, he may look in miserable health, whereas his sweat will proclaim the soundness of his body.

Here are Negroes who have come a thousand miles and not been granted even one bath on the journey, or as much as a dab of oil for their dry skins. Here are others, fresh and healthy-seeming, who have come but a hundred miles or less. Here are all ages and conditions: warriors, iron-workers, farmers, rulers, slaves. Some, like Babouk, had been struck from behind, on the back of the head, and had lain for weeks in the wet bottom of a leaky dugout before they came to this factory.

Now tell me which are genuinely strong and healthy. Which are good buys? On which will the captain be sure of making a profit for his employer?

Perhaps a native trader has doctored up a sick slave. The taster's tongue discovers the drug in the sweat. Perhaps a Negress's graying hair has been rubbed glossy black with oil and soot to make her appear young. But how will you change the feel of her skin?

Rotting teeth may be filled with white clay, but the Negro-taster has his nose close to the captive's mouth, and you cannot conceal from him the characteristic odor of decaying teeth.

Yes, the nigger-taster is a genius. And yet his method is old. Were not the rules for the choice of a nurse to a royal prince of France similar?—Her breath must be sweet. Her feet must smell sweet. The sweat of her brow must be pleasant to taste and smell.

And these captive Negroes whom the white man selects to go across the sea and be his slaves in that marvelous land, they must be as perfect as man can be. Each one must be a physical marvel such as only the hot breeding grounds of Africa can produce in such profusion.

But you might ask: "Yes, but why does he spit out in their faces?"

What? Are you, like Babouk, asking trifling questions?

What else would you have him do? You would not want him to swallow it, would you? The wine and tea-tasters do the same.

But why in the very faces of the Negroes?

Come now. Would you force him to turn his head aside, here on this burning rock of Goree, where even the sea breeze cannot temper the fierce African heat, where each move is an added strain to the overburdened human machine?

And how else express that contempt that the white man feels must follow and destroy a vile contact that too closely resembles a caress?

It was late in the day before the traders had agreed upon a price for the selected Negroes. The latter had but little conception of what was going on. Here were some who had been assaulted in the dark, and since then had never beheld the face of a relative or friend. They brooded, sullenly, in the midst of the bustle about them.

Here were others, Ibo warriors all, glaring fiercely about them. The king of the Gallos had made war upon them, and business success had smiled upon this African chieftain. He had taken a hundred Ibo captives and had kept them tied to heavy blocks of wood in an enclosure that was like a pigpen, until a white factor had come twenty days' journey up the river and bid and paid for them.

Bars of iron, glass beads, bolts of gay cloth, cheap muskets, swords of bad steel, had passed from the white man into the hands of the king of the Gallos. And the factor had led his chained file, like a long snake, to Goree.

And others were here. Habitual gamblers, who had gambled themselves into servitude. Their relatives had grown tired of redeeming them. And here were men who had always been slaves. For generations they had been slaves of this or that ancient Negro family.

They had not minded their serfdom. Their masters worked beside them in the fields. They ate and wore what their masters ate and wore. They lived in his house, and he might not sell them, except in an emergency, to settle a debt.

Excellent loophole, that. And now that the price of slaves had risen to such unprecedented heights, since the white man demanded hundreds of thousands every year, debts were likely to appear where none had been before, and an emergency arise where none had been suspected a moment before.

Two families might agree to owe each other money and might further agree to settle their fictitious debts by giving each other their slaves. Such slaves, then, which were really not of your own family, you might very well dispose of, and a profitable business it was, too, and no violation of any custom either.

And here and there, too, was a wretch who, contrary to all laws and customs of Africa, had been sold by his own relatives. For the price bid for slaves was really irresistible.

Often, however, despite the high prices, despite the attraction of the glittering articles offered by the Europeans, the number of slaves brought to the coast was entirely too small to meet the demands of the planters. Then it was the duty of the whites to spur on the native kings to make war upon each other in order to create a greater supply of captives.

For these poor ignorant blacks have no conception of the needs of industry, of commerce and competition. No more than most savages. You could not, for example, make the natives of the East Indian spice islands work at all. Lazy folk that they were, they deemed that their fruit trees, growing wild, provided them with all they wanted. Why should they work?

In vain the whites tempted them with beads, with guns, with alcohol. In short, there was nothing left to do but cut down every fruit tree on the islands and force the natives either to die of starvation or to work for wages that would buy the foods that the whites generously imported and sold to them.

Such were the hardships that the white man had to overcome in order that the nations of Europe might prosper and progress. And Europe did prosper and progress. It became studded with castles, and the walls of the castles were gay wih tapestries and the rooms were bright with gilt or polished furniture. And fine paintings and sculptures decorated these palaces. And books with marvelous contents were on the tables and along the shelves.

All the world was forced to marvel at the art and culture of the European. All the world was forced to beg at the door of Europe for a little of that culture so that they might not be objects of the European's contempt.

"See our castles!" the European cried proudly. "See our museums stuffed with works of art!"

And the world pleaded: "Give us just one painting. Give us just one statue. Let us have a little culture, too."

And Europe was generous. For a million dollars she would part with this fine daub, and for another million she would bid a tearful farewell to this or that naked woman in stone. But even as she parted with it, she sneered.

"Do you think you can buy culture with your money? How ridiculous!"

Ah, if these blacks, huddled together, some still in chains, others free, but all under the close surveillance of armed guards, but knew that they represented European culture in its first stage, how justly proud they might be.

But they knew nothing.

They watched the whites in terror. What were they doing now?

A charcoal brazier had been set aglow and a silver blade was bent into the shape of the four letters: P D N C. The first two letters were meant for the ship: the *Prie-Dieu*. And the second for the captain of the ship: Nicolas Collard.

And the silver blade was set in the charcoal until it glowed cherry-red when brought into a dark corner.

Then the first of the purchased slaves was brought forward. He shivered. His knees gave way beneath him. He fell to the ground and shrieked.

A white man lashed him with a whip made from the spinal nerve of a bull. The interpreter screamed unceasingly at the wretch:

"No harm is intended you! You are to receive a beautiful decoration!"

He was dragged to the brazier and made to lie down on his back. Then his heaving chest was rubbed with lard and a waxed parchment was held over this area of his skin and the hot silver blade was brought into proximity and maintained there until the heat that came from the edge made the breast sputter up in a line that followed precisely the line of the silver letters.

Parchment and branding-iron were removed and on the black chest rose the most beautifully curved welt imaginable.

The fright was erased from his face. The onlookers burst into relieved laughter. The patient touched the blistered pattern on his skin. Ai! that was painful. But then, it was artistic, too. And ennobling. In his tribe, only the noble families whose genealogies were chanted by the poets were permitted to raise decorative welts on their skins. Why, the white man had made him a nobleman.

Yes, all the slaves were agreed upon this. The pain was after all a small matter. Were they not accustomed to much worse, suffered in securing effects that were not half so pleasing or immediate? They were in the habit of poking thorns under their skin to distinguish themselves, or of making incisions which they would rub with salt lest they heal too rapidly.

Truly the white man, or the red man, as most of the Negroes described his color before they learnt better, was a man of power and ability. His skill, his magic, were unequaled. Here was proof of it. Here was something delightful, exquisite, indicative, as the interpreter took care to point out, indicative of the marvels to come. The most incredulous were now almost willing to believe the tale of a wonderland of food and clothes and dancing to which they were destined.

There were no more howling savages to be dragged to the brazier. Each one wanted to be first to receive the decoration. Many showed by signs that they wished to be branded in more than one spot and they indicated suitable expanses of black skin. The surgeon, Le Petit, laughed in good humor as he directed the work, and the Negroes laughed with him.

"What great big, stupid children!" the surgeon observed to the captain.

"As long as they are happy," said the captain. "A happy cargo is a healthy one."

But in the evening the Negroes were neither so happy nor so noisy. They were silent, pensive, dreaming of the huts they had left behind.

There, too, they would be gathered about fires, cooking rice or yams with a sauce of meat or fish and spices. And they would eat, all dipping into one pot with the right hand, sign of cleanliness and good-breeding, for the left must be reserved for ugly but necessary bodily offices. And they would be happy, but not noisy, for excessive noise is a sign of ill-breeding, and everyone strives to be considered a good, or gentle, man.

Nevertheless they would be happy at home. There would be anecdotes related of a recent hunt; or riddles to guess; or a discussion of a prospective feast.

Or a poet would chant to them, or an annalist would recite to them the deeds of their ancestors.

But what had they here? Behind them was the memory of ravage and desolation, and before them the terror of the unknown. And all about them was the blackness of the night.

As darkness fell upon the world, Babouk more than ever missed his love, Niati. There was not even the compensatory sight of another woman, for, once purchased by the whites, the sexes were kept far apart.

And Babouk, lonely, recalled to mind a verse he had composed some months before his capture, about a nightfall just such as this:

"The sky grows dark like dark blue cotton,
The fog grows milky, dripping dew of fresh milk.
The hyena bellows and the lion, ruler of the bush, replies.
How cozy then to sit in a corner, with a girl,
And whisper softly."

Slightly fevered by the burn of the branding-iron, the Negroes shivered in the evening wind and coughed dismally. They crowded closer to each other for warmth, their chains rattling as they shifted now here, now there.

"Tell us a story, Babouk," one of them begged. Then they all raised their voices:

"Tell us a story, Babouk."

"I am just a child," he retorted sullenly, recalling the insults of the morning. "My tongue can hunt duck and grow rice, but it cannot tell a story."

He was barely sixteen, and at home his arrogance had brought him many reproofs. He was *nama kana*, cheap trash, for he interrupted his elders and pretended to be a better minstrel than certain older men of established reputation. And yet the latter had often pointed out to him that he could not tell a story properly, and that in his recitations of the genealogy of their former great states—now, alas! laid so low—he made the most ridiculous blunders.

"Tell us a story, Babouk," he was begged again. Then he allowed himself to be mollified.

"Do you know," he asked, "that I would not be here if I had obeyed my father?"

"Please tell us," his listeners chorused.

"Do you know that if I had had but a needle to defend myself with I would not be here, but home with my people?"

"Please tell us," his listeners begged again.

"Very well, I shall tell you the story of the man who was captured by a robber because he did not obey his father. And I shall tell you how he escaped because he remembered the advice of his father.

"This young man used to go into the forest without any arms at all, not so much as a stick. And his father would say: 'My son, take some weapon with you. Let it be but a needle, it may suffice if you are attacked.'

"But the son only laughed. 'Who will attack me? And if I am

attacked, how will a needle serve me?' And he disregarded the advice of his father and went into the forest unarmed.

"And one day a robber took him prisoner.

"And the young man groaned: 'Alas! If only I had obeyed my father this could not have happened to me. He always told me to take at least a needle with me when I went into the forest.'

"The robber laughed: 'A needle? What good would a needle do you against my spear?'

"The son groaned: 'My father was right. If only I had a needle!'

" 'Come,' said the robber, 'you are as foolish as your father. What good would a needle do?'

" 'Alas! If only I had a needle.'

" 'Stop your groaning. Here is a needle. What can you do with it?'

" 'But this is a broken needle. Look, the point is off.'

"Then the robber bent down to see where the point was broken off, and the young man quickly plunged the needle into his eye.

"The robber screamed: 'Yi-ai! He has blinded me!'

"But the son ran home to his father."

And Babouk concluded with the ancient formula: "And the fable passed by here, and went out toward the sea. . . ."

A goodly number of the slaves had been able to understand the Mandingo dialect that Babouk spoke. Others profited by rapid translations. But many, of unknown races from the interior, depleted by their enormous journey, understood nothing, and fell asleep where they were, amidst the noise and clamor that accompanied Babouk's recitation.

Babouk himself, proud of the reception of his story, began to interrogate his fellow slaves: "What would you have done with a needle?"

The first few, caught unprepared, mumbled something about plunging the needle into their assailant's eye. But after that there were interesting variations, and the most alert among them prepared themselves for the moment when they would be called upon by Babouk to give an account of their prowess with a needle.

The audience found this vastly amusing. Some sleepy Negro would make a foolish response and all would burst into laughter, or another would think of something really clever that one might do with a needle. And then the audience would shout its approval.

At home the elders would have reproved this unnecessary noise. But here each one strove to drown his sorrow in as much laughter as he could summon forth.

Ha! They were brave, now, in retrospect. What wonders they might have done with just a tiny needle.

Babouk was made happy by the effect his story had on his audience. But when he noted how each man was trying to outdo his predecessor in boastfulness, and how those who could not boast were ridiculed by those who could, he determined to turn the tables on the braggarts. And he suddenly shouted: "You, yes, you are brave. Brave as the man who would not chase the striped fly."

At that the Negroes halted in their boastful talk. But, when Babouk said nothing more, those who were puffed up with big ideas could not resist going on with their invented heroisms.

Then Babouk said again: "Yes, you are as brave as the man who would not chase away the striped fly." And he pointed out the boasters one by one and said: "Braver folk than you do not exist."

There was silence for a while and a feeling of guilt on the part of the boasters.

"You are a very proud lot, and I am sure you are as brave as the young man who went into the forest with the young girl who was his friend and refused to chase away a striped fly."

"Tell us, please," the company begged humbly.

"Yes, you are brave," said Babouk, "You are as brave as this young man who refused to chase away a striped fly. Oh, he was brave!"

"Tell us, please," the audience chorused.

"Very well. This is the story of the young man who was so brave he refused to chase away a striped fly. Listen:

"A young girl was walking along the forest path and a young man came up to her and walked behind her, but she paid no attention.

" 'My friend,' he said, in order to impress her, 'you do not know that I am very brave. Why, in the last war I killed four men. And I made two prisoners. And I captured a horse. Why, I received eighteen wounds. Oh, there's none braver than I. Why, our people would not think of making war unless I consent to go along.'

" 'Really,' exclaimed the young girl, 'then your like does not exist.'

" 'Hey, hey! My like does not exist! I am the bravest of all!'

"But a hunter had hid himself in a tree, and, seeing them coming, leaped down before them. His great bow was stretched taut and a poisoned arrow was ready to fly. The young girl kept on walking, and the young man, who was behind her, would have kept on walking, too, only the hunter cried: 'Do not move or you are dead.'

" 'Why?' cried the young man.

"Then the hunter explained: 'Your people have often fought ours, and in battle your father killed mine. I have often hoped to see you in the battle line but it is not until now that I find you. I would kill you but for this young girl who might therefore never marry.

" 'Therefore, instead of killing you, all I shall ask is that you squat here and do your business. Quick! Down with you!'

"The young man did as he was told. And when he had done his business, he rose and would have gone on, glad to have escaped so cheaply, but the hunter still held his poisoned arrow in readiness:

" 'What? You would go on and leave this filth and all these flies buzzing about? Chase them away!'

"Then the young man waved his hand back and forth and kept the flies away. And when he grew lax, the hunter shouted:

" 'Chase those flies away!'

"And the young man bent down and waved his hand more rapidly.

"Finally the hunter said: 'Good. The filth is dry and no more flies come buzzing around. You may go on with that girl who has been so good as to wait for you.'

"And the young man went on, looking back over his shoulder now and then to see if the hunter were following. But the hunter was not following.

"Then the young man said to the girl: 'Did you notice that striped fly? Did you notice how I didn't chase away that striped fly?' "

Ha! What a story! The laughter of the listeners would not cease. And it was the turn now of those who had not been able to boast about their prowess with a needle to turn upon the boasters with shouts of derision: "You! Why you are so brave you would not chase away the striped fly."

The noise the Negroes made was so great that Captain Collard, who was supping with the Governor in the fortress, could hear them, and he nodded his head with satisfaction. "A happy cargo is a healthy one," he repeated.

Until late at night Babouk declaimed. Story after story, and poem after poem. And then long epics about the Mandingo empire. About the great conqueror, Soon-jato, the Lion-Prince, who went to the Holy City of Mecca with a vast invincible army. Of Soomanguroo who built the great capital city of Mali.

Finally his voice trailed off. He ceased talking, and there was no one to ask him to continue. Near-by he heard a group of Peuls chattering softly in their musical speech that is like the twitter of birds. He would have slept, too, except that he thought, with a stab of pain, of Niati, whom he would never see again.

What would Niati do, now that he was gone? Was it not to be regretted that he had cast such a powerful spell of love around her? He had spied upon her and knew when she bathed and where, and he had gone upstream and bathed too, so that the water that had washed his body should wash hers. Then quickly he had run downstream, beyond the point where she bathed, and had bathed in the water from her body. And thrown it into the air to fall in a spray about him. And cupped it in his palm and swallowed it.

They were bound now, bound by a tight web of love. Though she had never honored him with even a glance, and though he had been captured shortly after the spell, yet he knew she loved him now, and dreamed of him as he dreamed of her. Poor Niati, bound by a hopeless love!

2

We speak of the blood-cemented fabric of the prosperity of New Orleans or the Havanna: let us look nearer home. What raised Liverpool and Manchester from provincial towns to gigantic cities? What maintains now their active industry and their rapid accumulation of wealth? The exchange of their produce with that raised by the American slaves; and their present opulence is as really owing to the toil and suffering of the Negro, as if his hands had excavated their docks and fabricated their steam-engines.

—*H. Merivale*, Lectures on Colonization and Colonies, *1841*

The very next day, and all day long, the smithies rang with the blow of hammer on anvil. Two by two the captives were brought to the blacksmith, relieved of their old chains, and chained together anew, this one's right foot to that one's left. So that the pair could walk together by holding onto each other and propelling themselves forward with two outer, thin legs and one monstrous double leg between.

It was not usual for the captives to be hastened into chains so shortly after their purchase, so shortly after the removal of the wooden yokes of the caravan. In general, two or three weeks were allowed for a period of rest and restoration of energy and weight.

The captain, too, liked to dally a bit, fit up his vessel with a cool, thatched housing on the deck, and do a bit of profitable trading for his privy purse by the exchange of glass beads and iron bars for gold dust or ivory or beeswax.

It was important, likewise, to hire a *bombe* or two in order to instruct the Negroes in the art of dancing aboard a ship, the art of dancing on a heaving, shifting platform despite chains on one's legs:

an education that was very necessary since the imprisoned cargo
needed the relief of a daily bit of exercise.

Then, too, an effort was generally made to secure foodstuffs to
suit more or less the various nationalities of the captives. You could
not, of course, provide the Bambaras with the frothy milk, warm
from the cow's udder, that was their favorite food. Nor bananas for
the Aradas, nor fowl for the Ibos.

No, they would all have to get along with a couscous of guinea
corn, which we call Indian corn, yams, rice, dried fish, beans, and so
forth. But now and then, to ward off that most dreaded of all
diseases, melancholia, which decimates the blacks like a plague, it
was good policy to distribute various delicacies that would remind
the captives of their homes and cheer them up.

But all these considerations had to be secondary where there was
a possibility of a total loss of cargo.

England was at war with France, and there were rumors of an
attack to be made on the island of Goree. Indeed, but eight months
ago, an English fleet had passed by, but had sailed away when the
cannons of Goree had barked.

There were times when the island of Goree seemed lost, so far
away was it from the center of the world, Europe. Month after
month passed and not a sail appeared in the small sandy bay.

But Europe had not forgotten Goree.

This was Goree: A bare rock covered with fortresses. The Governor and the higher officers lived where the island's only spring of
fresh water existed, a spring carefully padlocked. The Governor,
Monsieur de St. Jean, could look down from the eminence of his
quarters and see every inch of his territory and even cross to the
continent of Africa, where giant baobab trees gave the unhealthful
coastal swamp a deceptively green and inviting appearance.

Three hundred soldiers, the very worst that France could spare,
lived in the island barracks when on duty and with their Negro
mistresses in the Negro town of the island when off duty, and there
gave rise to a growing population of mulattoes, half Yolof and half
Gallic.

The officers, however, chose mulatto mistresses, as being more in

keeping with their higher position in life, and kept them in their
own quarters, for the Negro town was beneath their dignity.

"The English imagine that they can dispossess me," laughed
Governor de St. Jean, and he was half anxious that they should and
he thereby be sent home to Europe.

"Don't run away," he pleaded with Captain Collard. "You're safer
here than at sea."

He pointed out the heavy batteries, strategically placed to fling
death upon any attacking fleet. He pointed out the recently constructed citadel of St. Michel, built *en barbet* and mounted with
great twenty-four-pounders.

"And here's a bit of suicide for your Englishmen," and he patted
the sun-warm metal of a bright brass cannon, an old-fashioned piece
of small bore.

Why a bit of suicide? Because near the touch-hole was engraved a
scroll in which was inscribed with a flourish: *Elizabeth regina*. And
in tiny letters: *Thomas Pitt made this pece 1589.*

Good Queen Bess!

"We'll shoot them down with their own ordinance," crowed the
Governor.

Captain Collard, good business man that he was, agreed with all
the Governor said. Yes, the island was impregnable. The English
would not dare attack so strongly fortified a position. No, no, of
course not. There was nothing to fear.

Still, privately he recalled that Goree had once been Negro property. And then had belonged to the Dutch.

And the English had ousted the Dutch.

And the Dutch had ousted the English.

And the French has ousted the Dutch.

Who knows? It might be the Englishman's turn once more.

So load in the yams! Load in the corn!

Hammer away, you smiths, and load on the cargo!

And off sailed the *Prie-Dieu*, and the Governor watched it go.
"When you see Paris, give her my regards!"

The Lord only knew how many months one might have to wait
for another visitor. Since the war the slave-ships had avoided Goree.
Cautiously, in the dark, they felt their way along the coast of Africa

and watched for fires set as signals by native chieftains and traders who had captives to sell.

Yes, Goree was impregnable, but it was not forgotten.

Forgotten? Not at all. For, the more impregnable is wealth, the more courageous grows cupidity. The more she schemes and plans to secure that wealth and make it impregnable in her turn.

For years England had been directed by a flood of reports, memoirs, broadsides, to realize that her interest demanded the conquest of the French fortifications along the coast of Africa.

"What!" cried these memorialists, arms uplifted in horror, "is not the ministry aware that in 1720 England supplied most of the world's sugar?

"And now, in 1759, France supplies five times as much as England!

"Yes, five times!

"Are we to be put in the shade by France? Must our merchants grow poor and our workers lack for bread?"

Intolerable thought. Conceive of it! The world uses French sugar and English pockets are empty.

"Gentlemen: The French must be expelled from the coast of Africa. For the sugar plantations of the French, particularly those in the French part of the island of San Domingo, require vast numbers of slaves. Prevent the French from acquiring slaves and their sugar culture must inevitably suffer, to the advantage of our planters. Furthermore, if the French are forced to come to English merchants for slaves, a price can be exacted that will cover the loss of the English position in the sugar until such time as we can regain our rightful place."

Come then, Mr. Keppel, take a squadron and proceed to Senegal and Goree, and strike the first blow for England's return to leadership in the world's sugar market.

And you Britons: Arise! To arms!

The dastardly French have done this and that. The cowards! The liars! The knaves! The traitors!

Kill them!

And brave Mr. Keppel arose and did as he was told. And the brave Britons arose and did as they were told.

And on December 27th, 1759, Commodore Keppel's four ships of the line, his frigate, his two bomb-ketches, dropped anchor as near as they might to the island of Goree, and at nine o'clock the action started.

Huzza! What a merry fray!

No less a personage than Reverend Lindsay, chaplain of His Majesty's ship *Fougueux*, has left us a *Succinct Account*.

The casualties were insignificant.

Shed a tear for poor Lieutenant West. A shot carrying along in its course an eighteen-inch bolt, torn loose from the timbers of the vessel, ripped out one of Mr. West's hips.

Applaud the heroism of an English sailor: "Being in the fore-top and having one of his legs carried away by a shot, with the heart of a lion, let himself down from thence hand under hand by rope, saying at the same time, *He should not have been sorry for the accident if he had done his duty: But it gave him pain to think that he should die without having killed an enemy.*"

Who could share this feeling better than Reverend Lindsay? Had he not had a brother, Captain William Lindsay, who had fallen in fighting the French?

Then did not this representative of God on earth cry out in anguish: "Would I were a soldier to revenge my brother's death!"

"Alas," mourned Reverend Lindsay, "my peaceful robes entangle my arms.

"But though by profession denied armed resentment, I have one method of revenge in store:

"I pray nightly for the confusion of France's politics from the very bottom of my heart and that our ministry may never sheathe the sword until an enemy so treacherous are on their bended knees."

Brave sailor who regrets death only because he has not killed an enemy!

Stout-hearted British clergyman, whose arms are unfortunately entangled by his sacred robes.

We may pass over the death of twenty nameless marines. They perished.

But let us recall an important death, that of Sayer, the master of the ship *Nassau*. He was struck by a bullet that tore him to pieces, scattering his bowels about the ship.

In fine, it was a magnificent display of British stanchness and ingenuity in warfare. Monsieur de St. Jean did not, it is true, surrender on his bended knees, but he surrendered nevertheless.

Through a rift in the smoke the British were aware that the French Governor of Goree had dropped his regimental colors over the walls.

The British marines marched proudly up to Fort St. Michel, and hoisted the British colors. And with three loud huzzas they took possession of the island.

In the evening the Negroes of the town gave a demonstration of welcome to their new masters. They sang:

> *"Frenchman a Goree,*
> *Go po-op—po-op—po-op—*
> *England a come! England a come!*
> *Go pop pop pop! Go pop pop pop!*
> *Go pop pop pop pop POP!"*

in which the declamation of the *pops* was designed to illustrate the quickness of the firing from the English ships compared to the slowness of the response from the French batteries on shore.

What a sweet revenge for the Reverend Lindsay! What a proud day for the sugar merchants!

How unfortunate, then, that this brave beginning should have terminated three years later in a peace treaty wherein, I know not in return for what concession from the French, the English gave back Goree.

I do not know what Reverend Lindsay said. Nor what the sugar merchants thought. I do not know whether the brass cannon of Queen Elizabeth went back to the French or not.

And I thumb my history books in vain to find out whether they gathered up the scattered bowels from the deck of the *Nassau* and returned them to her master.

3

I know that the blacks embarked on your vessel
are treated with as much kindness as humanity,
and, such being the case, I rejoice in having put
over an excellent stroke of business as well as a
good deed.

—Voltaire in a letter to his partner in a
successful slave-trading venture

Lying below, in chains, the Negroes felt all the motions of departure.
Heard the singing of the ropes, the complaint of the winches, the
pattering of the sailors' bare feet on the wood of the deck.

And then they felt the heaving of the ship on the troubled water as
the swift tide and a fair wind bore them out to sea.

They were off on a journey. On a journey to a wonderland of good
food and clothes.

They lay shoulder to shoulder, all around the hold of the vessel,
feet pointing toward the center, and not only chained in pairs, but
each pair attached to a great chain that passed through a ring
fastened to all the individual chains.

Could you conceive of a strength able to lift up this great chain
with all these Negroes suspended to it, you would have a gigantic
necklace of blacks. You would have more than that. You would have
three necklaces.

For above the hold, that is to say above the main part of the lower
deck, a platform had been erected dividing the height of this section
into two. And this platform, seven feet wide, buttressed to the beams
of the bulkhead, ran all around the hold and supported another
necklace of Negroes.

And there was a third necklace, separated from the two male
necklaces. For this one was a female necklace. Lift it up! See the
black women suspended by their ankle-chains, clutching desperately
at their children! There, Europa, my fair one, hang that around your
neck!

21

Silly imagery!

Who ever heard of necklaces of pendants of black slaves! Who would wear such a necklace? Why, the ladies of Europe wear only dainty necklaces of gold and pearls and diamonds.

Yes, a silly image! Besides, the black women were often left unchained. There was no revolt to be feared from them.

Captain Collard felt that you could not begin too soon. That very afternoon, seeing that the sun was shining brightly, he had one of the necklaces unfastened and unstrung and the paired pendants brought up on the deck.

"Line them up," Captain Collard shouted.

The Negroes, chilled by the ocean breeze, persisted in huddling together for greater warmth. It had been comfortable in the hold. Why bring them up here? Had they reached the end of their journey so soon?

"Talk to them, Gmara! In hell's name, why don't you talk?"

Gmara was doing his best, shouting above the noise of wind and sail. But how explain to these people to line up? They know nothing of lining up. They can walk or dance in file, but these scores of chained pairs, how are they to line up?

White men would understand at once. White men are always in line. Just go out and shout to them: "Line up, men!" and thousands of them line up. "Right by two's!" and right by two's they go. "Forward march!" you say, and off they march. And now it's up to you to march them where you please—to war, to death, to shout hurrah, or boo, to work . . . whatever you say goes.

But these are ignorant savages. They do not think or act in straight lines.

They stand there and gaze out to sea and wonder. They had suspected below that the rolling motion they experienced was due to the moving of the ship. But how were they to know? Now on deck they can see a cliff moving with frightful rapidity.

Babouk, ever forward with his knowledge, declared: "This is a bird.

"It has great white wings. Many wings, not just two.

"And beneath the water it has big webbed feet, orange-colored, like a goose. And that is what makes this boat move so fast, for it isn't a boat at all, but a bird. And after it has swum for a while it will leap from the water and go flying into the air, lifting itself up on its many white wings."

Amid a great clamor, Babouk's explanation was conveyed to all the slaves, being altered and translated as it went from mouth to mouth. Truly Babouk was wise. He knew everything, despite his youth.

"Break up those groups!" Collard shouted and cracked his whip.

It would have been easier, perhaps, for Gmara, had the slaves all come from the same tribe. But that is hazardous. An experienced captain would fear to load on a cargo of Negroes all of whom can understand each other. They would be sure to plot this and that together and even break out into open rebellion.

Not that they would be able, chained in pairs as they were, to do much damage, but the number of men in the crew was never more than a fraction of the number of slaves, and to be left short-handed might be trying, possibly fatal. And more than that: the death of a sailor could be borne, but the death of a Negro, of many Negroes—for such an outbreak must be put down unmercifully—would be an irreplaceable loss of capital.

No, it would never do to have a shipload of slaves all from one tribe. In fact, one must not even chain two from the same tribe together. For the first duty of the careful slaver is to prevent one black from striking up an understanding with another.

For that reason Captain Collard and his mates had taken care to note, from the very beginning, where two blacks seemed to be friendly. They were parted and chained separately.

And a big man was never paired with a small man. That too would lead to trouble, for the big man would naturally become the leader and the small man would perforce obey.

The trick was to match them from different tribes as evenly in size and age as you possibly could. Then they were not only born rivals, being from different tribes, they were not only prone to misunderstand each other for lack of a common language, but they were physical rivals, too.

There they lay, chained together and hating each other.

That was safe.

Safe for captain and crew. Safe for the cargo and its owner.

Safe for milady's diamond necklace.

No, indeed. Not every fool could be a slaver. So many youths of Europe thought that: I'll go into the African trade, too, and make my fortune. And they were lucky if they brought home their skins, and the poor dolts who had sunk their fortunes in such harebrained investments lost their good money.

"Gmara! Make them look at me!" Collard cried, and, seizing the second mate, he illustrated how the Negroes could manage to dance despite their chains by facing and holding onto each other's shoulders.

He signed to the two drummers to begin. The two Negroes selected for this task raised their drums, clasped between their legs, and began to beat on them. A dull, uninspired rhythm floated into the salt breeze and was as if tangled and shredded in the cordage.

"Gmara! Why aren't they dancing?"

Gmara shouted until he was out of breath. But the blacks would not understand.

The drummers pounded on their sea-damp drums, stopped to tighten the skins, and went on. But the effect was bad.

Only Collard and his mate were dancing, kicking up their legs.

Most of the Negroes did not even look. Or, if they did, it was with unseeing eyes. Though Gmara had explained a dozen times that the journey was not over, that indeed it had hardly begun, many were searching the horizon, thinking that this was already the wonderland, and bearing up cheerfully with the chill wind, comforted by the thought that they would soon be landed and could toast their frozen bodies around a warm fire.

"Every trip it's the same thing!" the Captain cried in despair, and ceased his dancing. "Whether you take a month or a day to teach them to dance on land, once they get on the ship they won't dance.

"Well, God damn them, they must dance!

"*Dance!* Dance, you black bastards! Dance!"

And Collard and his men went among the blacks, lashing out indiscriminately, forcing them into line, whipping their legs until they picked them up and danced.

The Negroes saw the whip rise and felt it fall. And they heard the word, *dance!* And still they did not understand. Why should they dance? Why the celebration when the heart is homesick and the body numb with cold?

But they were hustled into line and forced to get into action.

Under the rain of blows a long black centipede was formed. A centipede that twined about the deck and stamped and shrieked.

"Keep dancing! Damn you, keep dancing! You dance damn well all night long in your villages! You dance then until you drop! Now come on, dance here!"

And the centipede danced, chains clanking.

"All right, men!" Captain Collard cried.

A half dozen sailors moved down the line, casting buckets of freshly drawn salt water on the centipede. As they progressed, the dancing centipede shriveled up, sputtered, choked, gasped. The shivering Negroes let go each other's shoulders and clasped their hands on their painfully cold privates.

"Keep dancing!" Collard shouted. "Gmara! François! Jacques! Keep them dancing."

But the wet centipede had collapsed. To make matters worse, the sun was of a sudden obscured by a cloud, and a stiff breeze blew.

"Get out the rum, or they'll be dying of congestions!" Collard ordered.

Rum! Ah, that was good. It lit a little fire right in your belly, where you needed it most.

"Get the next batch up," the captain commanded and helped himself to a stiff pull of rum. Lord, what a job! A man who could stand this deserved every penny he earned.

In the bustle and confusion occasioned by the arrival of the second necklace, one bold Negro determined to escape. With a hoarse cry he seized Babouk, to whom he was chained, and, lifting Babouk in the air, began to run with him to the gunwale, where he would surely have leapt overboard had not a sailor barred his way.

The powerful black lowered his head and butted the sailor. The latter groaned and doubled up, but, bent as he was, he had the wit to draw his cutlass and strike at the rebellious Negro's leg. The blow cut the man's Achilles tendon. The blood gushed forth and the hamstrung leg crumpled up.

He and Babouk rolled on the blood-slippery deck.

Captain Collard came running up and dealt the sailor a cuff that knocked him headlong.

"You fool! You ruined the man for good!"

"Here you, cut that chain!" An ax did the job.

"Throw him over!" And the useless Negro was pitched into the sea.

Babouk, his face blue, his eyes popping from his head, saw the pitched Negro fall splash into the water. Heard him let forth a cry as if of triumph, and saw him swim vigorously toward shore.

He might really have made it, and brought himself back again, hamstrung but alive, to the African continent. That is to say, if anyone had thought to bind his leg up to prevent the loss of blood.

As it was, he swam but a few strokes, when his vigor began to diminish. But he could be followed swimming shoreward, even when his head was submerged, by the pink tangled ribbon that his gashed leg tossed off.

The planks of the hold, where the slaves lay, had meanwhile been washed down with vinegar, and vessels of ginger and other incense had been set to burn, in order, as the expression went, to perfume the quarters.

The platform necklace was now brought up on deck and the first necklace was returned to its place, the pendants made to lie down, and the great chain strung through the rings on the ankle-chains.

Lying here, in the warm hold, with the strange odor of vinegar and incense, lying here in the dusk with the smoke of the incense pots swirling through the gloom, lying here was almost cozy.

The numb bodies of the blacks grew warm, their numb souls expanded. But the misery and terror of their lot overcame them. They moaned or sang childhood songs and wept at the thought of what they had left behind.

Above them they heard the tramp of bare feet and the clank of ankle-chains as a new centipede was being instructed in the art of dancing.

Babouk lay, a single man, among many pairs. And he moaned along with the others and thought of what was missing on the end of his ankle-chain.

Now the sea grew heavy and the black bodies were tossed from side to side. The planks bruised their shoulders and their hips. The chains caught the flesh of their ankles.

The two small port-holes were closed against the poisonous night air. The darkness was complete.

Above, the sailors were amusing themselves with some of the Negresses. One man was plucking a zither. And the laughter of the company was heard by the moaning captives.

The tossing of the ship was beginning to affect some of the blacks. Their bowels grew watery. The food in their stomachs revolted and forced them to retch.

Now there were, at intervals, certain pails and pots which could be handed along, and the use of which had been repeatedly stressed upon the men. But to some of this men this repeated stressing had been done in a gibberish they could not be expected to understand. For when Gmara was confronted by an unknown tongue, and this was frequent, for of the hundred or more languages which were spoken by the various tribes brought to the trading posts he knew only a score, then he spoke a gibberish that deceived the white man without enlightening the Negro.

Again, many were incapable of breaking the habit of a lifetime.

Still others feared witchcraft. What other motive could be ascribed to this pail? Why should one want to put into a pot that part of one which the body ejected and which was therefore self-evidently good for nothing?

Instinctively man craves to hide away his dejecta. But where could one hide anything on this ship, where there was neither bush nor forest?

Another difficulty was the chain, and still another, the fact that your neighbors did not understand you.

True, certain commanders, captives themselves, but selected for their qualities of leadership, had been designated to supervise. But as yet they did not understand their duties, nor had they been freed of their chains. This would not happen until they had shown their fitness for the post.

What wonder then that, confronted with so many difficulties, surrounded by so much that was new and terrifying, the prostrate Negroes emptied their bellies where they lay?

The floor was soon slippery with filth. The close air grew heavy, fetid, and sour.

And from the platform the nauseous matter dripped down upon the wretches below.

"We are on the ship of the dead," groaned Babouk.

"We are on the ship of the dead," he repeated.

And the Mandingoes and allied tribesmen took up the lugubrious cry: "We are on the ship of the dead."

"We are dead," Babouk declared. "We have died long ago."

"We are dead," the assistants echoed. "We have died long ago."

"We are on the boat that takes the dead to N'koolango, where the dead reside."

On either side Babouk's neighbors slept. Snored and stirred in their sleep, dreaming perhaps of the freedom they had lost, clasping tightly in their fingers some familiar amulet.

"We are on the boat that takes the dead to N'koolango, where the dead reside."

Here and there was a Mohammedan Negro, a Fullah or Toucoulor, who, suspecting that the hour of sunset had come, knelt as best his chains allowed, and faced toward Mecca and repeated the al-fatiha:

"In the name of God, the compassionate compassioner.

"Praise be to God, the Lord of the worlds, the compassionate compassioner, the sovereign of the day of judgment. Thee do we worship and of thee beg assistance.

"Direct us to the right path, the path of those who have thy grace, in whom there is no wrath, who go not astray."

"We are going to the kingdom of the dead," Babouk chanted.

"We are going to the kingdom of the dead," his listeners chorused.

"We shall see our dead ancestors. And all the animals we have slain, and all the food we have eaten, and all the pots we have broken, will pass before our eyes again, as in a dream."

4

A people called Negroes, a people of beastly living, without a God, without laws, without
religion or common wealth, and so scorched and
vexed with the heat of the sun, that in many places
they curse it when it riseth.
—*Description of the Africans by one of the
earliest London slave merchants*

"Tell us a story, Babouk, please tell us a story."

They would have gone completely mad if Babouk had not told
them stories. As it was, half of them were ill with grief.

As if the horrible seasickness were not enough, homesickness
came further to weaken their bowels.

Day after day the Negroes had watched the changing coast and
wondered where they were to land. And even those who realized
that they were not to land on this coast at all clung to its sight,
feeling that as long as it remained visible they were not completely
torn away from home.

But one night the ship found her way into the tradewind, and the
next day the coast of Africa was blown out of sight.

There was no dancing that day, no matter how hard the whip fell,
no matter how hard the drums were beaten, no matter how gayly a
sailor twanged his zither.

Gathered below in the hold again, they gave way to their bitter
grief. Under the pressure of a pain that was keen as a toothache, they
moaned and howled. Some sang out wildly, in cracked, tight voices,
snatches of the songs they had learnt to sing as children. Others
dashed their heads against the beams of the boat as if a good
straight physical pain could obliterate this mad longing that tore at
them from within, they could not precisely say where.

But others, members of tribes that believed in the transmigration
of souls, finding their present existence unendurable, calmly put

29

themselves to death, confident that their souls would be reborn as babies, back in their own tribes at home.

In the midst of the general clamor they remained silent, until the moment when they chose to expire. Then they forced their tongues back into their throats and thus stopped up their air-passages.

Day after day and night after night the wailing continued, until even the whites on deck nearly went mad at this perpetual dirge that rose from below as from a grave in which living bodies had been immured.

The almoner, a miserable wretch who had sunk to this, the lowest of all ecclesiastical jobs, because of his addiction to liquor, could not sleep, drunk as he was.

And a young ensign, one of several lads of noble family, sent aboard the ship to learn the art of the merchant marine, after searching the whole vessel for a quiet spot to snatch a brief rest, came knocking finally at the almoner's door.

The almoner did not answer. Whereupon the ensign pounded madly. Then the captain came out of his cabin near-by and queried angrily: "What is this? What is this?"

The ensign had sunk to his knees: "I want to pray," he pleaded weakly.

"Yes, yes," said the captain blankly. "Pray, pray, by all means."

"Tell us a story, Babouk, please. Tell us a story."

And he would tell them one story after another. At first he spoke only to the few who were close enough to hear his voice, which did not penetrate the general moaning and wailing very far. But the little pool of quietness around him grew gradually, until one day the entire hold remained silent to hear him relate the tale of the most virtuous bed.

"Have you heard tell the story of the most virtuous bed that ever was?" he asked. For of late his mind ran to stories of that type, and such stories were best appreciated by his audience, too.

"No, we have never heard of it," the captives chorused politely whether they had or had not.

"Then I shall recount to you the story of the most virtuous bed in the world."

"Tell us, please," they begged.

Then he began: "Yakuba and Djima were neighbors." And he stopped, for, before he could continue, his words must be carried around the hold and the platform above the hold, and be repeated and translated a dozen times. Babouk did not mind the interruption. He sensed that he held his audience, and the longer he held them the prouder he was.

"Yakuba and Djima were neighbors. And Djima loved Yakuba's wife so much that he would not sleep with his own wife any more, but would save his vigor instead and would listen from his hut for the sound of Yakuba's wife making a great noise among her pots and crockery, for that was a sign that Yakuba had gone and Yakuba's wife was ready to welcome her beloved Djima.

"But one day Yakuba returned home unexpectedly soon, and his wife, hearing the rhythm of his steps, pushed Djima under the bed.

" 'Wife,' said Yakuba, 'why aren't you in the millet field?'

"Thereupon Yakuba's wife took a basket and went out as if to take care of the millet, but she did not go very far or stay very long, for she had not finished her embrace and her body was troubled.

"Meanwhile, Djima's wife, missing the company of man, since Djima no longer cared for her embraces, went into Yakuba's hut and, finding Yakuba alone, she thought to allay her thirst for a man.

"Yakuba was very willing, for his wife had not been kind to him of late. But Yakuba and Djima's wife had not time to finish their embraces when they heard Yakuba's wife coming back from the millet field.

"Quickly Yakuba pushed Djima's wife under the bed.

"And that," Babouk explained, as if in conclusion, "is how it always happens with those who try to steal their love. They are always punished in the end. And so neither Yakuba, nor Djima, nor their wives were able to finish their embraces, and they were like those from whom you snatch the cup just as their lips are about to drink."

The captives commented upon this conclusion: Decidedly it was just that people who steal love should not be permitted to enjoy it.

But this comment was mere politeness. And after a little interval one began to hear impatient clankings of the chains and a criticism more and more loudly expressed: "But, Babouk, you have not told us of the most virtuous bed."

"But I have, indeed," Babouk maintained. "Was not Yakuba's bed peculiarly virtuous, seeing that twice a man and a woman were prevented from stealing love upon it?"

Nor was this conclusion any more satisfactory than the first. But Babouk, gathering his breath, went on: "And consider too: What did Yakuba do, seeing that his body was troubled from not having finished his embrace? Would he not feel urged to say to his wife: 'Come, lie down here with me?'

"And she, would she not now be willing, seeing that her embrace had been incomplete, and that to complete it even a husband would serve?

"And so they lay down and loved each other as man and wife should.

"Tell me, now! Was not that a virtuous bed where husband and wife lay together?"

"It was that," the Negroes agreed.

"But it was even more virtuous," Babouk pursued. "For underneath the bed Djima and his wife, in their trouble, reached toward each other and embraced as wife and husband should.

"Was ever a more virtuous bed, where above and below man and wife loved as they ought?"

"Never, never," the audience laughed.

"Above and below the married couples embraced. And when they were through, seeing that their love had been as pleasant as any love can be, why, they embraced each other again.

"Yes, above and below they embraced each other again, and then surely there was no more virtuous bed in the whole world than the bed of Yakuba."

Loud laughter greeted the end of Babouk's story. But the noise subsided gradually as each man laughed more and more to himself and retired to his own thoughts to conjure up a dream woman to solace his loneliness. Either the wife he had lost, or from whom he had been torn, or any woman from the multitude he had ever seen and craved.

On deck they had not failed to notice the diminished wailing and now they were surprised to hear even sounds of laughter.

"They are just children," said the surgeon Le Petit. "They forget their troubles quickly. It will be easy from now on."

And the ensign who had prayed felt relieved now because he could hear the Negroes laughing and knew that they were happy after all, even in their misery. So true is it that even a vestige of happiness left among the oppressed can furnish many ample cloaks for the oppressor's conscience.

"Step on him again!" cries the oppressor. "He's still happy." Yes, so he says, even when the man beneath his heel shows nothing but the grin of death.

This was the moment the captain had learned to expect. The moment when the natural joyous nature of the Negro would surmount his homesickness. Now was the time for the captain to come forward and show the slaves that he had their good interest at heart, and thus capture their easily won affection.

From long experience he knew that nothing was better for the health of the cargo than that the captives should learn to love him and look up to him as their protector.

He therefore summoned Gmara and had him go announce to the captives that the good captain, pleased to hear that they were no longer wailing for their homeland, when the good captain was taking them to a land of marvels—that the good captain, pleased at their laughter, declared that, if they continued to behave well, then they should dance with the women on Sunday afternoon.

And the captives were truly overwhelmed with joy.

Women!

They cheered the good captain repeatedly. Women! Women!

Only certain of the more discerning Negroes and certain warlike Senegalese refused to cheer along with the rest, but glared out angrily instead.

Babouk was thoroughly disgusted. Who but the captain had taken the women away from them? Why should they now be grateful to him for restoring what he had stolen?

It hurt Babouk, too, to realize that, though it was the laughter which his stories had evoked that had been the means of securing a dance with the women, yet it was the captain who was cheered for it.

But Babouk's time came again.

There were days when the deck was swept by cold rain. Then the captives had to remain below, often one long day after another, in the steaming heat of the hold.

During such times the sailors who came below to superintend

certain selected Negroes in the emptying of the buckets, or in the distribution of one or the other of the two daily meals, removed their clothes and labored naked. Such stripping, however, was beneath the dignity of Le Petit, the surgeon, who came, once a day, to order the removal of the dead for casting into the sea, and the segregation in the infirmary of the infectiously diseased.

He hurried through his task, holding a cloth before his nose, feeling the sweat run beneath his clothes, and his lungs so aching for a breath of clean air that he would not stop to listen long to the endless complaints of the captives.

"All they want is a drink of rum," was his opinion. "Now that they know that they can get a tumbler of rum just by complaining, they're all full of complaints," so he would explain to the sailors who assisted him.

"No, no, there's nothing wrong with you or you."

Hastily he passed them by, stepping over the chained legs and waving down with his hand the Negroes who half rose to exhibit their sores or to cough lugubriously for the doctor to hear what misery they had in their throats and chests.

"Nothing wrong, nothing wrong," he would repeat, and would skip more and more rapidly over the chained legs. Finally he was back to the incline that led to the deck and could stumble out of the hatch and receive the fresh cool buffet of the sea-breeze full on his face.

And the blacks were alone again in their dark prison.

And soon, too, their voices would be raised, wheedling, to Babouk: "Tell us a story, Babouk, please. Tell us a story."

"Surely the good white captain knows more stories than I do," Babouk would retort. "He will soon tell you one that will make you cheer as you never cheered my poor efforts."

"No, Babouk. Do not say that. We know very well that it is you who know stories and not the captain."

"No," Babouk insisted in a surly voice. "You must go to the captain. He knows many fine stories. I am sure he will be glad to come down here and tell stories to keep you happy."

"You would not say that, Babouk, if you were not angry at us because we cheered the captain."

"You are mistaken," Babouk declared innocently. "And you were right to cheer the captain. Does he not give you back your women for an hour or two each week? Must you not be grateful for that?

"What if he should not let us see them at all? Even an hour is much for the white men to part with our women, for you know that the white man is hungry for our beautiful women.

"In their country they have no women. And that is why they come to our land: to get women to sleep with and men to eat."

"But there must be white women," someone objected, "for I have seen young white boys. They must be born of white women."

This argument, however, was soon cried down. For everyone agreed with Babouk that the whites were born out of the sea-foam that washes up on the sand of the beach. And these white creatures made of sand and sea-foam must go to the Negroes to find women to make love to.

And the proof of it was that, as one could see among the sailors, these white men sometimes made love to each other. That habit comes from the fact that in their country there are no white women and nothing to embrace but men.

The group around Babouk discussed this matter for a while, but such a subject for intimate debate did not satisfy the great throngs of captives who were too far away to take part in it.

"Babouk," they pleaded. "Babouk, tell us a story. You know we only cheered the captain out of politeness."

"Politeness? Politeness, indeed!" cried Babouk. "And do you think it a virtue to be polite?"

The blacks were, many of them, shocked. All their lives they had been taught to be polite.

"Do you know," Babouk insisted, "that of all animals the lowly crab is the most polite?

"Are you all crabs, that you should be polite to the white chief? Do you think that, if you could only ask him with sufficient politeness to take off your chains, he would do so?

"You are all crabs! The politest and lowest of animals!"

For the audience the sting of this insult was more than removed by the warm feeling that a story was impending. And swallowing meekly the insult of Babouk's scorn, they contented themselves with suggesting meekly: "Tell us, Babouk, please, why are the crabs the politest of all animals?" A request in which even those joined who already knew the explanation.

"Very well, then," Babouk relented. "I shall tell you the story of the politest of all animals, the crab, and what rewards he received for his politeness.

"You must know that, when God made the animals, He did not bother to make the bodies, for bodies are easy to make and such work could be entrusted to others. He fashioned only the heads."

And all about the hold one could hear the Negroes repeating in one language or another: "God fashioned only the heads."

Babouk continued: "And when a great variety of bodies existed and were already roaming the earth, but at a great disadvantage because they had no heads, then God called them all to come forward and receive each a head from the great basket of heads He had before Him.

"Now it happened that the animal nearest the basket was the crab. And immediately behind him was the elephant.

"And the elephant said: 'Crab, won't you be so kind as to let me get my head first?'

"And the crab, being polite, stepped aside. And the elephant received his head and went off trumpeting victoriously.

"But behind the elephant had been the antelope, so that now the antelope stood behind the crab. And he said: 'Crab, won't you be so kind as to let me get my head first?'

"And the crab, being polite, stepped aside. And the antelope ran off brandishing his horned forehead.

"And now the hyena was behind the crab and begged politely: 'Crab, won't you be so kind as to let me get my head first?'

"And again the crab stepped aside. And always he stepped aside. Until all the animals had received their heads and the basket was empty.

"And there stood the crab without a head. And the basket was empty, so that the best God could do was stick a couple of eyes He happened to have directly upon the crab's body and tell him to be off, now.

"And the crab did want to walk off, but look! he had become so accustomed to stepping aside, that he couldn't walk forward any more. All he could do, and all he can do to this day, is step aside politely.

"Yes, and that is how the polite man goes through life, without a head and stepping aside politely, for others to rush in and steal his share."

The worst storm of the voyage struck the *Prie-Dieu* about five weeks out. For four days she wallowed in a sea so mountainous and treacherous that it was only with the utmost effort that the iron pots of couscous were conveyed to the hold for the Negroes to eat. As to emptying the buckets, as to any cleaning whatsoever, that was out of question. The perpetual tossing of the ship, the constant danger of an unexpected blow from some tremendous crashing wave, stopped all work in this direction.

The blacks below were torn and pounded cruelly between their binding chains and the rough planks they lay on. And since the hold could not be washed down with vinegar, nor the air cleansed with incense, there where the skin was rubbed raw, often down to the bone, the wound festered and suppurated.

And they trembled with fear, too, hearing the impact of enormous masses of water flung against the ship by the tumultuous sea. They could hear the loose cordage beating a tattoo against the masts while the taut cordage whined like a harp-string, and the wind whistled past the reefed sails.

They were in darkness, in complete darkness, now, for not only were hatches battened down, but every other opening had been carefully sealed lest high waves reach it and pour in.

And thus they remained through four days and five nights, which to them, in their dark prison, were nine unending nights strung together.

When, at last, they were released from their chains and ordered to go out upon the sunny deck, many of them could not walk. Their legs would not sustain them. And then, too, the vision of day contained a curious dull glare through which one could not see, no more than through fog.

The men rubbed their eyes and cleared their vision for a moment. But the fog gathered again, and for some this fog was annoyingly speckled with brilliantly colored flies that dashed about with maddening speed.

The blacks blinked and shook their heads. These manifestations would stop, of course, once their eyes were accustomed to the light of the sun again. Yes, the sun felt good pouring down on the nape of one's neck. And good, too, was the fresh breeze. . . .

But the fog would not dissipate. Instead it grew heavier and the speeding flies massed themselves into dark angry clots.

The vision of the Negroes improved, however, when they found themselves back in the dark hold. The fog disappeared then, even the flies diminished. But their eyes were not comfortable. They burned.

And in the morning the lids could scarcely open because so much foamy, fatty substance had gathered in the corners during the night.

When the surgeon appeared for his morning round and as usual passed by hastily, muttering "nothing wrong," Babouk seized him by the leg and cried out:

"My eyes are dying. Doctor, my eyes are dying!"

The surgeon did not understand and would have torn himself loose and hurried on if all the hold had not taken up the mournful, frightened cry.

"Our eyes are dying!"

A few even shrieked: "My eyes are dead!" and struck angrily at the dry, opaque eyeballs that seemed to be the real obstruction to their sight.

Then Le Petit stooped, and seeing and recognizing the gray, lard-like exudation, he waited no longer but dashed back to deck and ran to the captain, crying out to him, all out of breath:

"We must not bring the captives up on deck any more. And none of us must go below!"

Captain Collard took Le Petit roughly by the sleeve, near the shoulder, and shook him. "What is all this? What is all this?"

"You don't understand," Le Petit cried, "the blacks are all blind with ophthalmy!"

Now Captain Collard understood. His cargo! His whole cargo became valueless! Who would buy a blind Negro?

He gripped Le Petit's sleeves so tightly that he forced the surgeon to his knees.

"Listen, you barber's apprentice! Listen to me! What are you hired for if not to see to the cargo's health? Now back to your work! Get down into that hold and cure those blacks!"

"No, no!" cried Le Petit. "No, no," he begged. "You can't make me go below. I'll go blind. We'll all go blind. We must abandon ship, take to the boats. . . ."

"So, so," said Collard quietly, still maintaining his grip on Le Petit's sleeve. "Abandon the ship, eh? And leave a million in slaves to die and the ship to become anybody's prize? You have very original ideas." He laughed. And then he muttered: "But I'll make you a doctor in spite of yourself!"

Then he thundered down at Le Petit: "Back to your work! Or I'll put you in irons on bread and water and keep you there until I hand you over to the port authorities in Nantes!

"Now, which is it? Irons or work? Answer me!"

"I can't . . ." Le Petit groaned. "Please. . . ."

"Take your time," said Collard with sudden gentleness, but he did not relax his hold on Le Petit's sleeve. "You're a bit upset.—Now, what is it?"

And Le Petit made his forced decision. "God help me," he said. "God help us all."

"Then back to work!" Collard shouted, and released the surgeon with a push that sent him sprawling.

Trembling in every limb, Le Petit rose and went off to his apothecary room to malaxate large quantities of mercury salve.

Now, either he made his salve too weak, or the disease was stronger than any salve, but the inflammation would not subside. It spread like fire in a dry bush. The slaves first, then the white sailors, then the officers. And at last the captain. As if nature were loath to lay violent hands on quality.

Le Petit himself, though he salved his eyes ten times a day, at last was going about performing his duty, his sight obscured by a gray fog spiked with bizarre flies. And though he knew that one of the symptoms of the disease was that one could see a little better in the dim light than in bright lights, still each evening found him hoping that his eyes had improved. But night, complete night, descended upon him.

Night descended upon all of them. The last man still capable of seeing dimly out of one eye held the wheel until that eye too was obscured. Then the ship plunged on through the night.

In the hold the slaves moaned incessantly: "Our eyes have died. Oh, white man, give us back our eyes." Then they wept, or shrieked, or sang, or were silent, as the mood of despair urged them.

Despair had taken hold of the crew, too. The sailors neglected their duties and sat together in corners and brooded angrily:

"Who does all the work if not we? Do we not load on the cargo, and feed it, and clean it? And what is our share? A miserable ten or twenty francs a month in addition to kicks and bad food. While the captain and the owners grow rich.

"What if we were no longer to work for them? Where would they be?"

"I tell you," said another, "that if there were ten men like me aboard this ship there would have been mutiny long ago. And let me tell you, a pretty piece of money we could get smuggling this cargo of slaves into San Domingo.

"Yes, and I tell you if there were a thousand like me in France you'd see the end of landlords and noblemen, yes, and bishops and the king too, for that matter. Pack of bloodsuckers!"

But when they heard the captain's heavy step they lowered their voices to whispers.

He strode about now with one slow decisive step after another, carefully inspecting every inch of the ship, and holding his whip ready.

He listened for the noise of a sail come unfurled, and the blind crew was lashed unmercifully if it hesitated to climb up and discover by the sense of touch what sail was loose and bind it tightly again to the yard.

He went into the galley and struck out with his whip at the cooks, who were lax in preparing the food. The sick cargo and crew, he declared, must have more food than ever.

And he beat Le Petit to force the latter, blind as he was, down into the vile hold, to creep from slave to slave and discover which, if any, were dead, so that the body could be removed and so that no decaying corpse should add a new infection to their present one.

Yes, and on Sunday, early, he lashed the drunken almoner out of his bed and made him say mass.

That day the wind seemed as if it wanted to sweep the world clean. It found its way into the badly furled sails, bellied them, and caused them to burst their lines. Then the hanging sail was ripped to shreds with a noise like exploding musketry. And the loose cordage lashed about and struck down crew and officers alike.

The following day, though the weather was calm, the despair of all had risen. But it is in the lowest depths of our misery that salvation seeks us out, or at least so it appeared when the men of the *Prie-Dieu* were startled to hear a faint halloo come across the water. They listened, and the halloo was repeated several times, and each time louder.

Then the blinded second mate groped for the megaphone and shouted back in a hoarse voice: "Ahoy!"

And now everyone heard plainly the response: "This is the *Sant' Iago* from Sierra Leone, bound for Havana with a cargo of blacks. As you love Christ send us over a pilot, for we are all blind here, man and mouse."

The blind second mate put the megaphone to his lips, but he did not answer. What words do the blind say to the blind?

Then the *Sant' Iago* hallooed again: "On the sweet body of Christ we beseech you. Send us a pilot! We are blind, one and all."

The second lowered his megaphone. No one spoke.

"For the love of God, send us a pilot! Where are you? Why don't you answer?" The *Sant' Iago* had now come quite close.

And still no one spoke. On the *Prie-Dieu* all was silent except for the moans of the captives.

"Why don't you speak? We are blind! Halloo! Halloo! Can you hear us?"

Then someone on the *Prie-Dieu* began to laugh. A low, meaningless giggle. But so infectious that in a moment they were all laughing. The captain too.

And the laughter grew into a roar. Some had to lie down on the deck, so weak were they from explosive bursts of laughter.

Then the *Sant' Iago* stopped hallooing. Instead she cursed. Her whole crew roared curses upon the *Prie-Dieu*. "Are you beasts," one of them shouted in a stentorian voice, "to laugh at our misery?"

No one bothered to reply to him. They laughed. And the laughter of the *Prie-Dieu* continued to answer the imprecations of the *Sant'*

Iago until the two ships had drifted apart and were alone again in their separate seas of darkness.

When the epidemic began to show signs of waning, though he himself was still blind, the captain had the slaves brought out on deck. Dancing was still out of the question, but the quarters could be cleaned up and those who had recovered could be segregated from those who were still sick, so that, as the disease ran its course, the rise in the value of the cargo could be noted.

Just as soon as the lard-like foamy secretions ceased to appear and the tear-glands began to function normally and wash the eye clean again, the disease was over. Then the fog disappeared from one's eyes and complete, or nearly complete, sight was restored. However, if, while the fatty particles ceased to appear, the tear-glands nevertheless did not function, and the eye remained dry, then the sight was lost, for the transparent cornea shriveled and grew rough, and the eyelid rasped against it and scarred it, so that, like a window that has been scratched, it ceased to be transparent.

But when the disease had reached its final stage and its ravages could be figured up with accuracy, it appeared that the financial loss was not nearly so bad as the captain had feared it might be.

As usual, the disease had been most fatal to the young. All of the eight Negro children who had come aboard with their mothers were stone-blind, along with one of the mothers. None of the other women was afflicted. Of the black men all but ten recovered.

Of the whites only one lost his vision.

One bright morning all the unsalable captives were brought upon deck, and, after a short quarrel with the almoner, who so strenuously insisted upon more than two *livres* for each case that the mercies of religion had to be dispensed with, the captain ordered the sailors to attach stones, pieces of iron, cannon balls, whatever weights could be spared, to the nineteen cases, and then they were pitched into the sea.

Some resisted and cried out. Others remained indifferent. But some were so willing that they assisted the sailors to guide them overboard.

The woman and her child made no disturbance except when an attempt was made to separate them.

In fact, there was very little trouble to speak of. It was Le Petit, the surgeon, the one white who did not recover, who created the greatest difficulty.

He kept insisting: "Throw me over, too. I'm not worth anything now, either." Consoling words would not help. He became violent and ran here and there, blindly, seeking to cast himself into the sea.

The captain finally ordered him locked up.

In the afternoon of that day the usual program was put into force again. But it seemed that the Negroes were aware of the fate of their blind fellows, for they obstinately refused to dance, and neither whip nor rum would awaken their enthusiasm.

The captain was beside himself. "After seven weeks," he declared, "they still won't dance." His anger knew no bounds.

5

You would never suppose that it is through Pity
that Slavery came into existence.

—*Montesquieu*

But there came a day when the whites no longer leaned so heavily
on their whips. The commanders relaxed their vigilance.

The blacks straightened their bent backs and forgot their anger
and their melancholy.

The captain ordered double rations of food and as much palm-oil
for anointing the skin, and chewing sticks for polishing the teeth, as
the captives might desire.

Whence came this new current of mildness that swept over the
floating prison, and softened the hearts of jailers and captives alike?

It was the odor of a continent, still invisible.

The ship was flooded with the sweet smell of land. She sailed
through a perfumed atmosphere. Crew and cargo, tired of the thin,
chill odor of the sea and the sour odor of the hold, sniffed at the
breeze, sighed, breathed deep, and sighed again.

The odor of America!

The geologic odor of America, a powerful and intoxicating perfume spread by thousands of miles of steaming earth and exuberant
vegetation, an odor that caused early explorers to sink upon the
deck, their hands clasped in prayer, tears streaming from their eyes,
their mouths babbling poetry.

This was the perfume of America, flower of continents!

This was the perfume of America, land of flora, as Africa was the
land of fauna.

Oh, continents, what has man done to you?

America, where is your perfume now?

There was, then, no further need to stint on rations for fear the
journey might last five or even six months, as sometimes happened.

44

No need now to repress every sign of independent volition on the part of the blacks for fear of revolt.

Time now to think of fattening them up, of making them recover their natural sleekness and gaiety, so as to command a ready sale and a high price.

And the blacks responded quickly to the new treatment, the new atmosphere.

Daily the perfume grew stronger, but as the ship approached and circled the island of Saint-Domingue, there was mingled with it another odor, a sharp, disturbing odor.

It was the odor of industry, the dominating scent being that of molasses steaming in the great sugar kettles.

And one evening, in the darkness, along the horizon, the sky began to glow with a strange red, in which sparkled dots of light.

The Negroes, who were being hurried below as the sun dropped suddenly out of the sky and the quick tropic night came on, had had time to witness this manifestation, and Babouk, who, to sustain his reputation as a wise man, could not afford to hesitate for an explanation, declared at once, oratorically, that this was nothing less than the death of the sun that had cracked up against the land they could see there and whose fragments were now strewn upon that distant shore.

The voyage was over.

There lay Le Cap Français, largest city of the French part of the island of Saint-Domingue, richest sugar island of the world.

The red glow on the horizon was due to the vast industry in smoking meats and fish, to the fires under the sugar kettles in nearly three hundred sugar refineries, to the constant activity of forty-some rum distilleries, a score of brickyards, ten or more potteries, and over a hundred quicklime kilns.

And on the following day the *Prie-Dieu* added its mast to the forest formed by some hundred or more ocean-going vessels lying in the generous port.

No sooner had the *Prie-Dieu* cast anchor than officials came to call upon Captain Collard. It was their business to see to it that the vessel was "perfumed," that is to say, that sailors or slaves afflicted with contagious diseases, such as smallpox, with incurable diseases, such as epilepsy and so forth, were removed, and that the hold was disinfected.

Formerly custom ruled that this perfuming be quietly and quickly settled with a cash gift of two per cent of the cargo's value. But complaints had emanated time and time again, both from the younger sons of the French nobility who occupied the colonial posts, and from the rich ship-owners of Nantes and Bordeaux.

Thereupon the king had forbidden the two per cent gratuity.

Since then the two per cent gratuity was out of order, and neither side dared complain.

The vessel now perfumed and there being no further let to business, Captain Collard received several slavebrokers.

These were not the agents who would handle the general sale of the cargo. These were adventurous business men, "plungers," who were anxious to purchase the sick and exhausted slaves at bargain prices and assume the risk of having their investment die on their hands, or get well and be salable at excellent profit.

This was important: they paid cash for their merchandise, and cash was rare in the sugar islands, purposely rare, so that the bankers of France could keep the colonial business in constant paper debt to them.

By this sale Captain Collard achieved two ends. One, he provided himself with some ready money; two, he cleared out his cargo, which, deprived of a number of eyesores, took on a much better appearance.

While these brokers were removing the sick (some having to be carried out in blankets, others walking with difficulty, their swollen bellies, their ashen skin, their ribbed chests, their haggard faces, and their melancholy coughs proclaiming their various diseases), the Captain arranged for the hire of a slavery where his more robust captives could rest up from their long journey and recover their spirits and embonpoint.

The landing of unsold slaves for the purpose of "refreshing" them, thus securing higher prices from the planters to further enrich the ship owners of France, was prohibited by the local sugar and coffee cultivators. This selling of the slaves in the hold, however, prevented distant planters from securing good slaves, the best of the cargo having already been claimed by the near planters, who could be on hand as soon as the ship landed.

The distant planters had then wanted to maintain an agent in the port to buy slaves for them. The near planters, who were in control, thereupon forbade brokerage in slaves.

But to a captain who was generous everything was permitted, for the noble custom officials had to live, and the royal treasury was often as much as six years in arrears with their pay.

All business details having been quickly disposed of, steps were taken to remove the Negroes at once to their new abode.

Even Babouk lost his tongue when confronted with the strange sights on the quay of Le Cap.

Fine scarlet and gilt coaches, drawn by six horses, dashed by, the bare-footed, but otherwise elaborately uniformed, black postilions and grooms swearing at the huddle of chained slaves that hindered their passage.

Naked Negro porters, with swelling muscles, trotted past, bearing gayly painted chaises.

Wagons, heavily laden with barrels or sacks, rolled slowly by, their broad, iron-tired wheels crashing noisily over the cobblestones, and then sinking softly in the quagmires of sand that checkered the wretched paving.

The newly arrived captives stared out so stupidly that the passing black workers, conscious of their superior culture, could not help casting an opprobrious word at these rude African bumpkins: "Bossales!" But the chained Negroes did not understand and only continued to stare.

What a crush of pedestrians! There were officers in white uniforms with gold galloons and clanking swords, and soldiers in dun brown. There were merchants and clerks. And all were busy, intent on this or that important purpose, whether it be to the tavern or the billiard room, to the market of the whites, or to the bath house.

The only people who were not rushing were certain mulatto women of warm yellow complexion, daintily dressed in silks and laces, and smelling sweetly of the flowers they carried warm between their soft breasts, and swaying gracefully on their hips as they passed by, their eyes seeking to capture a newly arrived merchant or captain who would take one of them to be his bed-sweetener and companion in the bath house for as long as he would stay in Le Cap.

There were Negresses of like profession, slaves these, who worked for the account of some master or mistress, and whose object was the lesser fry, the sailors and lower-class white who were unable to afford the fancier colored prostitute.

There were, in fact, women here for every class. Some so low in the financial scale that they had no bed, but shared their embraces in the daylight of the street.

When the slaves had all been brought to shore, they were lined up and marched to the slavery. Their progress toward the Rue Espagnole, to the outlying quarters, was impeded by a crowd that had gathered at the Place d'Armes to see the execution of two Negroes and a Negress convicted of having employed poison in the slaying of animals and slaves, and even of one white.

Had Captain Collard himself led his captives, he might have deemed it wise to spare them this sight. But he had delegated his second, and the latter gave the matter no deep thought, except that, inasmuch as he wanted to observe the execution himself, he did not hasten the march of the centipede past this point, but on the contrary slowed down as much as he could without actually stopping.

Three pyres of wood had been built up of crossed fagots, surrounding three stakes. To each stake, by means of iron chains, a black was attached, standing upon a small platform raised to the level of the highest tier of fagots.

The wood, dry resinous material from the mountain candlewood trees, had scarcely been lighted when great flames began licking upward, eating the melting resin with a loud greedy crackle.

Soon great purple and yellow plumes of fire curled up and gently brushed the bodies of the blacks. The great one-armed Negro in the center did not seem to mind much, though he winced and drew back as if he could find protection nearer to his stake.

He began suddenly to sing in a loud resonant voice that was distinctly audible above the shrieks of the Negress, who was perishing vociferously to one side of him, while to his other side the other Negro, his face set, burnt quietly as a candle.

> "Eh! Eh!
> Bomba!
> Heu! Heu!
> Canga. . . ."

He stopped, swallowed, his tongue worked in his mouth, striving to keep it moist. The smoke stung his eyes closed. His head, his neck, his vast pectorals ran with sweat that steamed and hissed as it met the upward climbing feathers of flame.

He opened his mouth again and chanted, shouted rather, in his deep bass:

"Aya! Bombaya! Bombay!"

He choked and gasped. Then he was silent for a spell, standing there, chained to his stake, midst the steam, the smoke, the curling flames, as if he were taking thought.

The other Negro had not made a sound or a move.

But the Negress caused a disturbance and some commotion in the crowd.

The burning of her legs gave her such anguish and produced such wild contortions of her body that she had managed to slip the chains down from her bosom and free one arm. Now, shouting unintelligible imprecations at the mob, she stooped and picked up blazing fragments of wood, and flung them at the mob of sightseers, who scurried aside with little noises of fright.

She bent and rose, again and again, picking cinders from the flames as one might bend to pick pebbles from a stream.

But finally she bent down and did not rise again from the sea of fire.

The great Negro in the center had resumed his singing. The melted oil and gum from his elaborate coiffure poured down over his face.

"Lama samana kana!"

His hair caught fire!

In a moment it was like a great red coal, a fiery sponge stuck to his skull.

Then he threw back his head as if to roar. His chest swelled like a great barrel, thrusting out each rib, hollowing his belly.

But no roar, no gigantic, earth-shaking, heaven-rousing bellow came from that corded throat where the Adam's apple worked convulsively seeking a moisture that had evaporated.

Nothing but a weak gasp. While the great chest remained inflated, the muscles swelled, the body looked as if it would burst with the distension of the gases within it.

But it did not burst.

The Negro was dead. Life ceased to buoy up that great frame but it did not collapse, for the heat of the fire substituted very well for the force of life. He stood erect, head back, belly slowly swelling.

On his skull the fiery sponge still glowed. And now his body burnt briskly, giving off occasionally a heavy dark smoke as new areas of fat flesh caught fire.

The enticing smell of roasted meat that spread over the Place d'Armes was ruined by the sharp odor of singed hair and nails. But all odors were soon swallowed up by the pleasant tonic odor of the resinous wood.

The flames from the fagots rose higher and enveloped the corpses. But behind the wind-stirred curtain of flame one could still see the bodies, blacker now than ever in life, or, when the surrounding flames diminished for a spell and the wind blew directly upon the corpses, glowing red then, like charcoal when one puffs on it.

And still the bodies of the two Negroes stood upright.

But at last they began to disintegrate. The muscles of the torsos curled away in ragged masses encrusted with charcoal and then dropped off into the bed of glowing ashes. And the greedy flames, finding access to the unconsumed interiors, licked their way in and devoured further.

Then certain parts, a forearm or a lower leg, losing its fleshly attachments, would hang first by a thread and then tumble away. But the chains, red-hot, still clasped the shapeless torsos and held them to the stake.

Nothing can be more revealing of the ignorance of the newly landed slaves, under whose feet the ground still swayed like the sea, than the opinions they formed of this sight.

There were a number of whom who were cannibals, accustomed to filing their incisors into points. But it was particularly their musky odor that made these Negroes poor sellers, for they infected the very ground they passed and left a heavy trail of odor that endured for minutes. And this was why few Mondongos and related tribes were ever imported. In the present shortage, however, created by the war, any slave was good; moreover some few free Negro planters were willing to buy and handle this dangerous commodity.

These cannibals, as they passed the pyres, could not help but wonder why the whites should cook their meat so badly as to ruin it for consumption.

Others, too, though not cannibals themselves, shared this critical opinion, for they knew the proper way to cook meat.

This, however, was not the uppermost thought in their minds. Their hearts sank at the realization that, all promises to the contrary, the whites did eat their slaves. Two months of association with the whites had not sufficed to dispel all their suspicions.

And, under the leadership of Babouk, they returned to their eternal question: "If the whites did not propose to eat them, what then was their purpose?"

They had no conception of the great commerce in sugar, rum, coffee, cotton, spices, dyewoods, that tied Europe to all the rest of the world, and their obtuseness precluded the possibility of any explanation.

Here, they saw plainly, was proof of the white man's cannibalism.

But others saw nothing of the sort. They had a ready explanation that fitted the customs of their tribes:

"These must be the two brothers and the sister of the new king of this country. In our land, too, the new king, in slaying his brothers and sisters, who might be rivals to his throne, burns them, for royal blood must not be spilled upon the ground."

And certain Mohammedans declared: "It is thus that the dogs of Christians sacrifice human beings to their gods."

And as the clanking centipede crawled past the Place d'Armes, it muttered and complained its deep ignorance.

Contrast the fortunate position of the modern educated white who can dip into old historical records and see that these burning Negroes are neither proof that the whites offer up human sacrifices to their gods, nor proof that they consume human flesh, nor proof that they do not know how to cook their meat.

Yes, fortunate is the student of history who, with documents in hand, can declare: Here in these three Negroes burnt at the stake is proof of the white man's indulgence.

Yes, the white man's indulgence.

Stop being sentimental. Don't let pity blind you. Your heart must not be your judge.

Study history objectively, from documents.

But you can't study the actual legal documents on this case for the official papers of *Saint-Domingue* were largely destroyed every few years. Time and time again we find an entry in the court records: "Burnt the papers relating to Negroes, along with other useless documents."

But we can go to the volumes of letters of Ordinator Lambert. In the hundreds of letters he wrote we will not find more than four or five references to the Negroes. You might as well search for references to oxen or any other animal.

Here, however, are the references we find: ". . . we condemned a Negro and a Negress to be burnt alive for having used poison. . . .

"Yesterday we did the same to another Negress, and also condemned a Negro to have his bones broken. . . .

"Last week we had a Negress burnt for poisoning and there are more in prison who will suffer the same fate."

That's all one can find in three volumes of letters, except for the following illuminating comment:

". . . we have reasons for believing that the cause of all this is the too many liberties allowed the Negroes."

There you have it! And contrast that intelligent analysis with the ignorant comments of the Negroes.

Since Ordinator Lambert does not trouble to expand his thesis, I shall do it here in accordance with the arguments developed by other contemporaries.

The indulgent white master promises a Negress who has borne him a child that he will free her in his will.

The informed Negress at once schemes to poison her kind master and thus hasten his demise and her freedom. For that reason testamentary manumission was frowned upon, and even legally forbidden at times.

Another indulgent master, an absentee owner, is going to Paris and will leave an overseer in charge, that is to say, a man who will strive to grind out a little extra profit for himself. Quickly a wise witch-doctor on the plantation poisons a hundred slaves, or a hundred head of cattle, ruins the good master, and prevents his departure.

No, one can't be good to a nigger. The niggers themselves say: "If you stoop to pet a dog, he'll lick you on the mouth."

Of course, there's the possibility that the white master did not die of poison. That the slaves or the cattle died of some obscure epidemic. But that's another matter and hardly worth going into, seeing that it would lead us astray into the whole subject of whether it's right or wrong to punish a Negro for a crime he did not commit, for example, to lynch a nigger who did or did not rape a certain girl.

I beg the reader's pardon. That was an anachronistic slip. This is a novel about an eighteenth century Negro. Today the black man is everywhere free and equal to the white.

6

His Majesty hereby orders, that any free Negroes who conceal fugitive slaves, shall be deprived of their liberty and sold conjointly with their families.

Moreau de Saint-Méry, famous eighteenth-century lawyer of Saint-Domingue and Paris, said of the Galifet plantation that its sugar was renowned for its sweetness.

Elsewhere he mentions the fact that the death rate of the Negroes on the Galifet plantation was higher than on any other plantation in the north of the island.

Could it be that the high death rate made the sugar sweeter?

Nonsense!

The high death rate had nothing to do with that. The high death rate was due to the fact that the Galifet plantation was low and damp, and, while the sugar cane grew sweet on its rich soil, the niggers died fast.

And yet, though the death rate was seven to nine per cent a year, there arose in the late eighteenth century a proverb: Happy as a Negro on the Galifet plantation.

Can it be that they were happier to be dead quicker?

Nonsense!

It was only that Babouk became one of the number, and that as long as their short lives might last, they were happier for his presence.

The Galifets did not live in Saint-Domingue. They lived in the center of culture and civilization, Paris, and were content to leave Monsieur Odeluc in charge, confident that their yearly income was safe in his hands, what with the sugar on their lands being renowned for its sweetness and no one being able to see or taste any nigger-blood in it.

Indeed, Monsieur Odeluc, young though he was, had excellent notions. He was imbued with the spirit of enlightenment and humanitarianism that characterized the second half of the eighteenth century. He used to say:

"You can never properly season a black that's over twenty-one. You can't expect to transplant a Negro who has perhaps already married and had offspring in Africa. Why, they die of melancholia!"

Monsieur Odeluc therefore bought only young slaves. And the Galifet Negroes did not die of melancholia. They died producing the sweetest sugar of the island out of swampy ground.

From Captain Collard's cargo, Monsieur Odeluc had picked out Babouk and three of the youngest Ibo warriors. And after ordering them branded with the Galifet initials, and signing the necessary papers, he drove back to Petit Anse, while two Negro commanders, mounted on horseback, were entrusted with the task of bringing the new slaves to the plantation.

It was raining down in great wind-swept sheets when the commanders reached the Galifet atelier. The four slaves, relieved now of all chains, walked along beside the horses, their black skins glistening in the wet, even as the soaked pelts of the horses. Slowly the cortège made its way through the silver rain and stopped in the muddy yard.

As suddenly as it had begun, the rain ceased. The earth steamed, and the yard was busy with the newly arrived slaves.

Despite the fact that the slaves had just been thoroughly showered by the rain, they were washed and scrubbed, for such were the orders that Monsieur Odeluc had left, and Monsieur Odeluc was always obeyed in his least behest. And after this cleaning a short pair of coarse, white trunks and a single white jacket were given to each new slave.

Now Monsieur Odeluc himself appeared and appraised his purchase. He was well satisfied. The men were healthy, there was no doubt of that.

He explored their teeth. All sound.

He examined their toes. No cracked skin.

He punched each one sharply in the belly. No, no rupture.

Excellent, excellent. One of the slaves in particular, Babouk, gave good promise. His toes, planted securely on the ground, were long as fingers. His slender legs, his long thighs, his flat stomach, his soaring, gently curving spine, his broad, bony shoulders, his short, powerful neck were so many anatomical promissory notes of many years of hard work. He was coated with muscles as with armor-plate, but muscles so supple that one could poke a finger underneath them.

Babouk's velvety skin seemed to shiver like that of a horse beneath Monsieur Odeluc's touch. And when Monsieur Odeluc awarded him the white planter's highest sign of approval, that is to say, spat in his face, Babouk ducked sharply. His head seemed to want to tuck itself into his body, turtle-wise.

Not that he thought of Monsieur Odeluc's sharply propelled saliva either as an insult or as a mark of approbation. He construed the entire examination differently. He had not forgotten the nigger-taster, nor the roasting blacks on the Place d'Armes.

Monsieur Odeluc, however, paid no attention. He had moved on to examine the Ibos.

Here was a special case. Ibos made excellent workers. But many planters did not care for them because they were prone to commit suicide on the slightest provocation, believing that death offered them an easy passage home.

But a system had been worked out to prevent that, a system so efficacious that Ibos, long held in disfavor, were coming into demand again.

You simply explained to them that, when they committed suicide, their heads and hands were cut off. And naturally no Ibo would want to go back to Africa headless and handless.

Of course, the Ibos just stood there blankly and didn't understand what Monsieur Odeluc was trying to convey to them.

"Haven't we got a single Ibo who can talk to them?" he asked his assistant, and shook his head with annoyance.

"You know," the latter replied, "that no Negro who has been here even six months will acknowledge that he knows any African language. They all want to be taken for Creole niggers. . . . It's a higher caste."

"How about Médor?"

But Médor, when he appeared, shifted from one foot to another and grinned foolishly: "Non, Monsieur," he repeated.

Annoyed, Monsieur Odeluc let him have a cut of his whip just to urge the black on, though he knew already that it was of no use.

"Well, bring out the heads and hands and see if we can make them understand."

From the storeroom where they were kept for that purpose were brought out several dry heads, stuck on pikes, and dangling therefrom a number of hands, tied in bunches.

The three Ibos and Babouk, too (for how was he to know that the show was not meant for him?), looked on uncomprehendingly.

But the lash of the whip and Odeluc's gestures and stormy words may have awakened some train of thought in their bewildered heads. Some train of thought such as this: this then is what these whites do to the dead blacks. Alas! Then neither in life nor in death is there any return home. . . . They stood there, one frankly weeping, the other two smiling, not knowing what else to do. Babouk squirmed.

From this state the three Ibos were aroused by a general burst of laughter from the old hands, who were looking on.

What passed in Babouk's mind is not hard to surmise. He had never worn trousers before. Surely he knew better than to soil himself. No, that wasn't it at all. He had more than likely laboriously reasoned out that anything else would be a *faux pas,* and that was the last thing he wanted to commit.

But the coarse burst of laughter that greeted the sight of water dripping from his new culottes made him at once aware of his mistake, and he was deeply shamed. He ached for the laughter to subside quickly, but it would not stop, for these Negroes who surrounded him had been through this same moment. They knew the shame and agony of it, and this was their compensation: that they could now look on and laugh while someone else had the pain of it. And this compensation they meant to enjoy to the full.

Monsieur Odeluc now appointed four men, four steady hands, who were to take charge of the newcomers and induct them into their new life.

The following days were a great trial to all four new slaves, but not equally to all four. Two of the Ibos, with the natural ebullience of youth, found themselves at once in this atelier of slaves.

The new Negroes, being of course an unknown quantity to the

women of the plantation, were fair game for all. In most African tribes such looseness would not have been tolerated. But under the rule of the whites, immorality was encouraged. It was a sport, a relaxation, that the whites could well afford to give to their slaves, for it cost them nothing (at least so they figured), and in return it so occupied the spare time of the blacks to the exclusion of all else that it kept them out of mischief, such as rebellion or flight.

There was, therefore, a rush of the female sex upon the new men. This did not please the old slaves at all, for women were scarce on all plantations. There were decidedly not enough bodies to satisfy all the male appetites, especially when the white men, too, had to be supplied, and of course selected the youngest and most vigorous.

Fights, verbal mostly, but some coming to blows, were in order around the fires that evening, but the women had their way, at least with the two Ibos, who, plied with stolen liquor, actually grew jolly and managed gradually to wean the third Ibo away from his sorrow and into the play along with them.

The women would have fought, too, and even more especially to see who should have Babouk, but by his demeanor he made it so evident that he wanted none of them that, in pique, they left him severely alone.

Médor, his tutor, was supposed to feed him and see to his comforts, but Médor had his own troubles. And Babouk was a difficult problem.

To begin with, he would not drink any liquor. Nor would he touch any food. When urged, he attempted a bite or two, but his throat was painfully constricted and he could not force the bolus down. At last he spat it out and, squatting, his back to the wall of a hut for protection, he looked out warily and mournfully toward the hills.

The scalloped outline of the hills, now melting into the evening sky, deepened his homesickness. The profile of the ridges, though sharper and higher, was nevertheless so reminiscent of the profile of certain hills near his home that for a moment he wondered if he might not be close to his own folk.

He could picture, beyond those hills, his familiar native village, the evening fires, the homely tasks, the banter, the boasting . . . and

Niati, moving about now in the light of the flames, now in the darkness. . . .

An old, white-polled woman, seeing him so forlorn, took pity on him. She squatted near him and grinned over to him with friendly invitation. Her face was wrinkled like old leather, especially around her lips, since her teeth had all dropped out, except for three or four worn yellow fangs, still leaning this way and that in her mottled brown and pink gums.

She held a salted cod in her sweaty palm, a delicacy she preferred above all things, and for which she had often given her body in the days when she had something more to give than crushed brown bags for breasts and a spine and hips too stiff to squirm in the act of love.

But being kind-hearted she was very willing to share her fish and even offered the new slave the head half, the best part of all.

He would have none of it.

Perhaps at first his refusal pleased her, for she worked hard at the market on Sundays, her one day off, to buy herself her beloved fish. But suddenly she caught sight of certain small cicatrices on Babouk's cheek, and her memory began to stir strangely.

Many, many years ago, as a little girl, she had come from the same tribe as this man. She began to rack her brain in vain to remember the words of polite greeting she had once been taught to use. And try as she would, she could not remember a certain song. . . .

She covered her face with her hand and meditated. Not a single word could she form. But the effort evidently brought back a flood of memories, for she sat there for a long while, the two halves of her salted cod clasped in one hand, the other hiding her face, and she did not move.

Then she clicked her tongue impatiently against her bare gums. There was so much she would have liked to ask this man. Embarrassed, sensing perhaps that her failure to remember her childhood speech was a matter of some shame, she began to mouth meaningless phrases into the palm of her hand and grin through the bars of her fingers.

And again, generously, she brandished her fish toward Babouk, but inasmuch as he made no motion to accept it she pushed out the tip of her tongue between her fingers and passed her fish over it. The crystalline deposit of salt was refreshing. She smacked her lips, craved more, and was soon frankly munching away at her delicacy.

To Babouk nothing was right. If only someone had begged him to tell a story. If only his lungs could find here a breath of the odor he craved. An odor of home. The familiar air he had breathed all his life.

If only he could believe what Gmara had so often assured them: that he was not to be eaten. But why then this latest proof of the white man's intention, this poking about in his flesh, this spitting in his face, this exhibition of heads and hands.

He minded neither work nor death. Of work, such as he was to experience here on the Galifet plantation, he knew nothing, but of work, lazy, slovenly work as he knew it in Africa, he had no great fear. Neither did he fear death, for he knew that his soul would survive. Indeed it was because he knew that his soul would survive that he feared to be divided into pieces and consumed by different persons, who would greedily absorb various bits of his soul.

That worried him, and the more he thought it over, the more constricted grew his reasoning, the tighter his gut, as if each thought about his fate laced itself around his intestines and knotted them.

Médor, a mild and willing black, to whom Babouk had been assigned, showed his pupil into the hut which they were to share, and pointed out the woven mat heaped with leaves and rags which was to be his couch.

But Babouk could not sleep.

As for Médor, he had private and important business. He had first to scrape lightly over the damp ground and gather up the thin layer of white salt that exuded therefrom. This saltpeter, gray, even brown, from the dirt that was picked up with it, he swallowed greedily.

A number of the slaves practiced and taught others this habit, though many more warned them against it, pointing out that the first symptom would be the inability to embrace a woman.

But those whose despondency was such that the attraction of women could no longer cure it resorted to earth-eating.

Then one no longer hated the morning gong. One rose and went to work.

And work was no trouble. One performed one's tasks diligently, albeit slowly.

Hunger and tiredness were things of the past. One labored on, caring for nothing, lacking the desire for either food, or rest, or woman.

No longer did the commander's lash fall on one's back. On the contrary, one was praised, although now and then the master stopped suspiciously and wondered at the lack-luster eyes, the skeleton body.

"Here, there, you! Look at me! Are you eating dirt?"

"Oh, no. Oh, no. I never eat dirt."

And so one worked on, until one day, not many months later, one did not wake up from sleep.

On many a plantation one could see these emaciated figures. Their eyes were dull and unseeing. Their skins were hot in the sun, cool in the shade, never wet with perspiration. The dust clung to them and they did not crave to wash it off.

The night did not bring them any great desire to sleep. They dozed, or walked about. And yet in the morning they were not tired.

From the presence of these dried, dusty skeletons walking along, shoulders bowed, arms dangling, children fled in terror. "Zombie!" they cried, remembering the tales their elders told of horrible men that were neither alive nor dead, but corpses dug up from graves and made to work.

"Zombie!" A creole corruption of the French meaning "the shadow of himself."

That was what Médor was. A zombie!

In the morning Médor should have begun Babouk's gradual introduction to work, which would last one or more months, but a gang of rowdy slaves wanted to amuse themselves with Babouk, and Médor lacked the will to resist.

So Babouk was brought to the brick pile and made to transport bricks in a wheelbarrow.

He stood dumbfounded before this instrument. He had never before handled anything that rolled on a wheel, and he could not understand how it worked, nor how to work it.

He had to be shown a hundred times, amidst the laughter of the onlookers. And surely he was not so stupid that he could not have learnt quickly. But each burst of laughter cut him. He was made so conscious of his inability that his mind simply ceased to function.

He was in mortal terror. He rolled his eyes, and licked his dry lips. Gingerly he placed his fingers around the handles and lifted up. Then he felt the load move away from his pressure so that it seemed to him as if the bricks were bent on escaping, and his first impulse was to rush after them, but that only caused the devilish device to move still faster.

A score of times this process ended in a crash and an upset. Patiently he loaded the bricks back, under the supervision of one of the commanders, for he had no conception of how to load bricks, these strange stones that fitted upon and against each other.

The worst of it was that suddenly, while the wheelbarrow was running away from you, it stopped, having encountered an elevation. But how was Babouk to understand that?

He pushed and pushed and slowly forced back the invisible demon who was holding it back.—And suddenly the load rushed away from one again.

Or worse still it suddenly turned upon you and attacked you!

The commander laughed until his belly hurt. Médor grinned feebly, uninterested.

Passing blacks stopped to cry out: "Look at that bossale."

Until Babouk had enough of it. Terror and shame lent him strength. He stooped low and caught the loaded barrow upon his head and hands and forced it up from the ground, his muscles likely to burst, his upper teeth threatening to crush the lower ones to dust. His nostrils bellied and flattened as he snorted in and out. But up came the barrow, slowly at first, until, half-squatting, he could rest it on his knees, then, getting a new purchase with the heel of his palms under the full weight, he succeeded in jerking it overhead.

This method of transportation, the method of the basket, that he understood. So now he had it, at first precariously, then well-balanced, reposing firmly on his black, wooly head. And he trotted off contentedly, expecting to be praised, and meeting to his surprise with jeers and howls.

The uproar ceased suddenly. Monsieur Odeluc had appeared

with his whip. The Negroes shuffled off as if they could escape without being seen.

That evening Babouk still meditated upon his fate. Though he had been set to do this and that easy task all day long, he had as yet no conception of the fact that he was working for the whites, nor the remotest suspicion that his work was in any way profitable to them.

He was a bit puzzled by the variety of small tasks he had been asked to perform, but still firm in his belief that the whites must be aiming to derive some advantage from him. What could it mean but that they wished to eat him? That answer did not satisfy, and yet it seemed the only plausible solution.

If only now he might hear his chained companions in the hold crying: "Babouk, please tell us a story," he would have dismissed his cogitations and allowed his soul to expand in the warm feeling of power he derived from swaying an audience.

But here there was nothing but biting laughter and shame, and exclamations that were evidently rude jests aimed at him, but expressed in a language he could not understand.

No, he would not eat. He could not touch any food. He brutally dismissed all overtures of friendship.

Then, when he was left alone, he looked on blankly while the slaves ate and danced or played at a kind of dominoes with shells, and he worked himself further and further into his nostalgia, his fear, and his despondency. So that again, as on the night before, he expected momentarily to be seized. But he was determined to fight, and to that end sat with his back to the wall of Médor's hut and glowered.

And again, as on the night before, he was overcome with the feeling that beyond those hills must be a path he knew well and which would lead him to his village. No, not more than two days' journey would be required. . . .

He should not have allowed himself to be deceived, for the hills of his homeland were surely not so steep as these. But all his hopes conspired to make him feel suddenly certain. Yes, one crossed that ridge, and then went up another, and then followed the divide for a day's walking. That brought you to the big river. Once across that and you were on familiar ground.

For the first time in days he smiled, and straightway the constrictions loosened in his belly. What, he wondered, would his people say when they saw him return? What stories he could tell them! He lost himself in dreams of a great feast in his honor, of Niati awaiting him, trembling like a dry leaf in the wind.

He was able to find sleep that night, but awoke long before dawn and slipped out of the hut.

About him all was dark, the many huts of the four hundred or more Negroes of the plantation were tightly locked against the clouds of mosquitoes.

Babouk made straight for the hills, plunging boldly through fields of tall green sugar cane, ripping his way through hedges of candelabra cactus, and then on through muddy fields of indigo, through swamps planted to rice, then through higher ground where ragged banana leaves soughed in the night wind and on until he came to the foot of the slope.

As he pushed his way upward, now through easily traversed coffee plantations, now through dense vegetation where his passage was obstructed by lianas and thorny branches, he was overcome with a feeling of unreality, as though he had died long ago, and were walking in spirit land.

For never had he seen such a bark, for example, associated with such a leaf, or such a flower grow on such a plant.—Why did the crocodile he had seen slip in the ooze of a swamp have so blunt a snout? Whence came this strange odor that he had never smelled before? And the familiar profile that he had seen from below, why had it dissolved into these rugged hills that were nothing like the true hills of his native land?

The joy of escape, the feeling of approaching home, had at first loosened the constrictions of his intestines, so that once again the long pent-up juices of hunger began to gather and rumble freely in his belly. But he did not dare pick up anything to eat, for all the plants were somewhat strange to him, and he would not dare cull any, nor venture to eat them, for it was increasingly plain that these were all magic plants, as all this forest was a magic forest, a realm of magic power cast like a net over him by the white enchanters who were angered by his escape.

If he trudged on, it was only because he held to a remnant of hope that he would yet manage to reach a familiar landmark. That would break the white man's spell, he would finally reach his home, and no white man would ever catch him again. So he stumbled on, footsore, hungry, breathless, unaware that he was three thousand miles from his home, unaware that on all the earth there was not a single spot of ground upon which the ubiquitous white man had not cast his enchantment, not a single spot of ground which he had not ringed with a magic spell.

Toward evening, as he was crossing a forest valley, Babouk came upon a clearing, and his heart bounded, for it was just such a clearing as they often made at home.

The jungle had simply been burnt down for a space, and among the fallen charred logs a vegetable garden grew. Though the plants here, too, were a trifle strange, the general impression was good. And included in that was the round hut, built of thin logs sunk into the ground, and surmounted by a conical roof of palm leaves and grasses.

It was the hut of an aboriginal Indian, one of the half dozen or so left on the island, their existence almost unknown to the whites, who supposed them all extinct despite a rare rumor to the contrary.

The owner of this hut, a scarlet man of delicate appearance, sat indolently by his fire. His dark eyes, mild and dog-like, the eyes of a love-sick youth, looked up without astonishment and without fear at Babouk, who, faint with hunger and exhaustion, came reeling across the open space.

This Indian had seen runaway Negroes before. He did not know who they were, nor whence they came, nor whither they went when they left him. He was content to know them harmless, although hungry for food and sometimes for his wife, both of which he could spare.

Babouk might have hesitated at the sight of this startlingly red man of an unknown tribe, but the smell of baking food was too inviting to be resisted. Moreover, the color of the man was certainly not white.

He stumbled across the remaining space and fell down by the fire. Two naked brown children with strange conical heads screamed

and ran toward their mother, who looked up from her work of
pounding manioc, and, seeing an unknown black man in torn white
clothes, herself ran at once into the hut, calling out loudly:

"Hatuey!"

But Hatuey paid no attention to her. He had eaten already, and
plentifully, from the first batch of cassava cakes, and had consumed
a small turtle and a piece of roasted parrakeet, too. Now, quite
satisfied, he sat resting, and fingered some tobacco leaves, which,
shortly, he would throw upon the ashes in order to breathe up the
smoke through his nostrils by means of a Y-shaped smoking tube.

Yes, he was contented now. The season of plenty was at hand. In
the off-seasons he would not be any less satisfied, even though his
family might not be able to find anything better than spiders and
worms, bats and snakes, to live on, which, with bark and clay,
would still suffice to fill their bellies and give them at least a feeling
of repletion if not a sense of nourishment.

Hatuey's mild eyes looked up from the smoldering tobacco leaves
and saw Babouk, but gave not hint of emotion. His calm features
belied the savage appearance of his head, which in his youth had
been flattened by pressure between two boards.

And so he appeared now, with a high retreating forehead, nostrils
wide open, teeth stained brown from tobacco, and long blue-black
hair falling all about his head. For the rest, he was not only entirely
naked, but absolutely hairless.

His anxiously chattering wife, who now reappeared with her two
children peeping round her thighs, was, except for a tiny apron,
naked too, but her marvelous sleek hair, black as coal, and shim-
mering with a metallic blue, enveloped her in a cataract of darkness
down to her hips.

Babouk spoke now, and the Indians answered, without either of
them understanding a single word. But they offered him food, which
he snatched at greedily, looking up now and then from his eating
with an expression of gratitude.

The Indian Hatuey had returned to the more serious business of
smoking. He laid more tobacco leaves on the fire, and as the smoke
curled up he sought it with the long end of his Y-tube and sucked it
up through his nostrils.

He retained the smoke in his lungs until his eyes glazed, and his

soft skin, even beneath the red oil with which he coated it to protect
it from sun and insects, could be seen to take on at the cheeks a
harsh, ashen appearance. Having reached the limit of endurance, he
expelled a great cloud of it, but at once sucked up some more.

Babouk watched, fascinated. His hunger having been satisfied, a
naïve curiosity took possession of him, and for a moment he forgot
his troubles before this mysterious manner of smoking.

At last, after ten or fifteen minutes, the smoking had its desired
effect. Hatuey's body fell sidewise, unconscious. His wife hastily
drew the limp form away from the flames, lest it be burnt, and
returned to her tasks. The children found a new sport in leaping over
their father's body.

Babouk, too, was weary. His body relaxed and a kind of stupor
took hold of his mind. Yes, he had lost his way and come upon a
strange, kindly people. He would rest and then turn back and
discover where he had strayed from the right direction, then he
would soon find his way home.

Yes, he had lost his way and come upon a strange, kindly people.
He would rest and then return and. . . .

And so his mind went flapping idly, up and down, up and down,
like a palm frond in the breeze.

7

A land flowing with milk and honey. . . .
—*Columbus, describing Saint-Domingue*

It was not without reason that God permitted their
destruction, for they were incorrigible.
—*Oviedo, Spanish chronicler,*
writing of the aboriginals of Saint-Domingue

Around the neck of the stupefied Indian was a string fashioned from the fiber of the aloe, and attached to the string was a pierced copper medallion.

An ancient copper medallion, so old that the worn face of one side no longer showed the image of the Virgin Mary in stiff Gothic robes dandling a little naked manikin: Jesus, whose head radiated a nimbus.

The reverse of this medallion no longer revealed the coat of arms of Castille.

But centuries ago, when the copper had been freshly minted, the images had been clear and sharp, and this coin had hung around the neck of an ancestor of Hatuey, and this ancestor prized it above all possessions in the world. In fact, he had given a thimbleful of gold dust to certain Spanish officials, who in return had given him this medal, and that signified: this Indian has paid his quarterly tax and may be permitted to live.

This was the new law of the land as instituted by the Great White lord Guanikinna, whom we call Christopher Columbus.

A few years before this new law, Columbus had reached this beautiful island, only to be chagrined to discover that the vast hordes of Indians dwelling there were an indolent and peaceful lot, content to let nature take care of all their wants, which nature did with abundance, though she failed to provide them with a single luxury: there were no pearls, no silks, no jewels, no spices. Nothing but a few golden nose-rings.

The tragedy of Columbus is altogether touching. Was it worth while, then, to have struggled all the way across the ocean with a boatload of convicts released from the prisons of Seville in order to find hordes of contented natives?

What would they say of this at home?

Would not the courtiers whisper to the greedy and miserly Ferdinand: "Look, Sire, there's that boaster Columbus, who promised you so much and now returns with empty hands."

There was, then, nothing to do but force the natives to help the Almirante keep his too hasty promise. They must strip themselves of every bit of gold and point out, too, where more of it was to be found. And since they did not themselves cultivate sugar, the Almirante would bring some cane from Europe and show them how.

More than that. For he and his Castillian galley-slaves would not only teach them how to work, they would in addition force them to work.

In less than a decade the island was covered with plantations worked by Indian slaves and lorded over by jail-birds who now styled themselves Dons and traced their mythical descent back to ancient houses of nobility.

And, true to their new caste, they had themselves trundled about in palanquins borne by the Indians, and other Indians ran alongside and fanned the air cool.

And so many of these Indians were there that many planters did not bother to feed them, for if they died there were new ones to take their places. When the Spaniards had finished dining the famished natives threw themselves under the table and wrangled like dogs over a bone cast there by a conquistador.

These Indians were not really good workers. For generations the meaning and necessity of work had never touched them. They danced, they played, they feasted, they smoked, they made love.

From this useless life the Spaniards rescued them so well that a dozen years after the first landing of Columbus over a million had died.

And the rest were dying so fast that the plantations that had flourished for a few years were soon in ruins for lack of laborers.

Bands of Indians, tortured beyond endurance by the Spanish order of gold dust or work, revolted, and had to be exterminated.

Smallpox, measles, dysentery cleared off the remnants.

It must be admitted that the natives were heathenish, slothful, ignorant, sexually depraved, and had to be cleared away before the advance of the pure whites.

Their ignorance is delightfully illustrated by the story of how the Spanish missionaries were unable to teach them the necessity of clothes to hide their nakedness.

They pointed to the crucifix and wondered innocently: "And this naked man on the cross, he taught you that it is a sin to go naked?"

For a while the ruined planters sought to enlist workers among the Indians of Cuba and Puerto Rico. They pictured to these gullibles the unearthly delights that were to be enjoyed as servants of the Spaniards.

But such tricks could not last, for Cuba was too close to Saint-Domingue, and news of the real conditions leaked across the windward passage and were bruited about.

Then, it is said, though on poor authority, that the good Bishop Las Casas, disconsolate over the fate of his beloved Indians, advised that Negroes be imported from Africa.

The business world was ready to save the Indians.

The right to send Negro slaves to Saint-Domingue was acquired as a monopoly by Dutch capitalists, who sold the privilege to Genoese capitalists for 25,000 ducats.

And business was so brisk that eleven years later the island could boast of a Negro rebellion. The first on the soil of the New World.

And, properly enough, on the plantation of Don Diego Columbus, son of the great discoverer.

By that time the Almirante was dead.

On his tomb had been placed this sentence, not meant in dispraise: "For him the known world was not enough, he added a new one to the old, and gave to heaven countless souls."

Among these countless souls, the Indians of the island called Haiti, or Hispaniola, or Santo Domingo, or Saint-Domingue, were the first to knock at the gates of Paradise.

The French colonists often came across skeletons of them, or remains of their pottery or idols, when gangs of black slaves dug foundations for roads or houses, or opened up new fields by works of irrigation.

The Negroes spoke of the Indian skeletons as the bones of "vien-viens," and in their tales preserved the story of the last three hundred of them retreating under the leadership of cacique Henri to the fastnesses of the Bahoruca mountains, where they lived on for many years until absorbed within the swarms of Negro slaves.

Even in the late eighteenth century, at the time of Babouk, there occasionally appeared among the Negroes a child, usually female, with abundant sleek blue-black hair, with eyes full of a racial heaviness, expressing an inborn melancholia, an incurable nostalgia for a home and a folk that had perished three centuries before.

They were creatures of a beautiful symmetric shape, of graceful indolence. The Negroes called them "ignes," a word that like the "vienviens," is but another corruption of the French "Indien," and knew that they were born to wealth. For the planters appreciated these strange throwbacks as a change from the diet of kinky-haired Congo belles.

And these girls, priding themselves on their Carib ancestry, took on airs, thought themselves superior to the field-hand blacks.

Yes, that was all that was left of the two or three million natives who greeted Columbus: an occasional neat-looking throwback. And then such words as canoe, hammock, hurricane, calabash, and a few skeletons and bits of pottery.

The rest had been ground into gold and stored in minted pieces in Spanish coffers. It is said, too, that the sailors of Columbus brought back to Europe the disease later called syphilis, which they had contracted from native women, but that is probably false.

8

A poor mulatto is nothing but a nigger! While a
rich Negro: there's a mulatto!
—*Saying attributed to Acao, Haitian Negro
leader and rebel who preached a primitive
agricultural communism (ca. 1843)*

When Babouk awoke beside the dead fire the Indians were still
asleep within their hut. He gave them no second thought, but, filled
with new hopes for the day, plunged into the chilly forest, where
each tree as it was shaken by his passage discharged a little shower
gathered from the morning mist.

A whole day's tramping, however, brought him only to final
disillusion. Late that afternoon he worked his way down a dry slope
toward a vast plain, where, as far as the eye could see, there extended
a forest of dull green cactus covering a dusty yellow earth.

Babouk had never seen before such growths, those great columnar
cerei armed with innumerable barbs and those fat opunti bristling
with sharp needles. At first it had seemed possible to pass through
them without difficulty. But he avoided one plant only to slash
himself on another.

There was something malevolent about these strange and cruel
plants. In his weakness, in his excitement, it seemed to him that
these growths were so many guardians placed there by the white
man to prevent his escape. It seemed to him that they actually bent
down to plunge their needles into his body.

At last he screamed out loud and tore back uphill regardless of
the lacerations to his skin. There could not be any doubt now that he
was wandering under a spell, in a world of enchantment.

And thereafter he did not know quite what he was doing. He
stumbled back into the forest, went down into another valley,
crossed range after range, going now in this direction, now in that,
falling into a dazed sleep when it was dark and waking to stumble

on when it was light, while his mind still chewed over the last bitter
shreds of a crazy dream.

One day two black men leapt upon him, tied his hands behind his
back, and prodded him along a path until he found himself suddenly in the midst of an African village.

He was not surprised. He knew it was not real, but it was magic,
and magic more powerful than reality.

He would struggle no more.

He remained docile, hanging his head in silence, while the chief
and the elders of the village discussed his case and repeatedly
examined the great brand-mark on his chest to determine its fresh-
ness.

Yet precisely here he should have struggled, here he should have
pleaded, for here were men like himself, slaves who had run away
from their masters. Had he begged them, there was much they could
have done for him.

But he did not know that these Negroes were free men, slaves or
descendants of slaves, who had escaped to this region and had
resisted all efforts of the whites to force them back into slavery.

Maroons, they were called, and they were a natural accompaniment to slavery, being found in English Jamaica, in Dutch Guiana, in
Spanish Cuba. For wherever the whites were unable to slaughter or
recapture their fugitive slaves, they did the next best thing: they
agreed to consider the maroons as free and independent provided
they would cease their depredations on the white man's fields and
promise to return all runaway slaves that came their way.

In short, since it was too costly to reenslave them, they might have
their freedom provided they would not interfere with business. . . .

Secretly, of course, these maroons aided many an escaped slave,
particularly women. Among the male runaways they preferred to aid
Creole slaves who had no brand-mark and thus could be passed off
as old members of the maroon tribes. Or else they might enlist the
support of the plantation slaves, who would diligently spread a
rumor of cannibalism, vague stories of men who were eaten in
savage religious rites, and behind this veil of lies, which the gullible
whites took for truth, a slave might disappear without fear of too
much active search.

But of a recently imported slave, whose mark was so evidently new—of him the maroons determined to make an example of their loyalty to the white man's treaty.

And proudly they marched Babouk down to the very last range of mountains before the great Northern Plain and presented him to Lieutenant Macnamara, who with his company of mulatto soldiers was just then out on his weekly expedition, beating the countryside for runaway slaves.

Like some gay tropical bird was Lieutenant Macnamara in his uniform of white and scarlet and gold. With a little smile of tolerance he held out to the chief of the maroons his jeweled snuffbox. The lid, presenting a shepherd and a shepherdess in silks and laces flirting in an idyllic pastoral landscape, held for a moment the chief's nervously shifting eyes, eyes of which the whites had been tinted as with tobacco juice.

It is probable that his eyes, unaccustomed to focusing on miniatures, saw nothing. He shifted about awkwardly on his tremendous feet, his horrible, loathsome feet that were as broad as they were long, and the dark skin of which was cracked like that of some swamp beast.

And indeed for many years he had been a swamp beast inhabiting the swamp of a plantation and cultivating rice and indigo. And his corrugated back revealed clearly that he had not been a good slave, and that the commander had had to resort to the whip all too frequently.

One of the lieutenant's daintily gloved fingers touched a spring and the pastoral lid snapped back.

The Negro chief leaped backward, startled.

And the lieutenant laughed, exhibited the contents, and offered the chief a pinch.

Then the chief laughed too, hoarsely, and found in his great nostrils room for the entire contents of the snuffbox.

After several loud sneezes, he spoke out gravely: "We have brought you this runaway slave; we always do, for we obey the treaty we made with you."

And he motioned his men to deliver up Babouk.

Lieutenant Macnamara thanked the chief and ordered his men curtly: "Fasten him up there, at that post, next to the others."

His mulattoes, in coffee-colored uniforms, thereupon seized

young Babouk, forced his head down against the post until one of the men could reach the black ear and, holding it fast, could drive a heavy nail through it and thus affix it to the post.

A shudder traversed Babouk, but he remained silent. A moment later, however, he began to whimper, whimper like a puppy left out in a cold rain, whimper so dolefully that it became necessary to silence him with a couple of blows.

One of the two other runaways tried to explain to Babouk that by hugging the post in his arms one could prevent the nail from pulling on the ear: "See, do it this way," he explained kindly, "as I do."

But Babouk did not understand.

The chief and his men looked on and said nothing, but the manner in which they instinctively moved toward each other, as if they meant to stand back to back and sell their lives dearly, revealed their fear of the white man's unstable temper.

As soon as politeness permitted, they were off to their hills again, yearning deeply for the quiet and peace of their village, which to them seemed like an island of orderliness and safety amidst the perpetual disorder, the unceasing alarms, the constant strife of the white man's land.

Lieutenant Macnamara sent off a messenger to *la grande place,* the largest of the three Galifet plantations, to apprize Monsieur Odeluc that one of his slaves had been captured and was being held for him.

The lieutenant meanwhile went up to the habitation of a nearby coffee planter, proposing to drop in for a bite. He left his men to take their ease and consume what food they had brought along.

For a moment the mulattoes were silent, feeling still the oppressive presence of their lieutenant lingering about.

Until one of them exclaimed bitterly: "It wouldn't do to invite us up to his coffee planter. We're only the white man's bastards!"

That was the signal for them to open up their wounds afresh and exhibit all their festering sores dripping with the pus of hatred.

"This," they said, pulling with disgust at their uniforms, "is all that is allowed us. Condemned to be common soldiers forever."

"You forget that we can run brothels and stock them with our sisters who are so much appreciated by the whites."

"Yes, those are the professions open to our kind. To be whores and common soldiers. For the whites are mortally afraid of us and dare not let us be lawyers or doctors or teachers."

"Patience, friends, our day is coming. We are destined to rule here yet. Yes, the day is coming when that law which reads: 'If a free man of color dare strike a white, whatever the provocation, his right hand shall be cut off,' will be altered to read: 'If a free white man dare strike a man of color, whatever the provocation, his head shall be struck off!'

"Yes, his head!" he repeated vehemently.

"It will never come," said one of them, bitterly, hopelessly.

"Ah, but it will," the other exulted, "it will! Why, the thing is plain. We are destined to rule here and indeed in all these West Indian countries. For of the whites who come here from Europe the majority cannot stand the climate. Fever lays them low.

"As for the blacks, they die off so fast and reproduce so slowly that if thirty or forty thousand weren't imported every year there would soon be not another black left here.

"But as for us? We are long-lived, healthy, active, immune to fevers. And as intelligent as the whites.

"Our race does not come from abroad, but was born here, created here.

"This is our native land, our home. All the whites yearn to go back to France, and the Negroes long for Africa. But this is our country.—Yes, and some day it will truly be ours!"

For a moment the speaker was silent, under the spell of his own evocation. Then he growled: "Ah, then let me hear a white say to me: *relatives on the coast!* and, by God, yes, by God, I'll rip his eyes out! Tear his eyes out with a corkscrew, as if they were corks!"

The image was too vivid and too ghastly to permit anyone to say anything for a little while. Then someone gave a little snort of irony and remarked quietly, drily:

"Why should you be so terribly ashamed of having relatives on the coast of Africa, and not at all ashamed of your relatives on the coast of Europe?

"It seems to me, my dear fellow, that what we lack is money. Do not our wealthier colored Creoles go to France, to live in luxury and respect? Our trouble is not that we are part white or part black, but that we are poor. Yes, for if we were rich we would have power, and if we had power we would make the laws, and I assure you the laws we would frame would be in favor of ourselves."

Whereupon the discussion broke out afresh.

In the afternoon, after lunch and siesta, Monsieur de Bérigny, Monsieur Duplessis, and Monsieur Odeluc appeared at the coffee plantation. They chatted awhile with the coffee planter and the lieutenant, while papers were filled out and the various charges made by the state for the pursuit of runaways were taken care of.

Then they all went out to the line of posts where the culprits stood with their nailed ears.

The mulattoes came to attention, slowly, sullenly.

One of them, whose duty this was, followed the company to the line of posts prepared with his sharp machete to release the captured slave to the custody of his master. The releasing took place by the simple method of slicing off the ear that held the black to the post.

And by this simple procedure was the law, that punished a first attempt at escape by the loss of an ear, satisfied.

The first man, Monsieur Duplessis' slave, received his punishment without a murmur, though the mixture of salt and pepper that was rubbed into his wound made him screw up his face so tightly that tears were pressed from his eyes.

It was the second man, he who had advised Babouk to hug the post, who was making all the noise. Even before the mulatto approached him, he had begun to scream: "How shall I carry my *petun*? How shall I carry my *petun* when I am at work in the fields?"

And as the company came toward him, he whimpered to his master in a thin, high-pitched voice that threatened to break: "Souplé, Moussé, souplé. . . ."

Please, master, please! For where would he carry his *petun*, his little homemade cigarette, if deprived of his nailed ear, for already he had forfeited the other for a previous attempt at escaping. Where would he now carry that precious cigarette which he would take to his lips a hundred times, just for the feel of it, but without striking a light to it, for it was meant to be the solace of his two hours of rest, during the hottest part of the day.

"Did you hear that, Lieutenant?" cried Monsieur de Bérigny. "Haha! Where will he carry his *petun*?" He could not stop laughing and motioned Monsieur Odeluc and Monsieur Duplessis to come over and hear this rich story.

Lieutenant Macnamara said, with just a touch of severity: "According to law, you know, both his ears should have been forfeited at the first attempt, and branding with a fleur-de-lis and hamstringing are what he deserves for the second."

"The stupid law," declared Odeluc. "What good is a hamstrung slave?"

"Precisely," said the lieutenant. "And that's why I prefer to have the runaways claimed here, rather than take them to Le Cap, where the full law would be executed. And you know the damages from the slave-fund would hardly compensate you for the loss of a slave's services due to hamstringing."

"I suppose you ran after some nigger wench again, eh, Bonaventure?" Monsieur de Bérigny chided.

The Negro smiled, embarrassed, and hung his head as best he could.

"That's where England does it better," Monsieur Odeluc declared seriously. "They distinguish between the merely recalcitrant slave and one who is driven by his animal passion. And they punish the latter by castration, which cures the fellow without depriving his owner of his services.

"Former Monsieur de Galifet, when he was governor, petitioned the ministry for a ruling permitting us to do the same. At first it was a question of the Church objecting. When that was settled, then the king refused.

"Yes, England has always been far in the lead in the matter of colonial government. Take only the matter of holidays. With her Protestant religion England has so few interruptions to work. Here we've been petitioning Rome for years to allow us to cut the number of holidays, which, we pointed out, the Negro only employs in license anyhow. . . ."

During the discussion that followed, Bonaventure, still hugging his post, kept up his heart-rending whine: "Ah, souplé, Moussé, souplé. . . ."

Until finally Monsieur de Bérigny directed the mulatto: "Just notch the ear so it will slip off the nail.—There now, you have a place for your *petun*, Bonaventure. Haha! But no more tricks, do you hear, or we'll take it off for good."

The men laughed heartily. And it was indeed a capital story. It would be repeated all over Saint-Domingue. A hundred people would consign it to writing in their correspondence, and a dozen books would record it in print.

Haha! the Negro's sense of humor. Yes, the Negro is a funny fellow. Always good for a laugh. Dramatists, turn on a little laughter to lighten up your white man's tragedies! Just bring a Negro on the stage. Novelists, relieve the deep tragedy of your lovesick hero and heroine by introducing the comic love of a Negro cook for her shiftless nigger husband. Yes, and yes, throw in a mammy song to show the sorrows of the Negro.

Alas for Babouk. There was no rich story to him. Not the least little anecdote to save his ear. Just a runaway nigger. His ear was sliced off according to law, and lucky he was they didn't carry out the full law and slice off the other.

And salt and red pepper were rubbed into the bleeding root to prevent infection.

9

We must exact from the negro all the work he can
reasonably perform, and use every means to pro-
long his life. If interest directs the first, humanity
enjoins the second, and here they both go hand in
hand. Happy accord!
—*From Chapter IV, "Of the Government and
care of the negroes and cattle," of P. J. Laborie's
handbook,* The Coffee Planter of San Domingo

Babouk was no longer any trouble. Médor, the dirt-eater, had died,
and his new tutor found Babouk easy to induct. Babouk was docile.
When he was led to work, he worked, when he was led to food, he
ate.

No wonder the planter thought of his slaves and his cattle together. And the cattle had even this advantage that, according to the
proverb, you might lead the dumb beast to water but you could not
make him drink. Such insubordination was not to be expected from
a slave.

Babouk rose at four o'clock in the morning to the lowing sound of
a conch. Even the cocks were not yet awake. At first there was no
response. All the huts remained closed. But inside, the blacks
stirred, rolled over, scratched themselves.

And one by one the field hands, men and women, issued forth
into the chill, starry dawn.

"Hurry, hurry," the commanders called as they gathered together
in their groups and cracked their whips nervously.

"Can't hurry the sun," one of the blacks declared, and everyone
laughed.

Babouk joined the group to which he was assigned, received his
tool, and was marched off to the fields to work, munching his cold
breakfast as he walked.

If on the way there was a stream to cross, the group welcomed the
opportunity to bathe and to rinse their mouths.

Babouk went along with them, bathed with them, and, like them,

80

scrubbed his teeth with the chewed end of a twig, but he never uttered a word; whatever he did was done in silence and sullenness.

At work all the men and women sang, and their prods or hoes rose and fell to the rhythm chanted out by a leader who worked facing the group.

But Babouk did not sing.

Nor did Babouk laugh when the leader's improvisations aroused laughter.

Nor on Sunday evenings would he dance. He remained apart, and sometimes did not even look on while the others caroused. He let his dry cassava bread fall to the ground and his tired muscles pull him into sleep.

Thus days passed, and weeks and months, and still Babouk worked. Now a field was to be planted, and now the rustling cane was to be gathered and fed into the crushers.

But for all his submission, Babouk was not a good worker. Too often, for no apparent reason, he would stop in the midst of his work. Then he would remain idle, in the hot air, sweat pouring from his body, and he the while breathing softly through his half open mouth and looking down at the ground.

From the various fields came the high-pitched melancholy chanting of the Africans at labor, and from the near-by hills, still covered with rags of mist, floated the wavering melodies of the coffee-pickers.

What was Babouk thinking of?

Nothing.

Perhaps he had forgotten why he was working so fast, so hard. Perhaps he was waiting to see if that pressure that kept him bent over his task fourteen to sixteen hours a day was still there.

Yes, it was still behind him. He could hear the commander speaking sharply. But still Babouk did not move. Words could not force him to work.

Then the expected whip whistled around his shoulders. Once, twice, three times.

Slowly Babouk raised his hand and felt for his missing ear. Only when he touched the gnarled ridge of cartilage was he roused to action. His machete flashed again and the ripe cane fell.

He felt aligned behind him the vast mysterious forces terminating

in a man who wielded a whip or who cut off an ear if ever for but a
moment he tried to escape from work.

   Occasionally in the evening he saw men and women grouped
around one who was telling a story, then it was as if he suddenly
remembered something that had happened to him in a dream long
ago. He approached and listened for a while, though he could not
understand very well as yet. But already these French words pronounced with an African accent, these sentences constructed with
an African syntax, made an almost familiar language to him. He felt
that at any moment he might burst into speech himself. Shout out
something to this story-teller to show him that he, Babouk, was far
beyond him in that art.
   But his mouth was shut tight. And instead of speaking out he left
the group and went to sit by himself in solitude and sadness.
   Still, increasingly, as months and months went by, and as his
muscles began to act of themselves and even sixteen hours of uninterrupted hard labor could not tire him, increasingly there came moments when his brain strove to pierce the nature of the forces that
stood behind him and oppressed him.
   But how was he to fit into one picture the various pieces of that
disaster that had snatched him from his home in Africa and brought
him to this life of unceasing labor on *la grande place* of Galifet?
   Why had not only white men, but also brown and black men,
acted so viciously toward him? Surely they were not all angry at him.
Why should they be? Or had all these dark men only executed the
orders of the whites?
   And who commanded the whites?
   Was there not some horrible invisible monster, some implacable
spirit of malice behind it all? Surely it must be so. Was not the proof
of it to be found in the fact that not only earth and sea, but all that
grows on that earth and all the men, no matter what their color,
who inhabit that earth, had united to fling taunts and insults at him?
   "Babouk, you black dog!" so the world shouted at him.
"Babouk!"
   "Crouch! Down with you!"
   "Lower! 'Way down!"
   "Down with you, for you are the white man's slave."

"You are the white man's slave forever!"

Come now, Babouk, you who grovel beneath the white man's foot with your eyes stopped up with mud, come Babouk, look at the beauty of the stars, see God's mighty handicraft! Listen to the music of the spheres!

Let the poetry of Homer, the rolling metaphors of Shakespeare, the cadences of Racine fill your ears!

Come, first show yourself worthy of civilization, black man, if you wish us to admit you as an equal to the whites! Otherwise continue to fill the slavish duties which are yours by right since all higher things are so far beyond you!

Now and then the group of which Babouk was part was sent out to do corvée work on the roads. Then it might happen that a passing slave would rush up to him and embrace him, crying: *"Bâtiment, bâtiment!"*

It was someone who had come over on the same slave ship with him and who recognized him with the greeting that was customary in such cases: "Vessel, vessel!"

Thus he began to know himself as the vague member of a loose association whose membership covered the island and was not merely that of a gang of workers by chance imported together, but a real group of people tied together by a common catastrophic experience:

"We went through that together!" they could say proudly.

Yes, and they had not forgotten Babouk. More and more people knew of Babouk and his ability.

But Babouk could not speak to them. His mouth was still closed, his whole being was still shut up.

In fact, he spoke so rarely that he was known as the Silent One, and by extension the Serpent, for the serpent is silent.—But increasingly he listened. And when he heard something that reached into his heart he welcomed it, treasured it, repeated it to himself, improved it, and then craved to shout it out loud.

But instead he kept quiet.

He listened, however, to the stories that he heard related in the evening, he sitting as far away from the circle of listeners as he could.

The stories were of several kinds. First there were the clever tricks by which the little Negro Ti Malice manages to outwit the lordly Gros Bouqui.

It was under the guise of such stories that the slave revenged himself upon his master. All day long he had suffered keenly under the sense of his own impotence with respect to his all powerful white master or the white master's delegates, the black commanders. Now, in the evening, the slaves salved their wounded feelings by making Gros Bouqui ridiculous and glorifying the lean and wily nigger Ti Malice.

And there were other stories. Tales of strange magic, of horrible deeds of witchcraft. And these tales, too, were directed against the white master. For they opposed to the very real whip that he swung at them all day long a more powerful but invisible whip, the whip of sorcery that was active at night.

How else could a man live on if his pride was never to receive any balm at all? True, time and time again the slaves had seen their witchcraft fail, but to have believed in that failure was impossible. It would have meant abandoning the last refuge their minds possessed. After that they must resign themselves to being beasts of burden and nothing more! So by tales of a higher opposing sorcery they excused the failure of their ouangas, their magic incantations, to have effect on the white man's actions, and they waited for that exceedingly rare but nevertheless occasional striking success that made treasured history and national heroes for them.

And there were still other stories. Stories of death, grim tales of what the dead do at night. Stories of evil demons. But these were simply incidents of their own lives put into story form.

For these men dwelt among death. And they grew both eternally fearful and eternally familiar with it.

How could it be otherwise among these slaves whose death rate was higher than that of soldiers in the most terrible warfare? One out of every eight of them was claimed by death every year, that is to say, the death rate was higher than that of our hospitals for the very sick.

On the three Galifet plantations, on the big one presided over by Monsieur Odeluc, and on the two smaller ones, there were nearly a thousand slaves, and the rule was one or two deaths a week, or even more, since the death rate at Galifet was higher than the average of the island.

If these deaths were mourned, what a constant lamentation there would be, what an unceasing wailing, what eternal and impenetrable sadness. No, life was already hard enough on the living, and the dead were fortunate to be rid of their burden.

These occasions must then be made the excuse for a little joy, provided one could steal or beg some food and rum.

Then the corpse was set up as the guest of honor, and the slaves offered him food, danced in his presence, and bade him farewell, for he, happy fellow, was off to the land of Guinea, oh, happy land of Guinea, land of bright rivers!

Sad, yes, sad is the black man's lot, and that is why he must drench himself in noisy jollity every possible moment. For life, he says, is but a flash of the teeth; meaning, life is but a burst of laughter.

Babouk listened and learned, and his mind grew more and more active, but he could not open his mouth. It was as if his mouth were an old wound, imperfectly healed, with green-yellow pus ready to well up from every break in the scab. If he were to tear open this great wound, what an ugliness of blood and matter must gush forth. . . .

Years passed, and his body grew heavy, chunky with muscles that had learned to function fourteen or more hours a day under a sweltering sun or under a cold, lashing rain. His feet were broad and calloused, his hands were enormous. His face was rimmed with a dark, sparse beard. A white lady, at dusk in the garden, sipping her cocoa from a porcelain cup under the sweet-smelling shade of blossoming orange and flamboyant trees, might well be frightened if she saw such a one confront her suddenly. But there was no danger of that, for the field hands were not allowed into the garden of the master's house.

Such was Babouk when one night he squatted lazily against a post and from a distance watched a crowd milling about under a bower of palm fronds. He looked with a sullen uninterested eye upon the antics of men and women dancing under the compulsion of drumming, shouting and chanting.

He was half asleep. The wavering lights coming from many splinters of candlewood had lengthened to luminescent bands in his eyes. He was about to shut them and doze off into full sleep when a simple but subtle drum beat called out to him, reached over to him with a beckoning finger, and then suddenly struck him, brutally, full in the chest.

He reeled and looked up, startled. The crowd was shouting and dancing as before, taking no note of him who was a hundred feet away and who was known to be uninterested in group festivities.

But out of that noisy crowd came that drum beat, rising clear from their midst, and reaching out to him, and knocking at his chest.

Oh, exquisite was the pain of it, tonic like the keen stab of a knife upon a dull ache.

Without knowing why, he heaved a great sigh and slowly let himself roll over on the ground.

A great nausea overcame him. He felt that he was about to vomit, and he did vomit, but what he brought forth was only noise.

He squirmed upon the ground, expelling the strangest sounds that ever were heard on earth.

From his painfully strangled throat, from his torn, distorted lips, issued not simply sounds but great aggregates of words. All the silence of years was being driven from him by the rush of a vast throng of long-imprisoned words.

He was aware that people had come running over from the bower and were now surrounding and staring at him. But he did not mind. His body continued to twitch and his mouth to pour forth a cataract of words and sentences, not merely in his native African language, not only in Creole, but in unknown tongues:

> "*Eh! Eh!*
> *Bomba!*
> *Heu! Heu!*
> *Canga bafio té!*"

All that his ears had ever heard, all that his soul had ever wanted to say, was now suddenly released from him.

All through the night his body kept pouring out its surcharge of words. Gradually the crowd around him diminished and went off to seek its sleep. Only a kind-hearted woman, Nara, remained near him and bathed his head with water, and now and then an old man with a round white beard came over to him and put an evil-smelling paste to his nose, which he hastily brushed aside. And still his body rolled, bent and snapped like a bow, and still words tumbled from his mouth.

Babouk's reputation was made now, and great things were to be expected of him. He who had been so silent for years now spoke fluently. He had been possessed by a spirit, and perhaps indeed by the greatest spirit of all, Damballah, the founder of mankind, he who reveals himself majestically in the forked lightning that splits the dark sky of a hurricane, and more humbly in the forked tongue of a snake.

Nara, the woman who had bathed Babouk's head during that long night when the spirit had held his body, thought herself entitled to consider Babouk as her pupil, for she was a priestess, a mamaloi, and she could instruct him in all the secret knowledge that a chosen vessel of the spirits should possess.

Under her tutelage then, he began to learn the names of the innumerable spirits that reside in all the visible world and who, while remaining themselves invisible, yet guide and control the world. And she revealed to him the many ways that a long line of priests and sorcerers had discovered for seducing these spirits into obeying the wishes of man.

From her, too, he learnt the names of the great men who had distinguished themselves in this field. Of Dom Pedro he heard, who had come many years before to fuse the numerous and conflicting tribes of slaves, many of whom had carried over to Saint-Domingue their petty inter-tribal feuds, into one vast organization that all over the western world should overthrow the domination of the whites.

Dom Pedro had taught a new way of worship. He was remembered, too, for a dance that stirred up one's courage, and for a secret way of compounding rum and gunpowder into a drink that would make the most timid slave able to confront his master.

And there was Macandal, the one-armed sorcerer who had plotted to have all the whites poisoned on one fell night, but who had been betrayed by the baptized slaves who expected to be admitted to the Christian heaven for saving their white masters' lives while sacrificing those of their fellow slaves.

Yes, Macandal and two of his accomplices had been burnt at Le

Cap Français, more than five years ago, accused of crimes they did not have the opportunity to commit.

Babouk was deeply stirred, for had he not landed in Le Cap precisely on the day of that execution? Had he not seen the one-armed Macandal burning, his hair glowing red-hot, his chest ballooned with heat?

Nara, too, had been there, for planters from miles around had brought to the execution those of their slaves who seemed to have power among their kind, to witness the punishment the whites inflicted on rebels and to bring back its lesson to the ateliers.

Boldly, as he was dying in the flames, Macandal had sung the song of death to the whites. *"Eh! Eh! Bomba! Heu! Heu! Canga bafio té."* Babouk, too, had sung it on the night of his possession. Where had he learnt it?

"Macandal told us that he would never die, that the whites could not kill him," said Nara, "but that his spirit would pass into that of a mosquito and that he would never cease to torment the whites."

And Babouk remembered, or thought he remembered: "There were clouds of mosquitoes about. I recall it well. We were constantly slapping ourselves."

"I would rather think," said Nara, "that he meant that the whites could never kill our desire for vengeance. And I would rather think, too, that his spirit passed into you, for you sang his song without ever having learnt it."

But as a pupil Babouk proved to be a disappointment. He tended to rebound from his former sullenness and struck out to enjoy the life of a slave who has accepted his lot and makes the best of it.

He no longer frankly stopped work in the fields when his thoughts weighed upon him. Instead he managed to break his tool and was allowed time off to repair it or to fetch another. Or else he counterfeited illness.

If discovered in an intrigue of this sort, he accepted the resulting beating as a natural hazard to which he had exposed himself.

He no longer glared darkly at the hated commander. He smiled and bowed to him, but only to revile him when his back was turned.

In the fields he was no longer silent. He sang with the rest, and even louder than the rest, and relieved his feelings against his master by thinking up cleverly veiled, spiteful things which he could sing against that man, things he could never have dared to speak out plainly.

Thus Babouk learnt the fundamental lesson of slave work: that he who works honestly tires himself out to the point of being unable to work and receives a reward of lashes, while he who is clever enough to labor hard only while the master is looking can hold out to the very last minute of daylight. Thus he earns the master's praise, which, though worthless, is at any rate unaccompanied by a beating.

Babouk learnt, too, another lesson of slave work: that one can prevent one's desire for revenge from piling up and choking one by a policy of daily acts of petty revenge. During weeding, for example, one might deliberately slash a promising stalk of cane. Or one might watch out for a good moment and then urinate on a mound of raw sugar. The sun would dry it up, of course, but a sense of satisfaction would continue to emanate for some time from this secret insult to the master.

Certain slaves found such petty actions insufficient. They had to set fire to fields or huts, they had to poison cattle or slaves. And there were midwives, for example, who would plunge a needle into the fontanelle of the children they helped bring into the world, whether white or black, and two weeks later a child so treated would sicken and die of a disease that closely resembled tetanus or jaw-fall.

Oh, well advised indeed were the whites who burnt, killed, and maimed their blacks for the slightest crime. For slaves were despicable beings who had to be ruled with a rod of iron else they would not work. It was a mistake to be kind to them, for they were only looking to take advantage of your kindness.

To the outlet a slave found thus were added the pleasures of sex. At night Babouk roamed about seeking a female body to embrace. He might have to travel miles to find a free woman, for women were scarce in Saint-Domingue, since the calculations of the planters showed that women, considering the interruptions of pregnancies and nursing, were a less profitable investment than men, and the slave ships therefore brought in fewer women. True, the females

produced children who might survive to become workers themselves, but wise planters had figured out that it was cheaper to
import fully grown slaves than to grow your own.

This, however, left the island deficient in the female sex, and this
deficiency was increased by the desire of the slaves for a home life,
which meant that wives had to be faithful in order to preserve their
homes. The result was that upon the small remnant of unmarried
women was heaped the task of absorbing the love of the remaining
large body of unmarried men.

Even on Galifet, which in this respect could boast of being among
the best, there were two or three unmarried men to every unmarried
girl, while on the newer plantations where nature, by births, had not
had the time to begin to equalize things, the disproportion was often
so great that the planters were forced arbitrarily to divide the men
into groups and assign one woman to each.

And then there was the planter. Formerly the mother country had
sought to satisfy his needs by shipping him the dregs of the Parisian
whorehouses. Naturally he had preferred the black women, and
even at this late date, when there were women enough of his own
class, the habit of reserving the choicest slave women for his bed still
continued. The climate was blamed for this.

There were, in addition, great gangs of slaves, entirely composed
of men, who were owned by contractors and were let out for the
construction of works of irrigation, for special help in clearing virgin
land or gathering in a large harvest. And these men had no other
recourse but to descend upon a plantation at night and, by liquor or
blows or seductive songs and dances, gain access to the women.

Indeed, the nights at Saint-Domingue were likely to be full of
angry, prowling men, laden with the burden of tropical fertility.

Such was the life that absorbed Babouk until he fell in love with
Elizabeth, and in turn found a chaste favor in her eyes. He had
reason to congratulate himself on his conquest, for Elizabeth was a
Creole slave, that is to say born on the island, and therefore baptized
before she could stand upright. That put her into a social caste that
was above the *baptisé debout,* that is to say the imported slaves who
were baptized upright, and of course all the further above a *bossale*
like Babouk, who had not been baptized at all.

On Sundays, then, Babouk and Elizabeth went to church, in starched white clothes that Elizabeth had washed the day before. They waited outside on the lawn, along with a great group of slaves, for the services for the whites to be over. Then the priest would come to conduct the lesser mass for the blacks on an improvised altar erected under the open sky.

Babouk always did his best to sneak up and get a glance into the great interior. The leaded windows through which came a magic rainbow light, the altar with its golden ornaments and its embroidered altar cloth, the painted statues of saints, and the priest himself in his dazzling stole made a great impression upon Babouk.

He was impressed, too, by the white ladies all dressed up in silks and satins, and the white men with their gay knee pants and their embroidered coats and waistcoats from which burst a lacy foam of collars and jabots, and from which dripped an equally lacy foam of cuffs. Black, bare-footed servants in mouse-colored velvet livery handed around trays of chocolate so thick that the spoon stuck in it.

Babouk waited impatiently for this great religion to be brought out to him. Of course he did not expect more than a part of it, for he knew already that he would not share in the deeper mysteries of it, involving the use of lace and silk and chocolate, and reserved for the white initiates.

Here, past this church at Milot, he had fled toward that familiar profile of hills. Such an incense he had smelled in the hold of the slave-ship. In the midst of this deep stir of emotions and impressions he smiled over to Elizabeth.

Inside, the ladies dabbled at their chocolate, admired each other's dresses, in whispers passed bits of scandal, took sly glances at the men, wondered with delicate blushes which of the light brown choir boys were the offspring of the priest and one or the other of his handsome black housekeepers . . . and finally the long mass and sermon were over and the congregation filed past the holy water and out into the sunlight where the carriages were being driven up to take them home.

For a while the priest rested up and reconsidered a few changes in the petition which he and his fellow priests of the island were presenting to Rome to demand the lifting of the vow of celibacy for the priests dwelling in the tropics, where the hot climate made obedience to this ideal costly to one's health.

And finally he appeared in the yard.

Babouk listened eagerly to the occasional Bible stories that fell from the lips of the priest. Certain sonorous Latin phrases he treasured too, but they were difficult to remember.

From long experience Father Sulpice knew that the Negroes loved miracles best, though he did not ascribe their love of miracles to the fact that deep in their hearts they realized that nothing but a miracle could save their blasted lives. He ascribed it to their low level of intelligence.

And of all miracles the one that attracted them most was the one that promised them a heaven after death provided they had been good on earth.

Yes, and nothing less than the heaven of the whites should be theirs if they were good on earth.

Yes, the heaven of the whites.

The mouths of the slaves were agape. Their eyes were wide-open, and over many a cheek tears flowed and mingled with the sweat that the hot sun drew.

Yes, on earth the whites had more, but to God that meant nothing. He judged only the human heart.

Had a black man been good? Then he deserved heaven.

And how was a black man or woman to be so good that God would take him to heaven?

He must love his fellow men, black or white.

He must obey his superiors.

He must work honestly.

He must not be vindictive.

He must not steal from the garden or the chicken flock or the orchard of his master.

He must learn to suffer, and turn the other cheek, for that was the example that Christ showed. Christ who died on the Cross to redeem all mankind, white and black alike.

After the sermon Father Sulpice devoted a little time to those of his flock who had special problems to bring to him.

"Ah, Babouk," said he, "I see that you have still not removed your idol. Come, give it to me now."

Father Sulpice referred to a small serpent of smoothly carved wood that Babouk always wore attached by a string to his neck. Nara had given it to him, and to it he attributed the fact that he had escaped from many a deserved beating, and he was convinced that it had procured him the love of many a woman.

"Give it to me," Father Sulpice said sternly. "It is a pagan, heathenish thing."

"It brings me luck," said Babouk and retreated a step.

"But give it to Father Sulpice," Elizabeth scolded.

Yes, for love of Elizabeth, Babouk would have surrendered his cherished serpent, symbol of the spirit that sometimes entered his body, except that, seeing the crucifix the priest wore, he had a sudden idea.

"May I wear a cross?" he asked.

"Ah, yes," said Father Sulpice, "and you should."

Then Babouk seized his serpent and broke it into two unequal halves and with the neck-string he fastened the lesser half across the greater, making a crude wooden cross.

Father Sulpice applauded. "Some day you will want a big brass cross, then when you have sufficient money you may come to me for it." Not a little of his income was derived from the sale of such holy objects to the Negroes; at times he was even willing to compete with the Negro sorcerers by writing out on parchment special prayers designed to secure a lady's favor, or to bring rain, or to restore a sick cow to health. He felt that by so doing he was not only attacking paganism, but also contributing in a slight way to Christianity, for these prayers were invariably addressed to Catholic saints.

In fact, the charms of Father Sulpice had a high reputation among the Negroes of the neighborhood and even at second or third hand still commanded a good price.

Later, thinking it over, Father Sulpice wondered if Babouk, by his making of a cross out of that bit of polished wood, had not imposed upon him. And he determined to confiscate the idolatrous object on the following Sunday.

But Babouk did not come on the following Sunday, nor ever again. Elizabeth went alone, stood alone during the sermon, with eyes that were bright with sorrow.

For it was on one morning of that week that Elizabeth was sent across the master's garden to convey a great crock of water.

She heard a whistle, but did not realize that the whistle was meant for her, and therefore did not stop until a second, more incisive, call brought her to a halt.

Slowly she turned her burdened head and her eyes rolled around until she saw Monsieur Odeluc at the window-door of his room, motioning to her to come over.

With trembling arms she lifted down her crock and put aside her ring cushion. Then she climbed up to the veranda and went over to the door. Monsieur Odeluc had retreated to the interior, but he beckoned her in.

She swallowed hard, but her obedient feet stepped in upon the cool tiles. Her eyes turned this way and that, estimating the possibility of escape should Monsieur Odeluc whip her too hard.

But he had no intention of beating her.

God, where did those black women get their velvety skins, always cool and refreshing even when they came in from the hottest sun!

What architect designed those perfect copper breasts, what sculptor those admirable limbs, those delicate ankles and wrists, those perfect curves of back and belly!

Ah, do not weep, Elizabeth. From your body is to come a long line of rulers, men who, some day, when the whites are all slaughtered and expelled from Saint-Domingue, will take up the white man's rôle, and despise and exploit your race.

And you, too, Elizabeth, shall have your reward. You shall come out of the ateliers and no longer do coarse work, but only cook and wash clothes and wait on tables, and now and then, as long as your fresh youth lasts, the master will invite you into his bed. For in this tropical climate the passions of men are quick and cannot wait. . . .

10

Pecunia non olet. (Money doesn't stink.)
*—Expression used by a Roman emperor
to explain that a tax on the collection of urine
did not taint the gold in his pocket*

Behold Babouk now, after many years of that hard labor for life to which his color had condemned him (according to the judicial codes of the whites, whose justice, blind as she is, has a keen eye for color).

Behold Babouk in the fields as he makes his fellow workers laugh with an improvised song.

Behold his crushed dark face that has no profile. Behind the deep wrinkles there, wrinkles wherein a constant scowl is seen to be lurking even behind a burst of laughter. Behold his yellowish eyes swimming with a moisture that drips over the inflamed red line of the lower lid. Already the black hair of his kinky head and of his wispy beard is mixed with gray. There are deep black cracks in the heavy blue of his swollen lips.

Such was Babouk.

He was up to his ankles in mud, and there was mud all over his body, for although the sun was out and the earth was steaming there had just been a heavy shower. There would be another one soon, too, and that is why the moment was opportune for the spreading of fertilizer over the fields, fertilizer consisting principally of stinking indigo plants from the putrefying pit.

"Oh, master," sang Babouk, "the devil has been good to you." Whereupon all the workers laughed, for it is well known that the devil's dirt stinks worst of all. But the men did not laugh too gaily or too carelessly, because they wanted to hold their breath as much as possible, for a whiff of the decayed indigo plants was enough to upset one's stomach.

"Oh, master," sang Babouk, "come here and smell how good the devil is to your fields." And the idea of the master coming out in his

95

clean white shirt and his white knee-breeches into this evil-smelling muck was so preposterous that the workers laughed again.

"But, master," sang Babouk, "we beseech you, come out here and smell what richness the devil has done for you. Master, it is all yours! All yours!"

But the master did not come out.

Then Babouk complained. In a high-pitched, tremulous voice, wavering like a thin thread ever ready to part, he complained of the hard work, of the rain and the mud, of the sun and insects, of the lack of food, and the evil smell of the fertilizer. "Ah, master, while you walk among the flowers of your garden, listen to our plaint."

Alas, the master in his flowery garden did not hear.

When, if ever, has the master heard? In all the history of indigo I search and cannot find that Babouk's plaint has ever been heard.

Did the master hear in the days when German woad supplied most of the blue dye of Europe? No, he sat in his *feste Burg,* surrounded by his wealth, and grew fat. It was not until the discovery of a sea-way to India that he seemed to have ears or voice at all. Oh, then he howled desolation against Indian indigo, while his impoverished farmers and his starving harvest hands went to swell the bandit armies of the Thirty Years' War. Yes, then he complained, and the chroniclers listened and dipped their busy quills. For it is not history until the rich man suffers.

Who heard the complaint of the Negro slaves when American indigo cut out India? Not until the planters in India began their campaign against the American planters and used anti-slavery sentiments as one of their best attacks, enlisting the church, the press, and sympathetic old ladies in the cause, did one hear of crimes against the Negro. For this was the complaint of the masters again, only disguised. Then history pricked up her ear and listened.

Thus India returned to indigo growing. Who heard now the complaint of the poor ryot oppressed by the English money-lending planter? Ah, but when a German chemist made artificial indigo, then indeed might you hear the wail of this so-called Indian planter, issuing loud and clear from his castle in Scotland.

Who listened then to the complaint of the worker in the German chemical factories?

But, Babouk, we have gone beyond your century. Your voice is lost in the past. Your wavering voice is lost in the steaming field of Saint-Domingue. It is lost both in time and space. And yet it cannot be lost altogether, Babouk. It cannot die in a void. Oh, no. All the wavering voices of the complaining Negro, be they of the dead or of the living, of Africa, or America, yet they will some day be woven into a great net and they will pull that deaf master out of his flowery garden and down into the muddy, stinking field.

The sun was now so high, the wet heat so terrific, that order was given to halt. The Negroes dropped their tools and retired to find a bit of shade where they could consume their frugal meal. For it was famine time, one of those ever-recurring periods when the white masters miscalculated on the amount of food needed. Then the governor had to open a port for foreign ships to bring in comestibles, seeing that France wasn't supplying enough. But for a while the governor hesitated, inasmuch as food prices were high and purveyors with stocks on hand wanted to make as much money as they could before prices dropped with the advent of an English or Dutch ship.

The planters complained and refused to pay exorbitant prices, and called upon the governor to hasten the opening of a port. But the food purveyors had called on the governor, too.

So the governor hesitated and the Negroes tightened their belts. In one such year of miscalculation eighty thousand Negroes perished.

When the noon rest began, Mozambique was never in a hurry to quit. The others could not drop their tools fast enough, but Mozambique was different.

"Stop work, Mozambique!" the blacks called out and laughed.

But Mozambique worked on.

"Come, Mozambique, throw down your tool! There are no whites about to admire you." So he was teased.

Then Mozambique, who had wished to distinguish himself, was shamed and went along with the gang. Day after day it was his habit to work a few minutes longer than the rest. He was no shirker, not Mozambique. And when the whites wanted a man to run an errand or do this or that special thing, they began to distinguish him: "There's Mozambique, he's a good fellow. He won't dawdle on an errand." And Mozambique, spurred on by this little compliment, far from lingering on an errand, would race until his tongue hung out of his mouth.

And now, at lunch, he would hurry through his washing and his eating and be at his work long before the two-hour rest was over. Yes, Mozambique was bound to advance in life. Mozambique was ambitious.

Few trees were to be found on the hot fields of Saint-Domingue. For the whites did not find them necessary, having trees enough in their gardens. A tree in a sugar or indigo field was plain waste of land and sunlight. Trees were altogether useless. The planters who occupied the hillsides simply burnt them down. The earth was too valuable and lumber could be imported very cheaply. If it occurred to them that bare hills would disturb the water supply and allow the soil to be washed away they dismissed the idea quickly. By that time they hoped to be rich and leave that worry to others. *Après moi le déluge*, says the exploiter.

Here and there, however, a few tall bushes grew and gave the earth a little shade. Around these, and up the wind of the indigo smell, the field hands gathered and pried off the splashes of mud that were drying and tugging gently at their skins. Some went off and returned with water, and all joined in washing hands and faces. Then they began to consume their meal of cold millet.

"Mozambique," said Babouk sagely, "you should not allow these fools to dissuade you from work."

Mozambique, pleased, grinned back. He was a good-natured Negro, anxious to please everyone, white and black alike. But he did want to move up in life. He envied the house servants, he envied the commanders. He had made up his mind to merit advance.

"These fools," said Babouk, "only talk because, like dry nuts, they rattle in the breeze."

Mozambique said: "Of course, of course," and felt the surge of a deep affection for Babouk for having thus taken his part.

"You know, Mozambique," Babouk spoke up, "if you worked through the entire midday rest, the white master could not fail to see that."

Mozambique's grin sickened a bit and then froze. Was Babouk making fun of him? But Babouk and those who surrounded him gave no hint of being anything but serious. Perhaps, after all, it was not such a bad idea. Yes, one really had to do something outstanding to attract the notice of the white master.

"You will advance, Mozambique," said Babouk and nodded his head.

Mozambique's grin relaxed a bit.

"You will go far," said Babouk. "Yes, and the white master will be proud of you. He will say: 'Of all the blacks in the land, there is no one like Mozambique.' And do you know what he will do?"

Mozambique sucked his breath in: "No," he said. "What?"

"Well, you can imagine that he will look around and say: 'Now how can I reward Mozambique?—He is my slave, true enough, but fifty slaves together do not do the work he does.' He will say: 'What if Mozambique should run off to the maroons? Why, I would be ruined.' And what will he do?"

Mozambique looked about and saw nothing but serious faces. But his suspicions were aroused. "What?" he asked hesitatingly.

"Why, he will say to himself: 'How can I keep this Mozambique?' And then do you know what he will do?"

By this time Mozambique was certain that he was being made fun of, and yet so great were his hopes that he asked yet a third time: "What?"

Then Babouk answered: "He will give you his white daughter to be your wife, and you will be the master and we will be your slaves, Mozambique." And quickly, before Mozambique could open his mouth, Babouk wailed piteously: "Oh, Mozambique, when you are master, please do not beat us. We promise to work hard for you."

And with that, all the blacks who had, on Babouk's secret warning, restrained their laughter, burst out pleadingly: "Oh, Master Mozambique, do not whip us. Be a kind master to us. You may have all our women to lie with." And some prostrated themselves before Mozambique.

What could Mozambique do in his embarrassment but join in with the laughter? But his heart was heavy and ached for days thereafter.

"Oh, Master Mozambique," cried one woman, "promise me that you will let me suckle your mulatto children."

And now, as if by common consent, they all tried to outdo each other in thinking up ways they might please Mozambique. This one begged to fan the air cool for him, and that one insisted that he could carry a pot for him to urinate in, for, since he had become a white, Master Mozambique will never want to urinate just anywhere. He will require a pot. And so they went on while Mozambique grinned feebly and did not know how to retaliate.

He munched his cold millet with disgust.

Babouk, seeing it, said: "You see, already he is half-white and cannot stomach nigger-food."

With that Mozambique lost his temper. He cast his millet at the group of guffawing blacks and ran away. But where should he run to?

He went back to his work of spreading out the fetid indigo. He stood alone, out in the field under the vertical rays of the blazing sun, amidst the stench, and he worked and sweated, and in work and sweat drowned his sorrow.

The others watched him for a while and misunderstood. But they made few remarks about him, for another subject had sprung up, suggested by Mozambique's marriage to a white woman.

The question, to which the company had various answers, was: "If a black man mate with a white woman, will the child be a mulatto?"

Babouk's opinion was listened to with respect:

"A white belly," he claimed, "cannot give color. The child of a white woman will always be white."

But Françoise, who gave herself airs because she claimed to have been a white man's mistress once upon a time, hastened to express a different opinion.

"The color of the child is always a mixture of the father and the mother," she insisted. "It is like cocoa and milk."

Françoise was avidly interested in society. She liked nothing better than to discover, by one means or another, what went on in the white masters' houses, and this society news she loved to report to the rest along with her explanations.

It was not surprising that she could rattle off volubly:

"A white and a black make a mulatto. A mulatto and a white make a quadroon, while a mulatto and a black make a griffe. A quadroon and a white give you a mestee, and a mestee and a white give you a mameluco, and a mameluco and a white make an octaroon, while an octaroon and white give you a mixed-blood."

And without a stop she pursued: "But a griffe and a mulatto give you a marabou, while a griffe and a black give you a sacatra, but a marabou and a black give you another griffe.—You see it is just like pouring more or less milk into cocoa."

Françoise looked around proudly as if she deserved applause for having proved her point against Babouk.

Others joined in and said this or that on the matter of the breeds between white and black, some agreeing with Françoise, others attempting to correct her, this last a hazardous procedure in the face of her rapid flow of language and example.

One man pointed out that whites, too, became black in the sun, and that it was for that reason that they avoided exposing themselves. All men were really alike, but the whites kept to their fine houses generation after generation, and so were now very white, while the Negroes worked in the sun and got blacker and blacker.

Another explained that he had seen a white man who was killed by the sun, for it burnt him so badly that he died.

Babouk let them talk on, for he had the patience of the truly wise before idle chatter.

But when he had had enough of this babbling to no purpose he cleared his throat. In the silence that followed, he spoke:

"There are many, many people who are neither fully white nor fully black, here in Saint-Domingue. Perhaps there are more of these *gens de couleur* than there are of whites. And there are a dozen blacks for every colored and for every white persons.

"But though there are many *gens de couleur* I have yet to discover one who has come out of a white belly.

"Yes, it is from the bellies of the blacks that all the mulattoes have come."

No doubt very few of the group understood the import of Babouk's words, but some of the feeling with which he spoke communicated itself to them. And their hearts were opened to receive his final words:

"It is not known yet what the belly of a white woman will bring forth if a black sleep with her."

What nonsense you talk, Babouk!

True enough it is by the millions that the Negro women raped by whites can be counted, but you should know that the terror of terrors is the Negro raper. It is of him that the newspaper headlines scream.

It is in fear of him that the white ladies close their shutters tight and lock their doors; and white husbands clean their guns.

Beware! The black raper is abroad.

The gorilla!

The monster!

Lynch him! Off with his brown testicles! For everything belongs to the whites. Africa and America! Asia and Europe! And women of all colors and countries.

Working in the sucking mud is an unusual exertion. When the sun is already behind the hills and sudden darkness is about to descend, then the commander gives the order to stop.

The men and women would like to droop and shuffle on the way back to their quarters. But that is not possible. They have still a task to perform. On the way home each one must gather a good bundle of grass and other herbage suitable for fodder.

They sigh and set to work.

"Bon dieu bon," 'the good Lord is good,' they mutter, and place their bundles on their heads.

The swift night gathers around them and brings with it a mild drizzle that they welcome since it will wash them clean from the odor of their work.

"It is raining in Guinea, too," they say, and look toward the west, under the misconception that Guinea lies in that direction.

And they stride off, freely, under their burdens, erect, a single file of kings and queens.

11

Twenty-five times before the War for Independence carried on by the States against the British, the Negroes of these States attempted wars of independence against their white masters and were brutally suppressed.

It was Sunday. No lowing conch, no clamorous bell roused the field hands from their beds of woven straw. But they rose nevertheless, all together, startled out of a sodden sleep by the moaning of an interior conch, by the clangor of a nightmare bell that struck as bronze on bronze, yes, a living clapper of bronze that swung with a sickening swing in their bellies.

They rose and cleared the night mucus from their throats and opened the doors of their huts to spit.

As if by signal, all the doors of the many huts swung out into the sunlight and men and women issued forth. For the rhythm of the six laborious days of the week was too strong and refused to retire before the gentle rhythm of the seventh day, the Holy Day.

The naked black children, too, tumbled out, dodging among the legs of their elders. There were few enough of them, despite the promise, signed by the King of France, giving an extra day a week off, to every woman who should give birth to six living children and bring them up to the age of ten.

One day each week. A royal day to add to the Lord's day.

One day each week, to which was to be added, every year, another day so that every slave woman who had given her master six fresh new slaves, all fifteen or over, might repossess her own worn-out carcass.

Yes, every slave mother who had reimbursed her master six times over for the loss of her own services to him, could, so to speak, out of her own entrails, manufacture a new American liberty for herself, to replace the one she had lost to certain white traders in Africa.

History fails to proclaim any Negro woman so unnatural as to take advantage of this offer, which from time to time was proclaimed anew. She preferred to abort herself with a decoction of the bark of the avocado tree.

Many of the field workers moved as if they would be off to work, and had to be reminded that this was Sunday. Then, their heavy muscles drugged with labor, their long arms slack with fatigue, they dropped down in the sunlight before their doors, and remained squatting there, hour after hour, without a sign of life except the slow rise and fall of their heads with the breathing of their chests, and the consequent tracings of their trailing fingers in the dust.

Others, either assigned to lighter tasks, or by years of effort inured to their duties and therefore less exhausted, squatted too, but awake, smoking cold on dead pipes stuck into their mouths, and blinking out into the world with that physical satisfaction that only those who rarely rest can find in complete inactivity.

Some, imbued with the hope of placing a foot at least on the first rung of the white man's economic and social ladder, passed grains of maize from one hand to the other and counted out again and again the sums of money that were due them and tallied them against sums they owed to others.

The hard grains grew wet and peeled in their sweaty, greedy palms. And the slippery seeds, in this fashion imitating real debts, popped out from their clumsy grasping fingers.

They had their accounts straight a dozen times and only began again because the pleasure was so keen that repetition could not wear it dull. Some day, they thought, hugging their wealth to their hearts, they would buy themselves free from the white master. Ah! the glorious life that would be theirs, then, with nothing to do all day but earn one's daily bread.

The women and children, and even many of the men, preferred to line up near the road to watch the procession of the rich on their way to church. Ah, here indeed was a sight to behold! For along this road to Milot flashed by the beautiful equipages of the planters.

As nearly as their wealth could afford it, they aped the Paris style, riding in a fine, elaborately paneled, carved and painted coach, swung on good springs and drawn by quick fiery horses fed sleek on guinea grass. For lackeys mulattoes were preferred, and they cut a fine figure in their brilliant doublets and galloons done in the family colors, with the family coat of arms repousséd on a silver carcanet around their necks.

Why not? Many of the planters were indeed noble, if not originally, then by purchase of a title when flush with money after a good harvest. And what prevented one, here, weeks away from the herald's office at Paris, from assuming nobility even if the contemplated purchase of a title had not quite been carried out? The purchase could wait until this or that mortgage was lifted, but meanwhile nothing easier than to add the ennobling particle *de* and various other initials to one's silver branding iron and stamp one's Negroes and cattle with ten inches more of burning scar tissue.

Little page boys, especially liked by the women, clung to the coach. They were dressed in fantastic Arabian Nights' style, with puffy pantaloons and striped scarves, and a gay turban with an aigrette. Nothing missing but the up-curving slippers, and that was not surprising since shoes were worn only by whites.

As these brilliant equipages rolled past the crowd of slaves, the coachman whipped up his horses. If the wind was coming from the direction of the ateliers, the women tried not to breathe and fluttered their perfumed handkerchiefs before their noses, exclaiming that the air was made intolerable by these hundreds of savages and their close huts.

The household servants, on the contrary, gazed their fill, and would gladly have lingered to exhibit themselves, their jewels, their silver buttons, their ribbons, their bright liveries or their starched white dresses.

There was a brief exchange of half humorous quips flung from field hand to servant and back, and then the gay church-goers had passed, and the slaves waited for the next carriage.

Between the carriages came, on foot or on donkey or on horseback, the higher category of slaves, the skilled artisans, the masons and carpenters, the supervisors of sugar or indigo extraction, the commanders. And these imitated the whites in their display of finery. There were among them a few so anxious to be in the class of the whites that they would reveal a plot to poison, whether true or false, in order to secure a reward sufficient to buy a length of fine muslin or velvet, or a set of gold braid and frogs.

Let us heap our just scorn on such despicable Negroes who go off happy with their reward while in the yard some hapless blackamoor, bound *à picquet* (that is to say, thrown flat on his belly and with arms and legs bound to four short stakes), squeals like a stuck pig and squirms and rears like a cut earthworm, while the lash comes up after each stroke with a bloody length of live skin that is flung off into the dust as the whip falls again.

Our just scorn on such low traitors who imitate the whites.

And with the sedate artisans and the crafty favor-seekers went their pious wives, proud of their affluence. These women, able with their natural gifts to act as mistresses or wet-nurses, were often the foundation of the family wealth. They attempted to imitate the *dernier cri* of Paris, as exhibited by the white ladies, by piling a dozen or more fine white handkerchiefs on their heads and a hat on top of that.

In their voluminous white skirts, their tight white corsets, their lavish white ruffles, the black faces looked out like flies drowned in milk. They passed by demurely, scornfully, or proudly, under a gay hail of derision from the field hands.

When the last of the worshipers of Our Lord had passed, the compound relapsed into its usual Sunday morning state, sodden, dull, spread out in the hot sunlight. Broad slashed banana leaves nodded gravely in an imperceptible breeze. And the workers rested.

"In the beginning," said Babouk, "there were no men, neither white nor black. There were only God and the devil."

He squatted within a half-circle of listeners all hanging on his lips to hear this, one of their favorite stories. For what could be more interesting than to know how there came to be blacks and whites in this world: white masters to command and black slaves to obey?

Now and then a mother might stop to suck clean the snotty nose of her child, in the manner of the European peasant, or to search its hair for lice which she would catch and eat without losing a word, two traits of primitive people who have neither 'kerchiefs nor combs at their disposal, and which, like their dark color, are surely crimes meriting hard labor for life.

"In the beginning, then," so Babouk spoke, "when there was

neither blacks nor whites, God had a big habitation called Paradise.

"Yes, God was a big planter and had a vast number of *carreaux* planted with sugar cane and indigo and great orchards of oranges and guavas and papayas and bananas, and gardens of manioc and of *ignames* and *patates*.

"But there were no workers to take care of that plantation, no blacks at all, for the plantation grew all by itself.

"Now one day God was on the porch of his house, and he thought it would be nice if there were a man who could eat all that fruit that was going to waste. So he took some mud and made a man.

"And when the mud dried it was white. And so Adam was white.

"Now the devil had been watching God, and when God had gone away with Adam, the devil took some mud and made a man too, and this man was white and exactly like Adam.

"When God saw that, he was very angry, and he cracked his whip.

" 'Devil,' he cried, 'why did you make a man just like Adam? Now how can I tell them apart?'

"The devil was frightened because God was angry and because God cracked his whip so loud, and he said: 'Why should you want to tell them apart? Isn't mine as good as yours?'

" 'He is not,' God cried, 'and so that I may tell them apart I'm going to paint your man black.'

"And that's how the black man came to be black."

Babouk looked around, craftily, and paused. And soon the disappointed listeners began to beg for more. Whereupon Babouk, flattered, continued:

"So God painted the devil's man black all over except on his palms, and the devil was very angry and he stalked away and the black man followed him.

" 'Don't follow me,' said the devil, annoyed.

"Then the black man hung his head and didn't know what to do, so he continued to follow the devil.

" 'I tell you, don't follow me! I don't like you now that you are black!'

"Then the black man hung his head again, but what else could he do but follow the devil? Where was he to go since God didn't like him either?

"Then the devil was very angry and struck the black man down. Struck him down so that he fell on his face and squashed his nose and his lips swelled up.

"And that's how the black man is to this day, with his nose squashed and his lips swollen."

Again Babouk paused to enjoy the tribute of his listeners' breathless interest in a tale he had told them a hundred times since the day he had first invented it.

"Now the devil was sorry for what he had done, and he picked the poor black man up and washed his wounds and tried even to get the tangles out of his hair, but he couldn't.

"And the devil thought: 'What can I do for this poor man, to make him happy?'

"And he decided to make him a woman, a black woman who would make the black man happy. Yes, the devil often has such very clever ideas.

"But when Adam saw what the black man had, he was jealous and took the black woman away from her black man.

"The black man cried because he already loved his woman, but God cracked his whip.

"And so the first mulatto was born.

"And that's how it has been to this day. The white man takes the black man's wife and so mulattoes are born."

Babouk paused and then began anew.

"When God saw that Adam craved a woman, too, he made him a white wife. Then the black man and the white man and his woman lived together in Paradise and were very happy. For in those days no one had to work.

"But the devil had not forgotten what God had done to his black man, nor had he forgotten that Adam had taken the black man's wife.

"Now, there was one fig-banana in Paradise that no man was to eat from, because it was God's own. But the devil changed himself into a snake and went to Adam and Eve and said to them: 'Why don't you eat from that tree?'

"And Eve tried one banana, and it was good, and she gave some to Adam.

"No sooner had they eaten from this banana than God cracked his whip and cried out: 'Who has eaten from my tree?'

"And God was very angry and he said: 'Now you shall have to live outside of Paradise where nothing grows of itself any more. You shall have to make your bread by the sweat of your brow.'

"So the white man had to work very hard, but the black man danced and sang all day and all night, and he did not work hard, for he lived in Paradise, in Guinea, where everything you want to eat grows very easily.

"But one day the white man built himself a ship and he forged many irons and then he sailed across the water, and when the black men were dancing he ran up to them and put chains on them and brought them over here where they have to work hard while the white men sleep.

"Yes, and that's how it is to this day."

And Babouk sighed: "Yes, that's how it is to this day. The white man's nose is not crushed. His lips are not swollen. The white man sleeps with the black woman, but the black man does not sleep with the white woman. He sleeps alone. And the white man does not work. He cracks his whip like God and the black man works for him. Yes, for the white man's God has said that man must sweat for his daily bread."

When Babouk had finished, the Negroes began to comment. One declared that he had heard it said that—"The whites are the children of God. The blacks are the children of the devil. The mulattoes have no father, nor any mother either."

There was a burst of laughter from certain women who knew by personal experience that many a mulatto child would not recognize its Negro slave mother, while on the other hand its white father refused to recognize it, too, so that it stood fatherless and motherless.

The Negress Françoise, who was so socially minded, insisted upon her having her say, too: "I do not believe that the black man's wife cared to sleep with the white man.

"The white man does not know how to embrace a woman," she instructed them with the air of a teacher who will impart valuable information if only the pupils will be quiet and listen. "They are all short and quick and cold."

The other Negresses had long been infuriated by Françoise's haughty attitude. "You never slept with a white man!" they cried.

Françoise turned upon them angrily. "I have so. At my former place my master used to want me every night."

"He must have had only one slave," someone suggested maliciously. "Yes, he must have been a very poor white." Everybody laughed at Françoise in order to force the point home.

"He was not!" Françoise lied. For in truth he had gone bankrupt, and his property, land, slaves and cattle had been sold. "He was very rich," Françoise insisted. "He had twice as many slaves as Monsieur Odeluc.—Yes, and, furthermore, I had all the black men I wanted, too." She lifted her head proudly: "We lived *à la matelote*." She meant "in the fashion of a sailor's girl," the term used to describe living with several men at once, the common arrangement on plantations where the number of females was but a fraction of that of the men.

"Did I have fun!" she guffawed and rocked herself back and forth, slapping her thighs. "I had to sleep during the day, I was so tired."

"You were tired from looking around all night for a man. They had all run out on you to find something with a little flesh on its bones. Yes, and you had to sleep with the dog."

Françoise was furious. Everybody was rolling on the ground, sick with laughter.

Babouk clicked his tongue in annoyance.

He did not like the conversation to go drifting away from him. He was very jealous of his position as the leader of all discussion, whether of a serious or humorous nature.

He sought about in his mind for something that would pull the crowd back to him. Now, it happened that he had been working over in his mind an idea for a new story. A good story, too. But could a self-respecting story-teller shout out to his audience: "Listen to me, I have a story to tell"?

No. That wouldn't do. An audience is supposed to beg for a story.

Yes, it was for that reason more than any other that Babouk shouted suddenly:

"Listen! Listen to me. You have not heard the news! We are all to be set free. Yes, it is true. We are all to be set free, and more than that. We are to be sent home. Home across the sea!"

Forgotten were Françoise and her love affairs. Forgotten was every-thing but this. The group shouted for more information. The news spread. Men and women hurried in from their little vegetable gar-dens. The atelier seethed with black shouting, pleading, weeping for more news. And Babouk sat, as unconcerned as he might, and let them plead until their tongues were almost hanging out for thirst to know how this miracle was going to happen, repeating only quietly: "Yes, we are all to be sent home. We are all to be sent home."

Finally he vouchsafed: "A great black king has arisen in Guinea. As great as the kings of the empire of Songhay. Greater and more powerful than the king of France."

Shouts of joy greeted this news. Those on the edge could not hear and had to ask their neighbors, who in turn asked those ahead, who, however, were too overcome to answer and only shouted, so that the hubbub grew with every moment.

At the least sign of any subsidence, Babouk threw another bit of news into the crowd, and the flames sprang up again, and ever higher.

"In the rivers of this kingdom there is so much gold that one man in one week can find enough to buy back one slave.

"And the king has therefore proclaimed it as a law that in his realm every man and every woman must spend one month every year hunting for gold."

The audience danced and sang. Tears flowed from every eye. Men and women and children hugged and slapped each other; even those who could as yet make no sense of the excitement joined in, for their hearts divined. . . . It was as if blind men had been told they could be made to see. That immense black cloud, perpetually stationary, that obscured the sun and blinded their lives, was going to be wafted away.

Only Babouk still sat on the ground. But he, too, laughed craftily, the wrinkles deepening around his eyes, his mouth thrown open so wide that the flat yellow tops of his white teeth were visible sur-rounding his pink tongue that lay quivering in its hollow.

"Yes, this king of Congo is going to build big ships, and he will come to buy us and bring us all back to Guinea. Oh, how we shall dance on that ship that is to take us home."

The entire atelier was sputtering like thick soup boiling in a kettle.

Great sobs had to force their way up through the laughter, making every chest and throat ache.

But as swift as the rise of these emotions, equally swift was the stop. It was especially those on the fringe, who had had their emotions roused before they could discover what the cause of the commotion was, who were quickest to discover flaws in the story. They pushed their way to the center where Babouk sat.

"Who will sail these ships?" one man asked.

"Whites will sail them," Babouk answered.

"Whites will never work for a black."

"They will. They will work for a black who has money."

"What is this black king's name? And why have we never heard of him even from those who have most recently come from Guinea?"

"His name is Tleeka," Babouk lied glibly. "King Tleeka."

"I've heard of him," one rather recent arrival declared quickly, wishing to distinguish himself. "He is the greatest king in the world."

"I've heard of King Tleeka, too," others hastened to declare in order not to be left behind.

Babouk only nodded.

But one skeptic still remained to question: "Where did you find out about Tleeka buying back the slaves? Why hadn't we heard of that?"

At that a mysterious shining blankness spread over Babouk's face. Slowly his eyes turned toward the hills. And then he declared incisively: "I have the news from the maroons. . . . Yes, the maroons told me that King Tleeka is buying up the slaves of the Spanish. Our turn will be next."

What could be more convincing? Who but Babouk should hear from the maroons? Hadn't he run away to them many, many years ago? Had not the whites recaptured him and cut off one of his ears? Yes, Babouk and the maroons were secret friends. One often saw Babouk wandering away at the fall of night and not returning until morning. Where did he go? Where did he go, off alone in the dark? Off alone in the precipitous *mornes,* unprotected except by his little wooden cross made up of the head-half and the tail-half of a snake.

Babouk did secret things. He had secret friends. Now and then at nightfall a stranger would come into the atelier and he would ask for Babouk. He had a letter for Babouk. A piece of paper, stolen, no doubt, from the whites, and on which were tiny magic characters. What was it? A charm? A prayer such as Father Sulpice wrote?

Babouk would hide the missive away until such time as he could steal over to Gosset, one of the adjoining smaller Galifet plantations. There was a slave who in Africa had been a learned priest, a man who knew the Koran by heart and who would not touch pork meat or take even a sip of rum, no, not even when the white master ordered it on days when the field hands had worked all day out in the rain.

This man could read the Arabic characters. Babouk and he sat together under a stick of flaring candlewood and spelled over the missive.

Their day would come! Yes, their day was coming. The day when the black man would rule in Saint-Domingue.

Meanwhile, let the poor folk believe in King Tleeka. How often had not Babouk dreamed himself to sleep with such thoughts! It was the task of the story-teller to pass such satisfying fancies on to those who could not think them up for themselves.

The white and their servants and the upper class of slaves should have been surprised not to see any Negroes assembled to watch them coming home from church. Perhaps they were only relieved.

The blacks had no thoughts now for the procession from church. The thought of Tleeka and their coming liberty was like a ferment in their minds. They could talk of nothing else. And the happiness it caused them remained glowing in their bodies so that, even when they spoke of other matters, involuntary smiles played about their lips. For no apparent reason, in the midst of some homely task that engaged all their faculties, they were suddenly impelled to leap into the air and shout like imbeciles.

Those who, in the afternoon, went to market with the produce of their vegetable patches or with the handicrafts of their off-hours, brought the news to town and from there it had spread to the whole district by nightfall.

Before morning, through the agency of those who went off courting to distant plantations, the news of King Tleeka, mighty African chieftain who was to free all the slaves of the world with the wealth he drew from the gold-bearing sands of his rivers, was well on the way to being known by all the island's blacks.

12

I once saw a Bambara negro receive a hundred
lashes. And though a strip of skin came off at each
stroke and his blood spurted in heavy drops, yet
he wasn't hurt. You mustn't judge by the effects of
the whip on the tender skin of the whites. The
Negro's skin is a kind of leather . . .
—*F. Carteau,* Soirées Bermudiennes, *1804*

"Liberty!"

"Freedom!"

"Another toast to freedom!" Monsieur Odeluc cried. "Why not,"
he challenged, "aren't the New Englanders free now? Why
shouldn't we be free? I tell you, France knows how we feel and for
that reason has given us the Dubuc reforms. But that's just a drop in
the bucket. We insist on complete freedom.

"We can't manufacture as much as a chair, though we grow the
best cabinet woods in the world. We can't refine a pound of sugar,
though without us half of Europe would not have sugar to put in its
coffee, nor hardly any coffee at all in which to put sugar. Why, we
have to send a bale of cotton to France in order to buy back a small
piece of cheap cloth. And yet we are asked to be grateful to Mother
France."

Monsieur Odeluc had touched off a source of such strong feeling
that for a moment there was a deep gathering silence. Then a wit
flung out slyly: "Monsieur Odeluc, we should be grateful that our
motherland allows us to make our own children."

Everybody laughed except Monsieur de Guimpffen, who was the
guest of honor, having recently come from France provided with
excellent letters of introduction. Monsieur de Guimpffen did his
best not to show his discomfort. But it was really extremely hot, and
the heat and the din were beginning to tell on him.

What a lot of noise to make over such a vague notion as liberty, he
thought, happy to know his own mind free from such fuzzy think-

ing. He tossed back his lace cuffs and put his index fingers to his throbbing temples. Really, conditions in this dining room were unbearable.

What a strange custom, so he thought, to have each guest waited on by two or even three Negroes, who, when they have nothing better to do, lean on the back of your chair and prevent whatever small circulation of air exists from reaching your burning nostrils. To say nothing of the heat and odor generated by so many savages.

He realized, of course, that it was all in his honor that his hosts were piling the table high with imported delicacies, that is to say, with precisely the ordinary foods of France from which he had fled in boredom.

But he, having fed his mind on Poivre and Bernardin de St. Pierre, rather than on Raynal, thirsted for those delicate tropical fruits, those peculiar native drinks and dishes, so praised by explorers, and the descriptions of which had always reminded him of the Golden Age.

Decidedly he would not be able to hold out much longer. The shouts of those dancing blacks were a bit too much. And that incessant booming drum. . . .

Why had they brought these poor wretches here anyhow? Just to enrich themselves? What a stupid desire when happiness was so plainly a matter of the spirit. He was glad to find himself above such sordid aims.

The jowly, red-faced Monsieur de Bérigny exclaimed: "There's no fortune to be made here now, Monsieur de Guimpffen."

"I have not the slightest desire to enrich myself," de Guimpffen retorted, heatedly, feeling himself surprised in his thoughts. "I have all a man of taste and education requires, and want no more."

"To be sure," said the other, half-apologetically. "I was only saying that there was once a time when you might say: 'Good-by, dear France, I'm off to America to make my fortune!' Those happy days are past. We are all reduced to penury now. The bankers and shippers own everything here."

The other guests concurred vigorously.

"Their method, you see, is very simple. First they keep the price of slaves so high that we remain above our ears in debt. To work off that debt we must produce as much as we possibly can. Now, what happens? Why the surplus produced gluts the market. Sugar falls. The best we can do is buy more slaves, plunge further into debt, produce still more, and hope somehow to catch up. But it is hopeless."

Monsieur de Guimpffen wished to ask whether they proposed to give up their plantations since they were only losing money, but, what with the heat and the steady pulsing of the drums through his body, he could not summon up strength for an argument.

In truth, the blacks were more than usually joyous this evening. Never, indeed, had they had better reason for utter abandonment to the impulses of joy. After years of forced labor they were going to be set free.

Freedom!

Liberty!

Another shriek of joy for freedom, another shriek for King Tleeka who was going to buy them all free and take them back to Guinea.

They were going to be as free as the whites. They were all going to have farms of their own.

Some already saw themselves dressed in knee breeches, and even in shoes, and lording it over rich plantations with hordes of slaves.

Yes, black slaves and mulatto slaves, yes, and white slaves too.— Why not? Turn about was only fair play.

Aya! How they would crack their whips. Yes, and pick out the prettiest white slaves to come into their beds at night.—Why not? Why should only the black women have the pleasure of experiencing the way of the whites in love? Black men wanted that, too.

Aya! But that made one's blood pound against one's temples! Aya! But that woke up your toes!

A demi-john of tafia had passed from mouth to mouth, had been emptied again and again and refilled each time from a stolen supply. Even the smallest children were allowed a pull, which made them splutter and cough with tears of pain in their eyes, but which also made them stick out their chests a moment later with the prideful thought that they were as good as their elders. And they, too, danced. The veriest babes danced, some as capably as their elders in

all the difficult lascivious motions, as if they had learned to dance
before they had learned to walk, as if they had begun to dance in
their mothers' bellies.

Four or five Negroes had caught great drums between their legs
and, squatting, begun to strike their instruments with fists and
fingers in a complicated rhythm of slow and rapid beats, varying in
sound according to the size of the drum.

Other Negroes, some taking part in the dance, others squatting,
shook rattles made of dry calabashes partly filled with grains of sand
or corn.

One talented Negro plucked at a crude four-stringed violin. And
thus, to the reverberations of the bamboula, the rattle of the calabashes, and the twanging of the banza, the Negroes danced.

They danced the calenda, and danced it again and again. Those
who danced themselves weary joined the circle of onlookers that
stood all around, hemming in the two lines of performers, the men
facing the women.

The cleverest improviser made up songs, one after the other, on
any topic whatsoever. The rest, clapping hands the while, listened
attentively, picked up the words quickly, and joined in vocally just as
soon as they could.

This evening, of course, all songs must refer to the approaching
day of freedom.

The dancers held their arms out loosely, and their hands and
fingers, completely relaxed, dangled freely to the motions of their
bodies. At first they leaped and whirled independently, each one as if
separately inspired and as if having excess exuberance to shed
before, on a change in the cadence of the drum beats, they could
bring their motions to coincide.

Now the two lines approached each other and then retreated to
their original positions. Approached and retreated again and again,
each time coming nearer and nearer, until at last the drums gave
permission. Whereupon, shouting now rather than singing, and
laughing and choking, and impatiently shaking the running sweat
from their foreheads before it dropped into their eyes, they moved
into the climax of the dance.

Male and female met in the center with a resounding smack!

It seemed that it was their bellies which thus slapped against each other, but it was their thighs. They withdrew, pirouetted, advanced, and collided again, and withdrew and repeated.

And as they warmed up to this procedure, the partners, or rather opponents, began to cast rapid jests at each other, hurriedly thrown in between the singing, males taunting females and females retorting, eyes sparkling, skins glittering with perspiration, chests heaving, haunches shaking, bodies near exploding with laughter that was uncontrollable and yet could not find vent, what with the singing and jesting and the necessity of keeping one's balance despite this perpetual whirling and these repeated collisions.

Nor was this all. Taunts and stinging comments were not enough. The hands, hitherto held dangling, began to make gestures that were at first mere hints, but that grew broader and broader until they were unmistakably portraying what was intended to take place when the symbolism of the dance gave way to reality.

And now the opponents ceased to be opponents and became partners for short intervals, their arms interlaced, their thighs still bumping in rhythm with a smacking noise that differed from any other noise that skin hitting on skin can produce.

Their faces met, they embraced. . . . Only for a split-second, however, then the merciless drums separated them. But the increasing tempo of the beat gave them time for scarcely a whirl and cast them back again into each other's arms.

And so on, and on, until the tired bodies refused and dancer after dancer either rolled to the ground and would not rise, and therefore had to be dragged away; or else slipped out of the line and took a place among the spectators, striving with popping eyes and twitching mouth to catch a breath of air, while a spectator left the ranks of the idle hand-clappers to take the place that was empty.

Again and again the calenda halted out of sheer lack of human material, as a fire must die down for lack of wood. The drummers were exhausted and leaned over, resting on their instruments. The dancers could not move another step, and the last group simply collapsed as if by common consent.

But after a brief rest, during which the fermented sugar syrup was passed around and dry throats were copiously rinsed, someone started the rhythm going again. It was irresistible. One after another yielded to its seduction. Or else the extemporizing poet would think up an especially good line. He must sing it. The others catch it up, take to hand-clapping, join in the refrain. The drummers put away their weed-cigarettes, their toes clasp the drums again, and soon the whole group is at it all over again.

Thus the day of rest wore on. The calenda, though the favorite, was sometimes exchanged for another dance, the violent Water Mama, which escaped or smuggled slaves had spread all the way from Guiana to Cuba.—Or else a group performed the minuets and other social dances of the whites. The parodying was excellent and therefore all the more ridiculous. The stiff mincing gestures of the whites, their lofty air of disinterest, their nonchalant show of elegance, their mannerisms called courtesy, all were perfectly imitated. A single banza, skillfully plucked, took the place of the nasal harpsichord.

This sort of thing could not be kept up too long. The performers injured themselves restraining their laughter, especially since the spectators, for their part, made no effort to restrain theirs, but rolled over and over expelling great belches of laughter.

The heat in the master's house continued terrific. When sharply warned, the young lads entrusted with the task of fanning the guests pulled away busily at the squeaking fan cords. But a moment later their tired eyes closed again and their heads fell over on their shoulders. A slave went about wetting down the canvas curtains to provide additional coolness.

A game of lansquenet was proposed, and the bankrupt planters, drawing out purses heavy with gold, began to play for high stakes, keeping up the while a sprightly flow of pornographic stories which, under the influence of good port, were appreciated far beyond their separate worth.

The two women who had been present at the supper table did not share in the joy of the gambling. They had retired to a corner of the room. And it appeared to Monsieur de Guimpffen not a little strange to see these two white women sitting on grass mats, with their legs crossed, or folded under, and thus enjoying the greater coolness of the atmosphere near the floor.

And enjoying, too, the pleasure of having the soles of their feet stroked and tickled by two black girls.

Every now and then the four of them, black and white, would put their heads together, twining their bare arms amicably about each other and whisper some naughtiness or other that would cause them to burst into high-pitched laughter.

When the merriment had subsided, the black *cocottes* would busily resume their duty of caressing their mistresses' feet.

Monsieur de Guimpffen, who took no part in the lansquenet, would have liked to engage the ladies in conversation, but he was frightened away by their rapid flow of Creole.

Suddenly he found himself queried by Monsieur Odeluc. "We have not yet heard your opinion on the Negroes. Are you, too, convinced that, though our labor here furnishes the livelihood of six million Frenchmen, we are nothing but a set of cruel beasts who force the naturally virtuous savage to labor for us?"

"I have not yet had the opportunity of observing the matter very closely," Monsieur de Guimpffen temporized. Then he gathered his courage together. "I must admit that I cannot heartily approve of the system of human servitude."

"Human servitude!" exclaimed Monsieur Odeluc, so aroused that the veins on his temples stood out. "Human servitude indeed! And what do you say of the workers I have seen in France? Those day laborers who can scarcely earn enough to add garlic to their diet of bread. Whose wives must give birth on the wayside. Whose children must walk barefoot in the snow. Who are so miserable that they call down blessings on the judge who condemns them to lifelong slavery in the galleys of Toulons! Have you seen any such misery here?"

"No, no," Monsieur de Guimpffen hastened to say before this stormy attack. "I certainly do not approve of that either. In fact I have long advocated extending to all Frenchmen the benefit of living in France as one family.

"Where can you see a family in which one member is treated to all the miseries while another is heaped with all the joys? Is not each member of a family treated according to his needs?" Finding himself uninterrupted, Monsieur de Guimpffen pursued:

"The small children should play and learn the rudiments of life. The older children should begin to help with the chores. Those in the prime of life should take upon themselves the necessary labors, while the ancients look on and offer the advice of their years of experience.

"As long as there is any food in the family larder, is any mouth suffered to go hungry? Are not the sick and crippled excused from labor?

"In a well-ordered state it should be the same. Upon reaching the age of puberty everyone, male or female, should receive a piece of land sufficient to the needs of one person. This land he may work alone, or, joining it to the land of his wife or family, work the whole in common.

"And so he ought to live, until death, when his land returns to the common heritage, with never a fear of destitution, with ample means to bring up his children, with a roof assured over his head. . . ."

The company had stopped their game to listen to Monsieur de Guimpffen. And he, flattered, strove to convince them of the beauty and superiority of this patriarchal and bucolic civilization of the future: families of gardeners living in peace, health, and abundance, side by side, on their little plots of ground; bearded elders in togas, seated on a podium, allotting to hardy, naked, keen-eyed striplings, about to enter life, the land which the state has just received from the aged who are about to limp into their tombs; and life in the fields and copses, the groups of youths and maidens, their hair twined with leaves and flowers, bringing in the harvest to the sound of song and flute, and preparing for a great village dance to celebrate the end of a year of healthful toil.

"Why," exclaimed Monsieur Odeluc, "it is the very system in force here. Precisely!—What! you doubt it? Come with me to the edge of the garden. You will see your own dream come true. And you will be able to go back to Paris and tell that infamous Society of the Friends of the Blacks just how these creatures really live who they think are being massacred, starved, and worked to death.

"Look at them at their dancing. Are they not happy? It is a proverb hereabouts: happy as the slaves at Galifet.

"Like the Frenchmen in your ideal state, each one receives his little bit of ground sufficient for his needs, which is his until he dies.

"What is his life? At first, as a child, in the bosom of his family, constrained only by paternal authority, he is as it were free. He plays, he learns what will be useful to him in the life he will lead; the master leaves him entirely alone.

"As he grows older and stronger, he is gradually inducted into work. But a new world of joy and freedom opens up to him at this moment. For it is the season of love, and certainly no master ever disturbs his absolute freedom there. Moreover, he is now a proprietor in his own right, for his master assigns him a bit of land.

"Yes, free, and an owner of land. What peasant of Europe has more?

"On his bit of land the slave plants his favorite vegetables and fruits. He adds in time chickens and pigs, and he disposes of his surplus produce as freely as any European farmer. Nay, more freely, for he does not have a host of taxes and imposts to pay. All these are paid for him by his master. He even sells his eggs and his vegetables to his master. And the master pays, for how could he dare confiscate them? Why, no slave would ever grow so much as a potato again.

"And thus he lives, in the field, in his family, among his kind; free, yes, free as far as any man can be, and prosperous, too, if he be thrifty; and to his wealth he adds the joys of dancing and feasting, and the consoling knowledge that in his old age his infirmities will be taken care of, and his children will travel the same happy career as he, without ever knowing worry or want.

"If you could but watch him, year in, year out, as I can, and see him at his dances, see him dressing up on holidays, see him spending his money for ornaments to bedeck himself, for he need never put by a penny for a rainy day. . . . For there are no rainy days for him; these come only to the masters who assume all the burdens and risks, for the sake of a possible fortune . . . that never comes.

"Thus, my friend, does the self-interest of the whites conspire to produce here, where you would least expect it, the perfect civilization of your dreams.

"Look at them! How happy they are. Have you ever been so happy? Neither have I.

"And their labor? Do they go into mines like your workers of Europe? Or climb steep roofs to clean chimneys? Or breathe the infected air of tanneries? No! They work in the sunny fields, or at the sugar mill, where the air is redolent and balmy.

"When you return to France, Monsieur de Guimpffen, tell your philosophers there that you have seen the natural man, the good savage. Tell them that he is truly as happy as they have always pictured him. Tell them that you have seen him and know this for a fact.

"And tell them that this happy man is none other than your mistreated slave of the Saint-Domingue planter!

"What do you say to that?" Monsieur Odeluc pushed home.

Monsieur de Guimpffen said as little as he could, for he strove to conceal his annoyance at having his beautiful Utopian pictures of classical youths transformed into hordes of ugly blacks.

Late in the evening, with torches lit, the dancing of the Negroes still continued. By dint of subterfuges they had laid by a little store of gunpowder. And these kernels, now ground into a fine powder and mixed with the tafia, provided the basis for a *Dom Pedro*.

The *Dom Pedro* was performed alone, each black intent upon himself, each one obeying his own internal rhythm and requiring no external urge to add to the fire of the absorbed tafia and gunpowder. And any step was good, provided only it satisfied the dancers. They threw themselves from side to side; toed in, toed out; twirled and twisted; bent themselves double, forward, then back; waved their arms, faster and faster, as if only the craziest and most rapid motions could overcome that internal itch, nay, that conflagration, that threatened to consume the wretched Negroes.

Wretched Negroes indeed, for this was not a dance of gaiety and laughter. In deadly seriousness, in earnest sweat, with eyes fixed and staring upon the ground, with grave and lugubrious shouting, or shrill chatter, the Negroes danced.

They danced themselves out of their senses, toppled suddenly and lay on the ground like overturned beetles, and continued to dance with their legs kicking in the air and their bodies whirling in the dust.

This frenzy was contagious. It attacked even those who had not imbibed the *Dom Pedro* mixture. Spectator after spectator found his throat expanding involuntarily; from tense lips explosive cries issued. One after the other they leapt into the midst of the dancers and danced as crazily as the rest.

The whole yard was full of Negroes rolling on the ground as if in epileptic convulsions. And that was true of several who were actual or potential sufferers of that mysterious disease. It was therefore not strange that the *Dom Pedro* should frequently result in a death or two. The convulsions led to a kind of hard, twitching cramps. The taut muscles refused to loosen and, with shouts that were usually misunderstood in the general shouting, a Negro passed on. His cold body was noticed hours later. Oh, happy man now home in Guinea stretching himself lazily in the sun!

It was because of this waste of life and energy that the *Dom Pedro* was strictly forbidden. Planters did not intend to lose a worker in such amusement.

Monsieur Odeluc, frightened by the unusual disturbance, sent out one of his house-servants to discover what the noise was about. It was time the slaves retired for the night, else the work on the morrow would suffer.

The house-servant came tearing back. "They are dancing the *Dom Pedro!*" he cried, his face a mixture of fear and cupidity. What would this information be worth? Surely a six-sous piece. Or dared one hope for more?

Monsieur Odeluc's face darkened.

"What is the *Dom Pedro?*" Monsieur de Guimpffen asked.

Monsieur Odeluc's dark expression broke. "Oh, let them have their fill of it for once."

At last, late at night, the Sunday of the negroes was over. It was a Sunday that they did not soon forget. . . . Neither the Negroes nor the planters. All over the parish and beyond there were signs of an unusual spirit in the ateliers. The Negroes would not obey promptly. The whip had to be used all too often to force them to work.

Why, there were cases of blacks daring to talk back not only to the commanders, but to the master himself. Such arrogance must be squelched at once, and radically, lest it get out of hand. For it is not now merely a question of present work suffering, but a question whether the cost of bringing the atelier back to order will not involve the necessity of a severity that will permanently render several good hands useless for further work.

Monsieur Piombé thought he had found the solution to the whole trouble. He declared rather savagely one day: "Well, let me tell you who's to blame for all this insubordination. We ourselves! Yes, indeed. It's all on account of our perpetual talk of natural rights and liberty and the good state. Such talk should be forbidden, and these traveling philosophers should be refused permission to land.

"No, no, I'm not referring to your friend, de Guimpffen. He's just a mild imbecile. But there have been so many others who have come over here to set us right. And we, too, are now full of complaints and talk of change.

"Why, there isn't a dinner table in the colony where the air isn't thick with so-called philosophy, and we planters, anxious to be considered as good as any scribbling Parisian, insist on taking part in these discussions.

"And, of course, the slaves listen in. Why, I even heard of one who was so bold as to interject a comment of his own. Not in my house, I assure you, or he'd have a back like a scrubbing board for the rest of his life.—And the house servants carry this talk to the field hands."

"I think you are mistaken there, my dear Piombé," said Odeluc. "Why, you can't get a house servant to talk to a field hand."

"Don't be deceived there," cried Piombé. "They are all secretly allied. They're all together in their voodoo business. I tell you, Odeluc, we are living on powder barrels and those philosophers from abroad are going to cast their famous torch of knowledge right in among us." And Monsieur Piombé illustrated with his hands the process of being blown up into the air.

Monsieur Odeluc laughed. "Come, Piombé, don't be such a pessimist."

The French employ the delicate expression of the inquisition for describing the process of extracting a confession from a prisoner. They say he is put to the question, which means that he is tortured with thumbscrew, with rack, and with whip.

In the parishes of Petit Anse, Acul, Limbé, etc., the royal officers and the planters met at a general conference in order to discover the cause of the recent growth of excitement, disorder, and insubordination among the slaves. And the above form of questioning having elicited the fact that the Negroes were spreading a story of a King Tleeka who was to buy all the slaves free, action was taken at once. It was decreed that any Negro heard bearing this story should receive twenty-five lashes. A second offense would cost him an ear. A third offense would entail the loss of a leg.

In addition, it was decided that an earnest effort should be made to trace this story to its source, for might not the author of it invent further disturbing tales? It behooved the planters to find this culprit and make a public example of him that should act as a deterrent to inventive minds. But the finding of this original culprit proved difficult, for Negroes do not sign their names to their stories, and by the time of the investigation King Tleeka in various versions had become part of the repertory of every Negro story-teller on the island.

Nor had Monsieur Odeluc any intention of permitting Babouk to be shouldered with all the guilt, for Babouk was still a strong and active slave and the fund for reimbursing masters for slaves executed by the state was for the moment very low. Had the guilty man been weak or old, Monsieur Odeluc would never have hesitated.

A lashing, then, would have to do. Babouk and several of his closest companions were therefore brought to punishment before the assembled slaves. And here is further proof of the delicacy of these French planters, for, there being among these blacks one who was a woman and pregnant, the earth was scooped away from the ground where she was to live to receive her blows, in order to accommodate her belly.

Some bore their lashes stoically. Others bellowed and whelped or whined, hoping thus to soften the heart of the executioner and cause him to lighten his vigor. None, be it insisted, cried out against Babouk, who was the cause of their suffering. Not that they did not know by this time that the tale of King Tleeka was false. But that did not matter. Had it not been a good tale while it lasted?

Evenings when one lay exhausted on the packed mud before one's hut, too tired to care for food, what greater comfort than to dream away of the gold-bearing rivers of the Congo and of King Tleeka who was to rescue his black brethren by finally stilling the white man's lust for gold?

No, no one bore a grudge against Babouk. What were lies for anyhow if not to cheer one before the misery of truth?

13

It is this defective hematosis, or atmospherization of the blood, conjoined with a deficiency of cerebral matter in the cranium and an excess of nervous matter distributed to the organs of sensation and assimilation that is the true cause of that debasement which has rendered the African unable to take care of himself.
—*Dr. Cartright of the University of Louisiana,*
proving that Negroes were designed to be slaves,
1860

The King Tleeka affair was not the first lashing Babouk had received, not by far. But it was the beginning of a new spirit of resentment and independence among the slaves, and, whenever this spirit grew shrill, Babouk was singled out for punishment.

For years he had not thought of running away. Now he began to think of it again. But the memory of the lash on his shredded back, the memory of his missing ear, had bitten deep into his courage.

Yes, the power of the whites, the vast, illimitable power of the whites. What can a poor Negro do against this power? The hand of the white reaches across the seas, reaches over the land, aye and up into the clouds.

April 10, 1784, was a great day for Galifet, for on that memorable day occurred the first balloon ascension in Saint-Domingue, and, indeed, the second in the New World, and it took place on the estate of Galifet in the presence of Monsieur Moreau de Saint-Méry, Monsieur Odeluc, Monsieur Mosset, etc.

In honor of this new victory of mind and science over the limitations placed upon man by flesh and nature, a great banquet was prepared for all the important whites of the region, and particularly for the nine subscribers who had furnished the funds. And under the spell of generosity that warmed all hearts the Negroes were called in from the fields to witness the ascension and were promised the afternoon off.

For weeks Negro seamstresses had worked on the great bag which was not less than thirty-five feet high. Great quantities of gum had been used to make the silk air-tight. And for added effect two French painters had been employed to decorate the sphere.

A special brick furnace piled high with straw and wool bunting had given off such a profusion of hot, smoky air that, four minutes after setting fire to the material, the balloon began to tug at its guy ropes. If these were not cut the balloon threatened to burst them of itself.

Hurriedly Monsieur Odeluc cast a squealing pig and a cock with a broken wing into the basket and the order for the release of the guy ropes was given.

Up leapt the balloon amid the shouts and cheers of the Negroes.

Majestically it floated on the air only a hundred feet above the heads of the crowd. The pig squeaked in terror. The cock essayed to fly. And then, suddenly, poised on the rim of the basket, it beat its impotent wings and crowed.

A slight breeze made the great bag tremble. It began to rise again, but slowly, turning meanwhile and presenting to all its painted decorations as if it wished the spectators to be instructed.

What, indeed, could have been more instructive than these symbolic depictions of air and fire which were, so to speak, the elements of a balloon, and what more informative again than these allegorical representations of chemistry and physics which were so happily united in man's conquest of the air?

Above these tableaux were shown the arms of the Galifet family as well as the arms of the lieutenant-governor and of the intendant of the colony. Finally, a variety of bright and colorful scrolls, cupids, nymphs, and acanthus leaves filled up the vacant spaces most decoratively.

The painters were acclaimed for the success of their work.

The Negroes cheered and danced.

The crowing of the cock and the squealing of the pig could still be heard, though the balloon was high indeed now and rapidly drifting off to sea.

The balloon rose and the cock and the pig looked down upon the island of Saint-Domingue. They saw 600,000 blacks. Here and there they saw a mulatto or a white.

"Those whites certainly occupy a beautiful island," said the cock.

"What do you mean, those whites?" cried the pig. "Can't you see it is occupied by blacks?"

"That shows how intelligent you are. Learn that this island belongs to those occasional specks of white you see down there, and they possess it in the name of France."

The balloon rose still further. The human globe lay below, warming itself in the glow of the sun.

"Now you see. There's France," said the cock.

"All of that?"

"No, stupid. Just that little piece. There, see. The rest is Prussia, Poland, England, Russia. Why, they are so different that they hate and kill each other."

"Really? And so differently colored people live in each of those parts?"

"No, no. How obtuse you are."

"Well, how do you know they're different?"

The cock didn't deign to answer. "There," he said, "now that's Africa. Soon it will all belong to those various parts of Europe."

"And what will belong to all those innumerable blacks down there in Africa?"

"Why, nothing at all," said the cock.

"Nothing?" queried the pig.

"Why, no. Nothing at all," said the cock and, full of enthusiasm, he crowed lustily.

The pig grunted philosophically. And then, very soberly, he commented: "Just like us pigs."

A group of Negroes gathered before the banqueting whites and sang a special song for the occasion. One agile fellow, keeping time with the singing, rolled over and over again to simulate a ball, and by muscular contortions endeavored to imitate the balloon tearing at its tethers. Suddenly he leapt into the air—a magnificent bound—and, with his feet off the earth, twirled around and crowed like the cock up in the balloon. He alighted, but only to repeat this trick again and again.

The whites applauded. The black performers, glistening with the sweat of earnest effort, their teeth and eyeballs sparkling with pleasure, were obliged to repeat their acts. Whereupon Monsieur Odeluc ordered kerchiefs distributed, one to each singer and an additional one to the dancer.

The guests, moved by this gesture of their host, contributed too, drawing forth small coins, kerchiefs, sacred images in bright colors, or whatever else of small value that they might happen to have in their pockets.

Only Monsieur Laborie, a coffee-planter, frowned upon such generosity, observing severely: "Monsieur Odeluc, I have never seen anywhere slaves so wealthy as yours."

Odeluc smiled. "Happy as a slave at Galifet," he said, and shrugged his shoulders.

Monsieur Moreau de Saint-Méry was busy taking notes for his projected volumes on Saint-Domingue, while Laborie discoursed heatedly on the growing arrogance of the Negroes, their increasing imitation of the whites, their open disobedience of the law, in taking a French surname, in learning to read and write, so that it was becoming more and more common for Negroes under suspicion to be caught with forged passes in their possession.

"I warn you, Monsieur Odeluc, you will yet regret your laxness. And I insist that your impunity is purchased by the just severity with which we other planters treat our blacks."

"Everybody is predicting misfortune to me," Odeluc laughed. "I assure you, Laborie, my Negroes work as hard as any, and my clear profit per slave is as high, if not higher, than anywhere in the colony, and the Marquis de Galifet is thoroughly satisfied. Does not our sugar command the highest prices paid? Is it not commonly said: 'As sweet as the sugar of Galifet'?"

"The original Galifet, when, nearly a century ago, he was lieutenant-governor here," began Monsieur Moreau de Saint-Méry, digging into his tremendous knowledge of colonial history, "was much concerned over the increase of Negroes here, and particularly over their increasing wealth. He feared an armed uprising.

"Well, now we have four times as many Negroes and still no armed uprising. For you can't count such minor affairs as those led by Michel, by Polydor, by Noël, by Telemachus Canga, or just recently by the brothers Isaac and Pyrrhus Candide over at Fort-Dauphine. Those are in the nature of banditry, and nothing more.

"There is, I think, a greater danger, and that comes from the increasing mingling of the two races, the offspring of which, in the female at least, furnishes our colony with its most seductive beauties.

"Did I not recently win a case in which my aid was solicited by the black freedwomen of Le Cap? They craved permission to sit in the theater, from which they were excluded except for the last row in the rear. I won the case easily, arguing that the mothers wished to sit with their fair daughters."

Everybody laughed; Moreau de Saint-Méry continued: "But the case I want to describe is that of Chapuzet, of whom you've no doubt heard something. Wishing to pass for white, he had himself insulted as a mulatto by one of his friends, pretended to be outraged, and came to court clamoring for damages. He won this pre-arranged trial and thus secured documentary evidence of being white.

"But when he wished to purchase an officer's rank in the militia, the esprit de corps of the guard was roused. It was discovered that his great-great-great-grandmother was a Negress.

"Chapuzet fought back year after year with one argument after another. He lost, again and again, until it occurred to him that his dusky ancestress might have been, not a Negress, but an Indian.

"He won his case on that. Today it's an everyday affair for a mulatto to have himself publicly insulted on the streets by one of his friends, to bring suit in court claiming Carib descent, and to have himself freed from his taint of black blood.

"Chapuzet's lawyer is making a fortune.

"And that's the danger. Armed uprising of the slaves is remote. But this insidious crumbling of the white man's prestige, there's a real danger. For between the white race and the black the gulf should be unbridgeable if our institutions are to survive, if the white race is to continue to command and the black race to obey. What then about the mulattoes? Are they to bear forever the stigma of slavery?"

"I didn't propose the question," said Odeluc, "and I needn't answer it."

"Then I'll tell you that those of mixed blood are only waiting for an opportunity to take signal revenge upon us!"

"Heu!" exclaimed Odeluc, "I hear nothing but warnings on all sides. And yet this was to be a day of rejoicing, for man has at last conquered the air. And I intend to put in a steam engine to crush my cane! Can science go any further?"

It was not a day of rejoicing for the Negroes. Unwittingly they felt that the hand of the white, ever increasing in its power, would only lie the heavier on them.

Was it not plain, they asked themselves, that we were meant to be slaves, we who cannot surmount the air like our masters?

They sat about Babouk and wished to be cheered.

And Babouk cheered them.

He recalled an episode of former days.

"The whites," he declared, "are dainty as flowers. A white woman, for example, never makes an ugly noise. Oh, she would almost die of shame if by chance such a noise should escape her.

"The white men are less careful, particularly when they are in the company of men.

"Now, one day I remembered that in Guinea I had been taught to make a powder that has a most amusing effect. The powerful sorcerer who was my master used to make it and keep it in readiness for certain occasions, as, for example, when a dance did not seem to want to warm up properly.

"You know how it is. The drummers stop in disgust, noting the weak response of men and women, and they say to each other scornfully: 'I guess we don't know how to beat the drum. Yes, that must be it!'

"They say: 'I suppose these people are accustomed to good drummers.'

"Then my master would sign to me to go fetch some of this powder, and secretly he would strew it about.

"Suddenly there would be a bang! like the popping of a gun, and everyone would laugh, and the guilty man would laugh too and look around as if he wondered: now who could be so rude? But his attempt to conceal himself among the laughers would only make him the more ridiculous.

"But then other guns were fired, bang! bang! And everybody laughed, and everybody felt guilty, and no one had to conceal anything. Then all present would loosen up, and men and women would dance with abandon.

"And the drummers, heartened by this unforeseen assistance to their drumming, had no longer need to be scornful of their powers.

"My master in Guinea," so Babouk lied, "he used to say: 'Men and women have drums of their own, and good drums they are, too. If you start those drums beating, a dance will always be a success.'

"Now one night two of us, namely Alexandre and myself, had gone to the big house to steal candles.

"Yes, that belongs to the good old days. For nowadays they use nothing but hard English candles that are not fit to eat. We used to have nothing but fine French candles. Soft and tasty, really excellent eating.

"We had hidden ourselves at the end of the veranda, near the white medicine storeroom, but we had chosen a bad night as it happened, for a lot of guests were coming up, and in the big room all the candles had been lit. Yes, all the fine French candles were just burning up, for the whites laugh at our notion of eating candles. Moreover, they have so many other things they eat.

"Alexandre and I watched the whites dance. We blacks would think theirs a very dull dance indeed. It was evident that the mood was cold. The ladies were seated on little golden chairs and the men stood and offered them chocolate in little cups.

"So we caught a young houseboy, one of the dozen who kept the fans waving, just as he was going out for a second to make water, and we promised him a calabash of rum if he would strew the powder we would give him on the floor of the room.

"If Alexandre were here now, he'd tell you about it. But Alexandre, who had all the rum he wanted, for he worked at the stills, came to the sugar house drunk one night when his shift was called, and stumbled over headlong into the syrup.

"They say it takes twenty breaths to drown a man in water, and even then he will often revive if pulled out and held upside down.

"But in syrup a man drowns in one breath and can never be revived.

"Yes, Alexandre would tell you how we watched through the curtains and how we waited, and how at first nothing happened. And Alexandre said the powder was no good.

"Then we heard someone break wind, not very loud, and a young girl rose from her golden stool and rushed from the room, picking up her skirt in order to run faster.

"Now there was one long bang after another, just like when hunters shoot at a flock of geese. And one could see how ashamed they were to be shooting geese when there was no call for it.

"Why, here they were acting no better than blacks, and having no manners at all.

"Some blushed and others murmured excuses. And some withdrew. And it seemed as if our plan to make them dance and be jolly like us blacks would fail. But no, fortunately a tall monsieur saved the day for us, when, after an explosion that was like thunder, he suddenly burst into laughter.

"No, I have never seen whites laugh as they did that night, and dance too.

"And I knew from then on that the whites are not so much different from us."

Babouk paused and then went on viciously:

"Why, if you whipped one of them, he'd howl like a black!

"If you stuck him, he'd bleed!

"Yes," Babouk sneered, "he may conquer the clouds, but he has a drum too, and can play on it as well as we blacks, if only he is properly started."

This story was received with gales of laughter. And the more serious-minded took its lesson to heart.

The noise had attracted other auditors and Babouk had to repeat. But since he never told a story without finding room for improvement, he expanded this new version to include a musical accompaniment which he performed with his mouth but which was designed to illustrate more accurately the noises of the human drum.

"Thus did our severe Monsieur Odeluc. . . .

"And thus the paunchy de Bérigny. . . .

"And thus dainty Mademoiselle Léontine. . . .

"And thus the old Madame who was drying up to a skeleton. . . .

"And thus the twins, performing in unison. . . .

"And thus all the little fan boys. . . ."

This improved story was so successful that Babouk was no sooner done with it than he had to begin all over again.

The squatting blacks slapped their knees, rocked back and forth on their haunches, their shoulders shook, their bellies grew weak, tears finally sprang to their eyes.—No, on no habitation anywhere was there so wise a man, so accomplished a story-teller, as Babouk. To the four quarters of the compass went his fame, and on Sundays his audience numbered visitors from a dozen or more plantations.

This story was certainly a pleasant one to hear. And the concluding line, "Yes, this sort of drum both whites and blacks have, and the whites can perform on it just as well as the blacks, once they are started," that was good to hear too. No, the whites are really no better than the blacks, even if they can send up a great bladder into the sky.

Yes, and it was good to laugh, too, and imitate the sound that this or that person should make.

"My master would do it this way," one visitor would say, "and my mistress thus."

And then each visitor in turn had to demonstrate.

Ha! what rejoicing there was on the Galifet estate. Yes, the slaves there were happy. Why, it was a proverb, passed into common speech: Happy as a nigger on the Galifet plantation!

Galifet! You nigger lovers of Paris, aye, all you nigger lovers of the world! Listen: let this sink into your heads crammed with utopian notions: The very blacks themselves say: Happy as a Galifet nigger. There, look at one of your fancied cruel masters: The Marquis de Galifet! Why the happiness of his Negroes has become proverbial.

Were there no blacks who wondered how much truth there was in this story of Babouk's? Surely there were! Though most were content to accept it as they had accepted the tale of King Tleeka.

Still, now and then someone would ask: "How do you make this powder that awakens the white man's drum?"

And Babouk was not at a loss: "Have you ever seen a horse

collapse, all in a sweat? Take this sweat and mix it with sugar. Dry it in the sun and then crumble it to fine dust. Strew it where people are dancing and where their feet will pound the dust into the air. Then, when they breathe it, they will have to break wind."

That was useful information. And while the story was in its heyday many were the Negroes caught beating a horse into a lather, whipping it unmercifully until the poor beast collapsed.

When a planter questioned such a fellow, would the black explain the reason for his cruelty? Of course not. He might reply evasively: "Horse is black man's nigger," and quietly accept the lashing he deserved.

But when such a powder was found to be absolutely without effect, except that the whites complained that the field Negroes were becoming altogether too arrogant and peering into the master's house every time there were guests, why, what then? Why, then, of course, you realized how truly sly Babouk was. He was not one to divulge his secrets to the first curious nigger who came along with an impudent question. Why, Babouk was just making a fool out of you.

And when by chance a white botanist came across this story, which in time had altered a bit so that the dried sweat and sugar were understood only as powerful magic able to control the white man, he put it down as another curious evidence of the Negro's ineradicably superstitious nature.

14

And still our political leaders expect to cure the
ills of the world by a play upon words.

It was decidedly a time of ferment. In France the king's ministers
fought against an inevitable bankruptcy. In general the rulers of the
land were divided in their emotions. They vacillated between sympa-
thy for the misery of the poor and anger at the very presence of the
poor, who grew tiresome with their perpetual insistence of the poor
upon food and shelter.

In the colony this same vacillation was observable. The planters
became humanitarians and declared for the amelioration of the lot
of the lowly. But that the lowly should dare demand such an amelioration, that would not be countenanced by the planters. The
slaves must learn to accept amelioration, if any, and be grateful for
it. Even the feeling that slavery was an evil which ought to be
abolished was rife among the planters, with the proviso that this
abolition could not take place before many centuries of education.
The dangers of immediate abolition were simply incalculable.

This desire to continue slavery despite the realization of its evil,
and despite the fear lest the slaves rise up and demand their own
rights, revealed itself in the whites' two-faced actions: they attempted
both to conciliate and frighten. With one hand they made a vague
gesture of showering kindness and with the other they actually
showered terror. For how can one be kind to a slave short of being
just to him? And since all their kindness was but renewed acts of
injustice tempered with more charity, there remained of the planters'
split emotions nothing of reality except more terroristic acts.

Some thirty miles, for example, from the Galifet plantation was
the coffee habitation of Nicolas Le Jeune. There, during the course
of twenty-five years, over four hundred Negroes had died of poisoning, at least so the owner claimed, for this was the excess of deaths
on his habitation over what might normally be expected. Surely all

this mass of slaves didn't die of overwork, bad food, or the unaccustomed chill of the mountain air.

In his anger, Nicolas Le Jeune began picking out this one or that one of his slaves as the criminal who was bankrupting him, and his fury was such that he must kill such a wretch by some slow or terrible means. At last his suspicions fell upon two Negresses, and, in order to make them confess, he tortured them by burning their feet and legs with hot coals.

Though he had warned his slaves never to whisper a word about him to anyone outside the plantation, on pain of immediate death, nevertheless fourteen of his slaves, by banding together and encouraging each other, were bold enough to go to Le Cap and accuse their master before the judges there.

An investigation disclosed the two tortured Negresses still alive but with their legs in an advanced stage of decomposition. Le Jeune declared that they had finally admitted their guilt and disclosed the nature and place of concealment of their poison, and he produced a box which when opened contained nothing but ordinary snuff and some rat dirt.

The humanitarian instincts of the whole colony were shocked. The planters were unanimously horrified and aroused over such signal cruelty. But when the court moved to punish the perpetrator, the mood of the planters suddenly changed. Delegations, letters, signatures thereupon poured in upon the governor. It seemed, so he wrote in surprise, that the salvation of the colony demanded the absolution of Le Jeune.

It was one thing to be humanitarian, but such graces must be laid aside when it became a question of standing solid before the institution of slavery. Either the master owned his slave, or he did not. There were no two ways about it.

Le Jeune went unpunished.

But the lesson of Le Jeune was not lost on the planters. They grew more and more worried. They stopped giving their Negroes passes to town so freely. They arrested all strange Negroes if they dared appear on their plantations. At night militiamen went about searching the Negroes for concealed weapons or poisons. They prodded the sleepy workmen out into the cold night winds and upset everything within the huts in their search.

And as the troubles in France grew, the planters waxed ever more cautious, proclaiming aloud their hatred of cruelty and even altering laws to show that the uncontrolled power of the master over his slaves had ceased, forgetting as they did so that previous restrictions had been made and never enforced . . . for a law must be enforced by a higher power, and here there was no power higher than the planter, and surely he was not to be expected to enforce a law against himself when he could ignore it with impunity.

Such laws are mere gestures to calm one's conscience or to deceive critics. And nowhere was this so plainly revealed as in the new law that was drafted to limit the number of lashes a slave might receive at any one time to fifty. Formerly slaves were given a hundred or more, which was often enough to kill. And this despite the fact that there had always been a law limiting the number of lashes to twenty-nine. The new law, therefore, really raised the limit. Moreover, who was to prevent the master from stopping at fifty and then beginning over again? Surely the groveling slave could not arise and say:

"Pardon me, sir, but is not this against the law? Methinks I counted fifty strokes already. Now, do you know that the new and kinder law allows you only twenty-one more than the old horrid law."

Yes, such is the kindness of the masters.

But behold! Over there in France light dawns. The revolution is on. The Bastille falls beneath the attack of the people who are arising to proclaim freedom, equality, and fraternity to all. Down with the white flag of oppression! Up with the red, white, and blue.

And what about the black man? The black men of the French colonies?

Yes, he too was to be included in the new freedom. The Society of Friends of the Blacks was going to see to that.

A test case came up when Saint-Domingue sent twenty representatives to the new National Assembly, figuring that she was entitled to that many in view of her population.

But Mirabeau met these slave-owning chevaliers and marquis with a scathing attack:

"Representation proportional to population?" he sneered. "Yes, but not according to live stock! Neither your slaves nor your mulattoes took part in this election.

"Now, either they are men or they are cattle.

"If men, they must vote.

"If cattle, then we too, here in France, shall count in our horses and cows in allotting our number of deputies!"

It was agreed, too, that the colonies should have a measure of self-government, and that all property owners should convene to elect representatives to their local governing bodies.

This ruling threw the colony into turmoil. For did it not mean that mulattoes could vote too? For there were large numbers of them who owned property, generally little bits of land sandwiched between the big plantations, little bits of land that were the gifts of the whites to their half-breed bastards.

These mulattoes clamored to exercise their right to vote.

The free Negroes did not dare raise their voices.

The slaves said nothing, knew nothing.

The whites, planters of course, were determined that no one but white planters should vote, and so interpreted the ruling of the National Assembly.

In France, the National Assembly herself, despite the efforts of certain hotheads, deliberately avoided the question as to whether their ruling that property owners could vote meant that mulattoes owning property could vote too. In short, was the French revolution for pure white blood only? Or was it for mixed white blood? And, if so, what was the proportion of white blood to black that entitled a man to share in the victories of the revolution?

And what about the black slaves?

The Assembly kept quiet until the case of Ogé and Chavannes bestirred them.

Ogé and Chavannes were two mulattoes who were fired with the spirit of revolution. They declared that either the mulattoes would be accorded citizenship or they would revolt. They gathered together a band of some two hundred of their kind and defied the government, repulsing an armed force of six hundred men sent out by the white rulers.

Thereupon the planters' government sent twelve hundred men against these furious half-breeds. When the latter saw themselves so vastly outnumbered, there were voices to urge that the slaves should be roused to revolt and help their fairer brothers. But Ogé was opposed. "They are not capable of freedom yet," he said.

Unsupported, the small force of rebels was doomed. Ogé and Chavannes and thirty-four others were brought to Le Cap in triumph. The rich encouraged the citizens to make a public holiday of it.

The chief accusation against the mulattoes, however, was precisely on that point: that they had plotted a slave revolt. Since the accused were given neither counsel nor a hearing, they could not very well deny it. They were found guilty, and sentence was passed upon them.

For the moment execution was stayed because the former executioner, a Negro slave, had turned maroon, that is, run away. Thereupon, according to a custom that obtained in the French colonies, the next Negro sentenced to death was given the choice between death and the post of executioner.

It was nothing at all rare to find Negroes spurning this means of saving their skins by killing their fellow Negroes. "I wish to die but once," one of them said; "as executioner, I would have to die every day afresh."

Fortunately the number of condemned slaves was sufficiently large so that a less sensitive candidate was soon found.

Thereupon, in the presence of the high judges, the court clerk made out the new executioner's commission, crumpled up the document, and threw it on the ground. The Negro, previously instructed, knelt and retrieved his commission with his teeth.

So great was the gulf between Negro and white that direct contact was unthinkable.

Thereupon Ogé and Chavannes, bareheaded and barefooted, clad only in their shirts, with ropes around their necks, were walked to the parish church and there were forced to kneel; and two waxen torches were placed in their hands and they were made to repeat in a loud voice, in a loud and distinct voice so that all the city's multitudes might hear:

"The crimes for which we were convicted were wicked, were rash, were ill-advised. We repent of them and ask pardon of God, of the king, of justice."

Then they were led through the hot streets, surrounded and followed by the clamor of the white mob, amidst the blinding dust raised by many feet.

At the Place d'Armes yet another insult awaited the mulattoes. For here there were customarily two places for execution, one side of the Place being reserved for whites and the other for blacks.

That it should be plain to all that the stigma of black blood, however diluted, could never be effaced, not even in front of death's door, the two condemned men were led to the scaffold on the black side. There they had their first glimpse of the two wheels revolving freely on upright axles which were to be the platform of their gruesome execution.

It is said that they met their doom bravely, but I find it hard to believe that they were not stricken to their hearts with shame at the thought that they should suffer death (which should be private) here in public on such a grotesque device.

The executioner, having practiced on a dummy, tied his two victims correctly to their wheels and then, with a heavy stick, broke their arms, their legs, their thighs, and finally their backs, going from one to the other after each bone-breaking blow. A physician stood by to certify that the bone was actually cracked.

The operation was slow and the men did not die of it at once. They remained twisting on their wheels and sighing miserably. That eventuality had not been overlooked in their sentence: it had been stipulated that they should abide thus, "as long as God chose to preserve their lives."

Some days later another mulatto rebel was thus executed. Twenty more were hanged and thirteen others were chained to the oars of the galleys for life.

Gingerly now the French Assembly approached the problem, delaying it until it could be delayed no longer.

What did the French revolution do for black blood? Did its principles stop with the whites?

Moreau de Saint-Méry delivered an oration in which he warned the government that the colonies would sever their connection with France if the Rights of Man were proclaimed there. Had not England lost her North American colonies by infringing upon the rights of the colonials to self-determination?

Abbé Grégoire, the great friend of the blacks, demanded that at least the tax-paying mulattoes should be declared citizens.

Malouet thought that the best the government could do was to investigate the conditions of the slaves with a view to bettering them. To do more would cause a revolt.

Lafayette and Robespierre spoke up for the mulattoes, too.

Then came the turn of the wily Abbé Maury. "It is beautiful," he said in honeyed tones, "to flatter the people and play to the gallery with high-sounding words of humanity and equality. But remember this: every mulatto has slave relatives! These slaves will come to power through the mulattoes and make laws against the whites. Is that your love of humanity and equality? To make slaves of the whites?

"I tell you we shall lose our colonies, for the mother country of these Negroes is not France but Africa. Yes, they will drop away from us along with the seven hundred millions of business that our colonials and shippers have built up!"

Robespierre shouted back: "Perish our colonies rather than sacrifice one of our principles of happiness, of glory, of liberty for all!"

Alas, these principles had already perished. The first sixteen beautiful rights of man proclaiming equality and freedom for all were repealed by the seventeenth and last right:

"Property rights are declared sacred and inviolate forever."

Yes, as a man the Negro was made free and equal to all, but as a slave, and therefore property, he was declared to remain the property of his master forever.

Yes, black blood was considered degrading in those ancient and benighted days.

That is why the court clerk crumpled up the document and threw it on the ground for the Negro to pick up with his teeth.

That is why the mulattoes were not executed on the site where white men died.

That is why Negroes must live in ghettoes, ride in Jim-Crow cars, and never dare enter our white men's hotels and restaurants or theaters.

For we still live in those ancient and benighted days. And the black race is still degrading and degraded in this land of democracy where all are born free and equal.

So the French revolutionaries played upon words, as if a play upon words could help the niggers laboring under the threat of the lash on the fields of Saint-Domingue.

Babouk was careful now to look around before he began a story, in order to make sure that there were no black or mulatto commanders about, nor any slaves who received presents from the master, such as an old coat, and who were therefore always on the lookout for a means to curry new favors.

Nevertheless, increasingly he was called to lie down on the ground with his hands and feet bound to short stakes and receive a whipping. The term used was *tailler*, really *notch* or *whittle*, like a knife slashing wood.

The most difficult stroke for you, Babouk, was always the first, for though you stretched your neck and twisted your eyes you were not able to catch a warning of its coming. But with the second the rhythm of the lashing was once fixed and you could set yourself to meet each stroke thereafter. The best way was to bite into the ground and feel pebbles and sand crunching under your teeth. That way, too, you avoided clamping your teeth down on your tongue which sometimes resulted in a tongue being severed in half.

Having your back rubbed with brine or lemon juice was necessary, since it prevented gangrene. That was not hard to bear since the pain of it was so keen that it was almost its own destroyer.

You could work still, in fact, you had to. And that is why the planter preferred the whip to imprisonment, which would deprive him of a man's work in the fields. But sleeping was another matter. At work, too, you had to be careful lest a sudden bent or twist rip up the wounds. Suddenly you would feel the warmth of fresh blood welling up and running down your back.

When the scab began to crack and crumble and the taut new skin to appear beneath, then the itching was intolerable. Yes, far worse than the lashing was this itch that made you bite your avid fingers lest with a sudden motion you claw off that hardened shell of scab and carry along the masses of spongy healing flesh with it.

After that, the lashing was really over except that, whenever you washed yourself and felt that rough and insensitive skin from which the feeling of life departed more and more with each whipping, then involuntarily you passed your hand over it again and again, striving to beat down the sense of a little bit of death, a little bit of death that had fastened itself onto you.

There was compensation, it is true, in having the girls look at you with wide-open eyes full of a world of pity, and stroke your wounded back with their delicate fingers.

But that consolation belonged only to those young men who had love to give in return. Not to Babouk. He sought elsewhere for relief of the bitterness that flooded his heart.

15

It is not advisable to introduce that so fertile and
so energetic African race into our colony: for since
these people lack neither military spirit nor skill,
they will seize the first favorable opportunity to
shake off our yoke and seize the power.
—*Cardinal Zimenes to Charles V, 1517*

The African Negroes will soon make themselves
masters of the island of St. Domingo.
—*Girolamo Benzoni,* History of the New World,
1565

For a week the rada drums had been announcing a meeting for the
voodoo worshipers. Back in the hills, in a woods that was formerly a
coffee plantation, the meeting was to be held.

Who had abandoned this rich soil once cleared at so great an
expenditure of labor and planted so carefully to quincunxes of
coffee bushes? Why did no one come here with gangs of slaves to
gather the precious double berries that the appetite of Europe might
be stilled? Here was a fortune! Why was it left to waste away?

The explanation is simple. It was a case of thieves falling out.
Theoretically the king of France owned all the land of Saint-Domingue, but generously permitted his subjects to stake claims upon it
and thus become the owners of parcels of a certain size. And,
inasmuch as there were no state surveyors, each prospective owner
hired his own surveyors and staked out his land and planted the
required border hedges accordingly.

Now, this manner of procedure resulted occasionally in an intolerable situation. It was not only that hired surveyors could be bribed to
survey wrongly and the state to approve a plantation that was
illegitimate, but two or more claimants might dispute a piece of
ground to which they had both laid claim in different offices, for the
whole country had been so miserably surveyed that the various
parishes could never be sure of the limits of their jurisdiction.

And then again, a piece of ground that appeared to be virgin might have been cultivated once and only abandoned for so many years as to appear virgin. The old owner might suddenly turn up and the courts give him the right to claim all the profits that had been extracted from his ground even though by the labor of another.

Here, then, was a plantation that was cursed. Since you could not be sure who owned it, better, then, not to work upon it at all, for the money you grind out of it with the labor of your slaves might not be yours but belong to someone else. So, until the slow-moving courts decided to whom the profits belonged, the land had better be given back to the jungle.

Nothing, therefore, could have been more suited to the congregation of voodoo worshipers than this piece of ground so strangely hallowed and blasted by the mystery of private ownership. Two angry men appeared in court and demanded that Justice weigh in her balance their conflicting claims and determine which one of them was the legitimate owner of this property that had belonged to an unknown race before it had belonged to the Quisqueyans, before it had belonged to the Caribs, before it had belonged to the Spanish, before it had belonged to the French.

Oh, marvelous balances of Justice, so delicately hung that you can tell by the weight of a subtle thought which of the many thieves rightfully owns this land. Scientific laboratories the world over! Gaze upon this marvelous device that puts your crude scales to shame! I call upon you, Gentlemen, gaze and admire. Here is the majesty of the Law!

And now a dark-colored people will gather on this disputed land and consider how they may become the owners of it. And you shall see how fast Justice discards her marvelously delicate balances and seizes the sword as the real instrument of ownership.

Day after day the drums had announced this important meeting. But the whites were unaware. They considered the drum only the passion for rhythm of a class of being having not much more than this, the lowest conception of music.

After his long day's work the tired savage swallowed a hasty supper and was off into the darkness, unafraid, since for all his superstitious fears he knew the truth of the proverb: in the dark there are no commanders. In a little bundle he had wrapped up the sandals that he would need when he stepped on the holy ground near the altar and also his offering to the deity and the priest.

From fifty plantations and more they come, men and women who were not appalled at a tramp of fifteen miles uphill and downhill to the site of the meeting, where they knew there would be cheerful fires waiting for them, and around the fires friends from other plantations whom they might not have the opportunity to see again for many months.

Priests and sorcerers were already on hand. They had slipped away from their work earlier than the rest at the risk of a beating. Some of them were painted in the fashion of their tribes at home, others were decked out in whatever fantastic costumes they could secure, but always striving to express their station, which was half-way between the seen and unseen world, the link, as it were, between matter and force.

Behind the altar, which was an old tree stump covered for this occasion with a red cloth, stood the queen-mother, Nara the prophetess, still a powerful figure despite her gray hair that was like steel wool. Ceremoniously she lifted from the altar a little hut of woven branches, beneath which she disclosed, in the light of the many fires, a green snake slothfully curled up.

A wave of emotion swept through the congregation, as when in the cathedral the miracle of the transubstantiation takes place to the tinkle of a bell. For here, too, was the symbol of the godhead, though it was nothing more than a harmless snake, a beast so mild and inoffensive that it often happened that a mother would wake up to find one sleeping by her side, replete with the milk it had drunk from her full bosom.

The congregation, squatting for the most part, repeated various formulae of allegiance to the voodoo snake, and Nara with extended hands acted as if she received these oaths in deposit.

Nara's eyes were off in the distance, her voice had a far-away sound to it. "My children"—so she spoke, ever so gently—"my children, there is nothing the voodoo will not give you if you will be true to him. You must trust him. What do my suffering children wish?"

A number of those present now rose and began to file past the mamaloi, the queen-mother, and placing their offerings at her feet they hurriedly whispered their requests. Nara did not look at them, she did not seem to hear them as they moved past her and begged for the return of their love or for the revenge of an insult or for the relief of an illness. Most of the pleas concerned the kindness of a commander or a master. Was not their fortune made if they could obtain his favor? Would they not have less work, as well as presents of cloth and food and even money?

One of the medicine men now took the still sleeping snake from the altar and placed it at Nara's feet. The beast, well-fed and contented, wanted nothing so much as to sleep. But now, disturbed and uncomfortable, his body rose stiff in the air and made as if to move this way and that, settled itself, only to rise again and repeat all the sinuous motions that a serpent will make when it is seeking to find a comfortable spot on which to curl up.

That was not the strange thing that the congregation was craning its neck to see. It was the curious way in which the body of Nara moved, bending this way and that, her arms and shoulders stretching in a lazy, snake-like motion, now here, now there, precisely following, as near as the human body can, the motions of the snake, as if the beast and the woman were one compound body, and the rhythm and the flowing muscles of both obedient to the impulse of a single brain.

And yet Nara's eyes looked straight ahead and the snake was at her feet. And before her was the congregation, each crinkly-haired head swaying to her rhythm.

Gradually the litheness, the smoothness departed from Nara's movements. She shivered as with palsy, her motions broke, grew ever more abrupt. At last she seemed as if attacked by violent cramps, each muscle, each limb, twisted in separate torture.

Suddenly her body remained frozen, as if turned to stone and adhering to the last awkward and unbalanced position it had assumed. Thus she stood stiffly, her head up, her eyes open, her eyeballs set as in death, her mouth drawn as in great pain, the cords of her neck protruding.

At her feet lay the snake, curled up, asleep.

She spoke. Her voice, strange and cracked, issued from her drawn mouth without a disturbance of her lips. And in this weird cataleptic state she remained until she had answered the request of every supplicant.

To one she promised everything, but to another she denied. This one she praised and flattered, while to another she was full of harsh reproaches. Now and again her voice grew loud as thunder and she showered some poor wretch with horrible imprecations. She ordered this or that to be done without fail, as being the law of the serpent that let break who dare.

The multitude bowed before her like a field of millet in the play of a breeze. They shouted their thanks or groaned their woe and repeated over again their promises of implicit obedience. Many had received answers that were vague or had a double meaning, and these poor folk bowed their heads with the rest and accepted what was given them though their bowels were tortured with fear lest they misunderstand the oracle.

Except for the black faces, except for the abandoned coffee plantation that served them for a temple, this was ancient Greece, and Nara was the Pythoness of Delphi. In truth, the resemblance would have been startling to anyone who did not insist that classic beauty comes always clothed in white. But such is the force of the black complexion that no one could credit these people with a religion that was first cousin to the Olympian, and the rare whites who stumbled on these ceremonies invariably deduced that the slaves were gathered here to worship the devil.

The Pythoness having answered the last request, her limbs slowly freed themselves from the cramping force that held them bound. She relaxed and leaned exhausted, breathing heavily, against the altar.

At this juncture, when as a rule the initiation of new members was in order, Babouk stepped forward from among the group of medicine men and, standing at the altar, he shouted:

"Who are we that should plead with Bamballa for the favor of the white masters? Have we not strength of our own?

"Did we at home in our tribes do nothing but plead? Did we leave our arms hanging weakly by our sides?

"Or did we not rather sing out a battle song and go out to die?

"Are we not men? Did not even the enormous elephant fall before our spears and dig his tusks into the earth?"

At the mention of that great beast, a heavy sigh arose from the audience. Even those who knew the elephant only from the tales of their elders joined in. Some groaned out loud at the thought of the great lumbering beast that they used to pursue so viciously but of

which they now thought with a strange sort of kindness. A nostalgia
rose in them for a sight of those enormous flanks heaving like the
sides of a tent. . . .

Babouk, seeing that he had struck the right line, insisted upon all
the other animals they would never see again, mentioning not only
those of the region from which he had come, the antelopes and
tigers and the lions, but also the giraffes and the river-horses of
which he had only heard.

But each animal as he mentioned it aroused groans. These things
were gone, alas. No, they could no longer cast their spears at game,
no longer burn the bush or lay traps. . . . But no, they had not lost
their courage for all that. . . .

"Is there not a better game than all the game that runs on four
feet?" Babouk asked. "Is there not the best game of all? The beast
that runs on two legs?"

No, no, they must not be silly as some had been and go on
fighting here in Saint-Domingue the members of their hereditary
inimical tribes of Guinea or Congo. Let all now unite and fight their
common oppressor.

Babouk suddenly brought forward a small earthenware vase that
he had put ready.

"Behold!" he cried as he pulled out a brown square of silk and let
if flutter in the breeze that was beginning to stiffen. "These were
once the owners of Saint-Domingue! The *viens-viens!*"

Suddenly he crumpled up the kerchief that represented the Indians and palmed it away. "Where are they now? Gone!"

And digging into the vase he whipped out a square of white.
"These are the present rulers of Saint-Domingue!" He let the square
wave in the wind for a moment, then viciously he ripped it to pieces,
and dramatically he drew forth an immense black kerchief.

"Here are the real masters of Saint-Domingue! Here are the
coming rulers of this island, when all the whites are gone!"

Triumphantly the black silk fluttered in the wind, lit by the first
flashes of lightning from the brewing storm, and accompanied by
the distant reverberation of thunder.

The audience was deeply impressed, but silent, oppressed with
the ingrained fear of long servitude. And Babouk, realizing that this
lesson must be pounded home again and again to drive out forever

that tendency of the black man to quail before the white, began to shout at them as if they were a parcel of proven cowards:

"You have been bitten by snakes, yes, but must you forever after that shy at earthworms?

"What are you afraid of? Do you think that the white man can resist us?"

And now Babouk brought forth a tall cylindrical jar of glass, filled nearly to the brim with black beans.

"Behold the numbers of the black people in this land!" he cried. "Behold now the few white who are on top of us!" And with these words he poured some grains of yellow maize over the black beans.

"Look!" he shouted, "the white on top of the black!"

All looked and saw that it was so. They were as if under an hypnotic compulsion, they followed Babouk's least motion with fixed eyes.

"But look now!" And with that Babouk, placing the palm of his hand over the mouth of the jar, turned it upside down and shook it up several times.

When he took his hand away and showed the jar to the audience the grains of yellow corn had vanished; dispersed among the great quantity of black beans they were effectively lost.

"What has become of the whites?" Babouk asked. And again he asked: "What has become of the whites?" He began to smile. "What has become of the whites?" he thundered. Then suddenly he burst into loud, raucous laughter.

It was the signal for the whole assembly to burst into endless peals of merriment. They had controlled themselves too long. Their pent-up emotions spilled over. They rose from their squatting positions and began to dance without any order, but slapping themselves and each other gayly, as though the whites were already drowned in the black sea.

The long-threatening storm had obscured the sky. The untended fires began to die down. The blacks paid no attention, filled as they were with the sense of a liberating emotion, that of hatred toward the white master.

While this mood was still uppermost, a grunting pig, wrapped in a cloak, was pushed forward to the altar, and Nara, swinging a great cutlass, began to dance and pirouette around the beast. She chanted, too, though at first her voice could not be heard in the general clamor. But little by little she captured the attention of the audience. She sang of the deeds of warriors and of that home in Guinea to which all who died in battle would return. She called upon all to swear to be loyal unto death, and suddenly her swinging cutlass descended and the grunting pig squealed a brief squeal before it perished with a slit throat.

A terrific crash of thunder followed so immediately upon Nara's stroke that it could not but seem as though the stroke of her cutlass had released the imprisoned storm. The spectators were as if glued to the spot, each caught in a whirl of shivers that traveled up and down his spine.

But the assistants at the altar were busy collecting the pig's blood in bowls, and the slaves, just as soon as they had freed themselves from their paralyzing emotions, rushed up to have a drink of blood or at least a smear to wet their lips, or paint a snake-line on their foreheads, and thus to pledge their undying loyalty to Babouk and the rebellion.

Though the rain began now to fall in torrents, the dance for new members was called. Each acolyte, provided with a bunch of herbs, dry once, but now soaked with rain, and with pieces of horn, and some hair from a gray-haired woman, all tied about with a human navel cord, were set to dancing in a great circle drawn in the wet ground.

Strong liquor was passed around, and the drums, their tones muffled by the wet, guided them in their dancing and in the singing of the chant of initiation:

> *"Eh! Eh!*
> *Bomba!*
> *Heu! Heu!*
> *Canga bafio té*
> *Canga moune de le*
> *Canga do ki la*
> *Canga li."*

What the words meant not even the singers knew clearly, but the power was there nevertheless. Like the words that were written in letters of fire at Belshazar's feast, the meaning may have been obscure but the portent was plain:

> *"Death to the whites!*
> *We swear to kill all whites*
> *Or be done to death by them!"*

Now Babouk called upon God to witness the oath of loyalty of all: the leaders to their followers, and the followers to their leaders.

"The god of the whites is thirsty for the water of our eyes," he thundered.

"Must we blacks then weep forever to satisfy that thirsty god?

"Is there no other god in heaven?

"Who is then the god who gave the sun its warmth? Who is then the god who lent the sea his anger and the storm his rage?

"It is the black men's god! The black men's god, who, from behind the cloud where he lies hidden, has seen the evil of the whites.

" 'Rise up!' he cries, 'rise up! and tumble the god of the whites out of his heaven!'

"The thirsty god of the whites shall die!"

The fiery mood of the assistants, even seconded as it was by the fiery tafia, yet fought an unequal battle against the chilling rain that had put out all the fires. The Negroes, tropical animals, shivered, and one by one disappeared from the company. Even a number of the witch-doctors, their stripes smeared and their regalia ruined by the rain, had gone off. Nara, too, her steel-gray hair glistening with rain drops as with diamonds, left the meeting, carefully bearing off her voodoo snake, snug in its hut of woven branches.

The few who remained were those whose passion for the coming revolt was beyond the reach of rain water. They sat in a circle, oblivious to the downpour, a score of Negroes and a couple of mulattoes. The steady rain cascaded upon their faces and made them twitch into grimaces. But they did not move. They discussed the question of arms and agreed that there was nothing to do but arm themselves as best they might and trust to their numbers and the surprise of their sudden attack rather than to their weapons. The revolt should begin at various points, fire on any one plantation

being the signal for all neighboring ateliers to rise and slay their
masters and burn the fields.

It was to be expected that commanders everywhere would be
willing to join the rebels. Already many of them were more anxious
than the lowest slaves. But if not they were to be slain unmercifully,
for nothing must endanger the rebellion.

Especially important was it to set the sugar cane fields afire at
once, for that was their strongest move, since even the most cowardly
slave might be expected to approve a policy that would relieve him of
those endless hours of labor about to begin again with the coming
harvest of the ripening cane.

Thus the revolt would spread as fast as the devouring flames.

Late at night the conspirators separated. Babouk hugged under
one arm his vase with its wet handkerchiefs, and under the other the
great glass jar from which the black beans and the white grains of
maize dribbled out as he made his way down the precipitous hill-
side.

16

The colonists slept upon a Vesuvius, nor were they
awakened by the first jets of its eruption.
—*Mirabeau*

Yet it seemed as if the slaves must be shown a hundred times that
nothing but universal revolt could remedy their situation. Degraded
by their condition of serfdom, and brutified by their constant heavy
labor, they awoke from their slothful apathy only to a brief explosion of rage, which, being unformed and unsupported, was speedily
extinguished and, of course, punished in exemplary fashion.

Thus, near Port-au-Prince, certain angry slaves ran amuck. But
when the incident was over they were no better off than before.
"General Caradeuz," so says a contemporary letter, "has just be-
headed fifty Negroes on the plantation Aubry, and that no one
should be ignorant of the transaction, he has affixed the heads upon
poles, in imitation of palm trees."

But Babouk bided his time. Under his direction the slaves secretly
fashioned spears and bows and arrows, and it was his intention to
wait until the cane of the fields should have reached its best growth.

On the night of August 20th of the year 1791, however, on one of
the lesser two Galifet plantations, that was called *la Gossette,* an old
Negro named Ignace, who on account of his age had been exempted
from labor, appeared in his master's bedroom just as the latter had
retired behind his mosquito netting.

"Who is it?" the master asked into the darkness where he saw
moving shapes.

"It is we who have come to speak to you," said Ignace.

Monsieur Mosset was about to raise the curtains of his bed, but
as he did so a couple of slashes of a machete rent the curtains to
pieces and the following slash struck Monsieur Mosset in the shoulder.

Mosset thereupon leapt from his bed and seized the spear from

157

the hands of one of the Negroes, who, too long accustomed to obey a white, could not summon his muscles to resist, and with this spear the overseer began to sweep the frightened Negroes out of his room and out upon the gallery, the door to which he thereupon closed and barred.

In the adjoining room a friend was staying over the night, and sleeping tightly despite the noise. Mosset awoke him and sent him on the run to the mansion house to fetch Monsieur Odeluc, while he, arming himself with a pistol, cried out that anyone who should dare raise a hand against either himself or his friend would be shot dead.

The intimidated Negroes awaited the outcome of this sudden defeat, crouching on the gallery and looking about glumly and in despair.

"You, Ignace!" cried Mosset, through the locked door, "have I ever done you anything but favors?

"Speak! For years now you have been excused from all work. You live in idleness, yet you are supplied with food and drink and shelter!"

"Nothing but favors," the black man agreed sullenly.

"Then why do you seek to kill me?"

"I have sworn to kill you," said Ignace darkly, "and I hope still to be able to do so."

Monsieur Mosset sponged up the blood from his wounded shoulder with an old shirt and shivered to hear such savagery from the mouth of a Negro upon whom he had bestowed so many kindnesses.

Ignace, out upon the gallery, tried to formulate in his mind the sentence that should clear up the emotions he felt, he who, after working hard for fifty years, had at last been permitted to rest his wornout carcase, and was expected daily to be grateful therefor. But his mind refused him the benediction of clear words and he remained pondering sullenly, his whole being blocked and choked by this dull, inexpressible resentment. At last, incapable of justifying himself, he began to feel guilty and before long was pleading for Monsieur Mosset to forgive him.

"Why should I forgive you?" Mosset exclaimed. "Why should I be kind to you again, when you have shown yourself to be a beast unworthy of anything but a kick?"

"Yes, Monsieur, yes, Monsieur," Ignace assented meekly.

An hour later Monsieur Odeluc had arrived, whereupon Mosset's friend and the three white men passed unharmed among the hundreds of slaves, who stood in groups in the darkness, not daring to come to action.

Before this, which they interpreted as proof of the black man's innate cowardice, the whites grew bold and scornful.

"Go to sleep!" shouted Monsieur Odeluc, much as one might say to an angry dog: Lie down! And the slaves turned away and made as if to be off to their huts, but as soon as Monsieur Odeluc had passed them by they returned and gathered together again.

Early in the morning, Monsieur Odeluc went to *la Gossette* again, and, taking along with him some slaves from the main Galifet plantation, slaves upon whom he thought he could rely, proceeded at once to arrest all those implicated in the affair of the previous night, along with their parents and their closest friends. Then he went off at once to Le Cap, and returned with the judge of the seneschal and twenty soldiers, and set to work to discover what was at the bottom of all this, for that there was a conspiracy of some sort afoot seemed reasonably clear from the way Ignace kept repeating: "I have promised to kill Monsieur Mosset."

"What! your benefactor! Kill your benefactor! To whom could you promise such a horrible thing?" the judge demanded, puffing through his blue, wine-swollen lips. The day being hot, he laid his wig aside and covered his bald scalp with a white kerchief.

But Ignace would not divulge to whom he had given this promise. The whites, however, continued to question and threaten, for much depended upon their securing the name or names of the men who had started this movement, so that swift punishment could nip it in the bud.

Now resort was had to an old trick. Ignace and his companions were separated and questioned independently, their memories being awakened with the whip. Then the judge pretended to the youngest and weakest of the slaves that the others had confessed, so he might as well give in and confess with the rest, unless he wished to suffer an especially severe punishment all by himself.

Nothing would have been easier now than to have proceeded to execute all the slaves mentioned by this youthful betrayer and thus put an end to the conspiracy. Unfortunately for the whites, the very ease with which this and all previous conspiracies had been stopped before going very far had made them feel a little too sure of their powers.

Monsieur Odeluc contented himself with ordering the locking up of Babouk and several others among the slaves of his atelier who seemed implicated, and he left it to the authorities at Le Cap to send off messengers to the other habitations to warn the planters of possible ringleaders said to be in their ateliers.

On the following day news came that a revolt had occurred on the plantation of Choiseul, which was near-by. The cane fields having been set afire, the tocsin was rung to call together all the hands of the district to fight the fire. Monsieur Odeluc went around in haste collecting the whites in order to organize a fire-fighting brigade. When he came to the plantation of the Fathers of Charity, he found the Negroes swarming about the cadaver of the overseer, who had just been massacred by certain enraged Negroes.

The twenty soldiers from Le Cap proved of little use. Frightened by the demeanor of the slaves and the vast numbers of them, they dropped their arms and ran off. Monsieur Odeluc was concerned, but still not frightened. He returned at once to Galifet to take new measures.

It seemed now, from the many columns of smoke ascending at various points of the horizon, that the whole region was disturbed. From all directions, distant and near, came the clangor of the tocsin.

Monsieur Odeluc felt that his first move must be to assure himself of the loyalty of his own slaves and thereafter to organize a group of whites who, with a regiment of black slaves provided with guns, would soon quell these isolated revolts.

He spoke this over with a Monsieur Daveiroult, a deputy to the colonial assembly, and the two, along with the three soldiers who remained from the twenty who had fled panic-stricken, went out toward the ateliers.

Things seemed utterly peaceful here. He heard his grandnephew crying in his cradle and the Negro nurse rushing to the infant with many motherly shushes.

But no sooner had the group stepped out into the garden than he saw his commander Mathurin coming up with a dozen or more blacks, all armed with machetes or pikes or staffs. Despite their truculent advance and their angry expressions, Odeluc suspected no evil.

"What's up, Mathurin?" he called out.

"I'm Monsieur Mathurin now!" cried the commander in a voice so thick with passion that his words coalesced into one hoarse shout.

"Mathurin, what's come over you?" Odeluc wanted to know. "You've been drinking again, and I swear that I'll relieve you of your position!"

Monsieur Daveiroult counseled: "No mercy, Odeluc. This impudence. . . ."

At that moment the group of slaves made a concerted charge upon the whites. Monsieur Odeluc received a cut of Mathurin's machete that laid his bowels open. The three soldiers were simply chopped to pieces, and Monsieur Daveiroult was so battered with machetes and pierced with spears that the black flagstones of the garden walk were flooded with his blood.

The atelier was alive with chatter. Everyone was interrogating himself and his friends as to their attitude toward the new conditions. Many were of the firm opinion that a great crime had been committed against God, and that at any moment now the sky must split open and all the white saints appear to avenge this deed upon their favorites, the white masters.

But others, overjoyed, could think of nothing except the fact that the cane fields were going up in smoke and that there would be no hated cane harvest from now on.

As for Babouk, now released from his prison, he was distinctly annoyed to find that the revolt which he had planned to lead to triumph had advanced so far without him and without the dramatic signal which he had intended to give to the whole plain.

He looked about in the confusion and sought for a point on which to reassert his leadership.

He declared for the immediate firing of the sugar cane fields. It had already been done.

Thereupon he wished to rush upon the mansion and loot it. The looting was already in progress.

Monsieur Odeluc's head must be exposed on a pike. It was already so exposed.

But there was still something undone. Léontine, Monsieur

Odeluc's niece, and her little baby were still alive. Some, indeed, had already attempted to lay violent hands on them, but the Negro household women had come crowding around their mistress and had prevented any attack upon her. For the moment, then, she remained somewhat of a prisoner in her own house and under the protection of her women.

Hundreds of slaves were swarming into the house. Some of them had seen it from the outside for forty years or more, and now were in haste to seize this unique opportunity to view from the inside those mysterious rooms from which emanated the terrible power of the whites. For the most part, they were disappointed. They had expected to see something vast and marvelous, something beyond all imagination. Instead they found only certain amusing chandeliers of crystal, certain oil paintings that were no better than the colored images which they could buy from the priest, and various rugs and upholstered furniture that were delightful to sit or lie upon. Otherwise there was nothing.

Babouk was incensed to discover that the household women were protecting Léontine.

"What do we owe to her?" he cried. "Is she any better than any other white? Will she not at the earliest opportunity betray us all?"

He roused up certain of his more vindictive followers, and together they raided the room where Léontine cowered, surrounded by her faithful servants. With their spears they prodded everybody out into the yard.

"We need a servant," Babouk cried above the excited babble of the women. "We need a servant to clean the latrines, and if Madame Léontine will do that work, then she may live. But first we shall put on her neck the collar of spikes which our own women had to wear."

This collar of spikes, sharply pointed, spikes a foot or more in length, was put around women who were considered too amorous and were thus arousing fights among the men. It was claimed that such women aborted too often because carrying a child interfered with their amours, and they were therefore condemned to wear this device around the neck, a device that prevented proper loving or proper sleep, until they should have given birth to a living offspring.

The slaves cheered Babouk, especially, of course, those of the atelier who had had experience in cleaning latrines and in wearing the spiked collar. The household servants, however, continued to plead for their mistress, but the will of the majority prevailed. Léontine was roughly pushed toward the privies. The young mother, overcome by her many miseries, sighed dismally and fell down upon the ground and would not move.

"Drag her to the latrines!" Babouk commanded. "No. First let her see her baby die."

"Don't kill the baby," the frightened servants whined. "Ah, don't kill the little child." Even the field women joined in this cry, yes, even the men.

Seeing that the emotions of the crowd were being swayed toward pity, Babouk brushed aside the women, seized the baby from the arms of one of them, and flung it on the ground.

"Nits grow into lice!" he vociferated wildly. And again he shouted: "Nits grow into lice!"

The child screamed hysterically; its face turned blue.

Then Babouk's spear pierced it through and through so that he had to dig the point out of the ground before he could swing it aloft with the baby spiked upon the point of it.

17

Queen Isabella wept to hear of the sufferings of the enslaved Indians. She was only consoled by the assurance that they were being speedily converted to Christianity so that if their bodies were being racked at least their souls were being saved.

Queen Elizabeth was touched by the misery of the Negro slaves. But being assured that no force was used to enslave the blacks, she erased the moisture from her eyes and accepted her share in the profits of Hawkins' slaving expeditions.

Queen Marie Antoinette could weep too . . .

With a wild cry of terror: "The savages have broken loose!" the planters fled before Babouk's band with its standard of a white child stuck upon a spike.

"The savages have broken loose!" they cried, and rushed toward the city of Le Cap. Some were accompanied by their whole atelier of Negroes, which they forthwith put into safe-keeping aboard some vessel in the harbor or locked up in some well-barred barracks. Many owed their lives to the faithfulness of their black servants, who had risked, or even sacrificed, themselves that their masters might live. But this was not a moment to inquire into the degree of loyalty of various Negroes. The great majority were locked up permanently, the very minimum of blacks were permitted freedom during the day in order to minister to the needs of their masters.

The news of the Negro uprising did not reach France directly. It came to France from England, to whom Saint-Domingue had appealed for help.

At first the terrible news had been discredited, for the spectacle of patience being tried, and tried forever and ever, tends to make one believe that patience will never succumb to any of its trials. But when mail after mail confirmed the sad story, the hall of the Assembly at Paris reechoed with accusations:

"This is the hand of the royalists. I have proof that royalist agents have incited this rebellion and that the revolting slaves cry out: '*Vive le roi!*' and display a white flag!"

The royalists rejected the charge as ridiculous; what possible benefit could they expect from such an insurrection three thousand miles from the royal palace? In their turn they accused the Society of the Friends of the Blacks. Had not Abbé Grégoire published his *Open Letter to the Blacks of Saint-Domingue* but a few months before?

Brissot sprang to Grégoire's defense: "I and my colleagues offer our heads to the scaffold if ever a single emissary, a single letter was sent to the slaves of Saint-Domingue."

No, no one could explain this phenomenon: Negro slaves demanding their liberty.

No, no one wanted the honor of having actually incited the slaves to stop the crime of slavery.

The Club Massaic, formed of the great absentee landowners of Saint-Domingue, some of whom had never even seen the land or the Negroes who for fifty or a hundred years had provided their families with prompt annual tributes, went into mourning for their incomes that had perished.

Sadly they donned deep black velvet and dull black silk. For they had been stricken deep in their most sensitive flesh: their pocketbooks. No, they would allow themselves nothing but a bit of black lace and the faint glinting of niello buttons and buckles to relieve the dense blackness of their sorrow.

And, thus attired, they moved in a delegation to lay their griefs before the king and queen of France. The Tuileries were still well guarded, though the tri-colored ribbon which had surrounded garden and palace to show the royal family that the nation would not brook another attempt to escape, had recently been cut.

Admitted before His Majesty, Monsieur de Cormier presented an engraved petition. Then the Marquis de Galifet, leader of the planters' party, took the word.

"Sire," he moaned lugubriously, "for three years revolutionaries have been sending delegates to our plantations in a vain attempt to stir up our faithful Negroes, whose good common sense, however, hitherto held out against the fancied promises and foolish notions of universal equality with which these self-styled philosophers tempted them.

"Now at last we hear that they have succeeded in perverting these simple folk and have caused them to fall back into that savagery from which we had rescued them with so much difficulty.

"Sire," Galifet declared, "our cause is no selfish one. Our cause is that of six million Frenchmen who derive the bread of their livelihood from the colonial shipping and commerce and manufacture.

"Sire, our plea is for all our American colonies, whose downfall is inseparable from ours.

"Sire," Galifet's voice rose dramatically, "our cause is that of the monarchy itself, to whose brilliance we contributed by our colonial wealth, to whose power we contributed by our marine commerce."

The fat monarch blinked and moved his arms in a gesture of resignation. He realized their plight but he was powerless to remedy it. Were not his hands tied? What could he do?

The black-clad delegation bowed itself out sadly, and then moved down the corridor and into the presence of the queen.

"Madame," said Galifet, "we have come to you in the depths of our misery, hoping to find in you consolation and an elevating example of courage. We colonists of France, who cleared the virgin forests of America and made the tropic ground yield wealth to France, appeal for Your Majesty's protection."

At that moment the little dauphin came running up to his mother and put his arms around her skirts.

"Ah, Madame," said Galifet, touched by this scene of domesticity, "we know you, too, are troubled. But your enemies are ours.

"Ah, Madame, conceive these simple blacks, as peaceful as were formerly our own Frenchmen, suddenly taking to pillaging and burning.

"Conceive of this once happy folk, for in all the world there were no people so happy as our slaves, so that ourselves used oft to envy them, conceive of them now with an impaled white baby as their standard, sawing people in half, tearing out their eyes with a red-hot corkscrew, forcing noble-born women to clean latrines and do other ignoble work until their hearts give way and merciful death relieves them of these tortures. . . ."

The queen leaned upon Madame Elizabeth: "Spare me further details, please," she breathed, and fluttered her handkerchief.

The delegation bowed its head and the Marquis de Galifet murmured excuses. There was silence.

Finally the queen steeled herself sufficiently to utter: "May my silence tell you more than any words." She could say no more, for her throat was choked with sobs and her eyes threatened to release the burden of their tears.

Silence again until the little dauphin piped up: "Mother, write down that last sentence for me."

"But, darling," said the queen, "what could you want with it?"

"I want to carry it here forever, over my heart."

Before this touching display of innate nobility, the delegation, with not a single dry eye among them, felt constrained to withdraw in silence.

My history books preserve for me the tears of the queen. They glitter on forever, cold, dry, imperishable, starring the pages of our heartless historians.

But what of the tears of Babouk and the other Negroes? Who records them? Who preserves them? No one! Not even the Negroes themselves. If the sun does not snatch them up, then it is the earth that sucks them dry.

They are lost forever. Only the tears of queens are considered worthy of being embalmed.

18

The dying ox bequeaths his misery to his hide.
                              —*Proverb of Negro slaves*

Our historians, who always shout reign of terror when a few rich
people are being killed and see nothing much worthy of comment
when poor are slaughtered by the thousands in the miseries of
peace, cry out unanimously: The pen cannot describe the cruelty of
these savages!

My pen is not so delicate; it can say, and it will never cease to say:
not over a thousand or so of whites were killed in this reign of terror,
while the legal and protected slave trade killed over a hundred
thousand Negroes a year. Buried its victims in Africa and America
and strewed them over the Atlantic Ocean.

One must be exact: the slaves revolted, and the reign of terror that
had lasted hundreds of years in Saint-Domingue stopped! Yes,
Candy heated his corkscrew to pull out the eyes of former white
masters, and Jeannot got ready his planks between which he tied his
victims to saw them in half, and that was peace compared to the
long reign of terror under the whites, from Columbus down.

But there were blacks as astute as the whites. Had they not gone to
a good school? There were leaders among them who ordered their
men to keep safe all stores of sugar left from previous harvests. And
they ordered their men to throw into heaps the loot of the white
houses: jeweled and enameled clocks thrown pell-mell with iron
pots, laces and blood-stained knives, surveying instruments and fine
porcelain, bearskins and silks and tuns of wine and fine furniture. . . .

And the smell of loot attracted the Yankee business man as the
smell of decay attracts flies. They brought their vessels into hidden
harbors and sent their agents to deal with the Negro chiefs. . . .

"We have good cod from Massachusetts and fine Maryland tobacco."

And the Spanish were even wiser. They brought fine uniforms

with braids of gold and great plumed hats together with parchments that appeared legal, what with great seals of scarlet wax and bright blue ribbands, and these they exchanged for gangs of slaves.

Why not? There were ateliers which had defended their masters and fought against the rebels. Very well then, if they insist upon having masters, then masters they shall have! And they were chained and sold into new servitude.

Jean Biassou and Jean François went about magnificent in their gold-bedizened uniforms. Their tents were filled with treasures. One styled himself vice-regent of conquered territories and grand Admiral of France; the other called himself Field Marshal of his most Catholic Majesty of Spain. And these men bickered with the whites, promising to force all their followers back into slavery provided the leaders were suitably compensated.

Babouk had nothing to do with these. Bearing ahead his grim standard of Leontine's baby, he carried the war up to the very suburbs of Le Cap, where hurried defenses had been thrown up by the whites.

Behind these defenses the whites waited, contenting themselves with repulsing the attacks of the slaves. But this very lack of enterprise on the part of the whites was most disturbing. What were they plotting back there in silence?

The Negroes could not be expected to know that the whites had been frightened deep down into the very marrow of their bones. Through centuries they had maintained their feeling of superiority over the Negro race only by constant proof of it through whipping and torture. The fellows did look so damnably like human beings that one must keep perpetually insisting on those minute differences of black skin and heavy lips and wide nostrils and kinky hair, as must the white masters, for that matter, be continuously insisting on the bad grammar and unwashed hands of their peasants and workers. In fact, one must call upon the Church, upon God, upon nature, upon science for constant reassurance, and even then only by stepping on the Negro a dozen times a day can one be really positive.

For several days now the blacks had awaited some decisive action on the part of the whites. The latter's constant retreat up to the defenses of Le Cap should have encouraged the Negroes in the belief in their own power. But there was something ominous about the attitude of the whites, as if they were only drawing breath for a mightier revenge.

In the camp of Babouk all were affected by this spirit of fatalism, and spoke in quavering voices of their miseries. Babouk himself was prey to this feeling.

One night he dreamed of his mother. She appeared to him not as he had last seen her, some thirty years before, but as an old woman, her face slashed with deep wrinkles, her rusty hair turned into strange yellow locks of wool, her body sere and wasted.

She greeted him without surprise, looking up from her household work. And her voice contained only a mild reproach: "You've been away long, son."

Beside her stood an elderly woman who did not in the least resemble that vivacious Niati whom he had loved and who had answered his passion. Yet he knew that it was she.

When he woke up, Babouk appreciated the significance of his dream. For how many years now had he not given as much as a single thought to his mother or to Niati? It was plain, therefore, that his soul was already tearing itself loose from his body and that he must soon die. Was it not plain, too, that his mother and Niati were still alive since they had grown old in his dream? They would outlive him.

But Babouk was weary and willing to die.

And he communicated this thought to his sad companions. "I shall die," he said. "Perhaps we shall all die. The sons of Abel will die and the sons of Cain will live on."

When he saw the pleading glances in the eyes of his comrades, he could not refuse them the story which most of them had heard before:

"You must know that all men were first created black. In those early days there was but one family of men on earth and that was the family of Adam. And Adam and his family were black, and so were his sons Cain and Abel.

"But Adam did not mind that his children were black. Eve and Adam loved their children, for the mother crow, as we say, thinks her baby crows are white.

"Now, Abel was a man of good, and he worked in the fields and the fields returned him plenty for his labor. But Cain would not work, and when he was hungry he took from Abel, and, when Abel objected, he whipped his brother.

"Now it happened one day that Cain whipped Abel so hard that Abel died. And his blood flowed upon the ground and the ground began to cry out to the sky:

" 'I am the blood of Abel. I am the blood of Abel!'

"And Cain was frightened and ran away and hid.

"But God had heard the cry of Abel's blood and called out to Cain: 'What have you done to your brother Abel?'

"And Cain was so frightened at the voice of God that his black face went pale with fear.

" 'Am I my brother's keeper?' he cried, his face now white with terror.

"Then God said: 'Cain, you shall be white henceforth, as a sign that you are not your brother's keeper. And your hand shall be against every man and every man's hand shall be against you.'

"And thus it is to this day: the race of Cain is not the keeper of his black brothers. And as a sign of God's curse upon him, his race is white."

Babouk shook his head wearily.

The men and women about him had expected that Babouk would be put into a story-telling mood by the relation of this one short one, and they were disappointed when he ceased. Babouk had used to tell such long ones, and now, when the odor of death was all about, one wanted long stories to pass the time.

But Babouk was tired. Wry saliva kept gathering in his mouth and he had to keep spitting it out. All about him, for miles around, fields of sugar were burning and the whole vault of the sky was like a bowl of hot smoke.

There was suddenly a commotion in the camp. The outposts had come running in to apprise the revolters that the whites were busy. White officers, in command of troops of whites, mulattoes, and even Negroes, were dragging shining brass cannon to an elevated position in order to attack the Negro camp.

At once all the Negroes began to prepare themselves for war, sharpening their spears or knives, looking to their bows and arrows.

While the men of mature years saw to their armor, anxious mothers called together their broods. The young girls and striplings did not wish to accompany their mothers. They wanted to fight alone, or, better still, alongside the men. It was not that the mothers intended to be left behind. But they wanted their children about them in order to keep an eye on them. Even little babies clinging to their backs left them their hands free to strike a blow at the white enslavers. Not even the aged and crippled were going to be left out: they hobbled energetically along with the rest. After all, were they not fighting for the same object?

The first step before entering upon battle was to prepare everyone for the coming conflict. This was the task of the priests, the n'hougans, who straightaway set to work to fashion those ouangas that had the power to protect against death or, failing that, at least to assure all those who died of being transported back to Africa at once.

There was some confusion in all this preparation, for among the priests were several who were not of the African spirit faith. There were some who had been Mohammedan priests, and they chanted from the Koran, in Arabic; and there were others who had been slaves of the Catholic priests, and who could and did sing in Latin. But this very confusion was inciting to the masses, who endeavored to sing along with the leaders.

Jugglers and acrobats, too, gave exhibitions of their skill to take the minds of the people off the dangers and to rouse all to do their best. And dancers stepped forward and with shield and spear performed mimic battles, striking war-like attitudes and making facial grimaces intended to intimidate the enemy.

These improvisations, whether of song or speech or dance, soon had their desired effect, for there was not a silent throat left in the multitude, nor a quiet body. All danced and shouted and cavorted, and the boldest sought to attract attention upon themselves by vowing to die in this battle and urging all others to do likewise; and brandishing their weapons they hurled imprecations at the foe.

The whites paid little attention to these preparations. They were busy with their own maneuvers. They had dragged their cannon into position on a small height and were soon ready to begin their attack on the Negro camp.

The blacks had indeed seen cannon before, and even seen them fired, and they knew by hearsay of the dreadful ravages that this weapon can make. But they were roused now to a frenzy that made them ignore all consequences. They ran in massed array across the fields that separated them from the whites and charged straight upon the great tubes that sparkled like gold.

The weapons barked like thunderclouds, and indeed a cloud of smoke did come out of each piece. And the iron balls plowed through the crowd and ripped a path through flesh and bone. To right and to left the dead and the mangled sank to the ground.

For a moment after this first volley the blacks stopped. Their warlike cries were now mingled with the howls of the dying and the whines of the timid. Then the bravest of them, Babouk, leading them with his standard with its white baby held aloft, dashed full upon the cannon.

Babouk, grasping a cannon in his arms and blocking the muzzle with his chest, called upon all to follow him: "I'll keep the ball from flying out."

Imitating him came others, some clasping the muzzle end, others stemming the openings with their shields. One tall fellow pushed his arm down into the bore, and feeling there the ball and confident that he could in his muscular strength hold it back, he exclaimed: "I've got it! Come on, all!"

Until the laughing cannoneers touched off the charge with a loud report. When the smoke had dissipated, there lay the mangled bodies.

Now the screaming women fled with their shrieking children, seeking safety in the mangrove swamps or in the bush. The men held out for yet a while, sacrificing themselves needlessly.

After the combat the whites had no trouble distinguishing the body of the rebel leader Babouk, not only because of his tallness, but also because one arm that hung to his body by a shred of flesh still tightly clasped that horrible standard in his fist.

It was the custom in all wars against rebellious slaves to sever the heads from the bodies of the fallen Negroes in order to string them in festoons about the white man's camps.

"That will intimidate those savages," was the feeling of the white officers.

But for Babouk's head a special fate was reserved:

He was brought to the Place d'Armes in Le Cap. To the side of the blacks, of course. And there his head was exhibited upon a pike. And a placard was placed at the foot of it, and it read:

"Babouk, chief of the rebels!"

And history tells us that "death had brought into relief upon his frozen countenance all the hideous cruelty of his savage nature. His eyes were still open and sparkling and seemed to be encouraging his men on to the massacre."

19

Divide and rule.
> —*Policy of the imperialists*

Black and white
Unite and fight!
> —*Modern rallying cry for world social justice*

The vast crowds of citizens and refugees in Le Cap trembled as they looked out from their retreat and could no longer see a horizon that was the dividing line between sky and earth. Instead, their startled eyes viewed a rolling wall of dull red fog that seemed to be advancing on the city with frightful rapidity. And indeed it was advancing, but only slowly. Thick vortices of smoke spiraled up from this wall and poured into the clouds, clouds that were not wet with rain, but dry with soot. The appearance was that of vast storm clouds. And the delusion was carried out by reverberations that were like distant thunder.

And from these dry clouds came flashes of lightning, a lightning that was only a brief view of the fire revealed through sudden rifts in the clouds.

Most curious: it seemed as if these dry clouds brought a snow. A strange snow that the hot wind hurled across the tropic city like a northern blizzard. It was the white ashes of sugar-cane straw.

Nearer and nearer to the city came the wall of flames, and the snow grew pink, and the wind hotter, until at last, when plantations were being fired close to Le Cap, then the pink snow changed into a rain of fire that poured down upon the town and down upon the harbor, igniting roofs and sails and burning the clothes of people, and scorching their wigs and eyebrows, and filling the air with a pungent odor of scorching.

The streets were covered with a silvery velvet, and the quiet harbor rolled a thick black scum.

For three weeks the day was obscured by smoke and the night was

made bright by flames so that the difference between night and day
was smudged away and people did not know when to rise and when
to sleep, and fell to acting strangely. With soot-caked hands they
smeared the sweat on their faces and looked out haggard, as if gone
mad, upon a world that had surely gone mad.

Yes, mad!

The first thought in people's minds was that the mulattoes were
leading the Negroes into rebellion. Certainly in the south the mulattoes, incensed by the execution of Ogé and Chavannes, were up in
arms, but here in Le Cap they had been quiet. Now, though the
whites would not openly admit that mulattoes had ample justifica-
tion for revolt, yet they unwittingly employed that thought in their
reasoning.

And acting upon such reasoning the wealthy planters encouraged
the sailors and other poor whites of the town to set upon the
mulattoes and to kill them. By the score they were slaughtered in the
streets of Le Cap. Hundreds found refuge in the Church of the
Ursulines, where they cried raucously for pity, swearing that they
had nothing to do with the revolt of the blacks and begging to be
shut up in prison, offering their wives and children as hostages to
prove that their intentions were honorable, and finally agreeing to
enroll in the troops to fight the Negroes if they were released from
prison.

Inasmuch as the thought that the Negroes might have rebelled
without the spur of foreign agitators was inconceivable to these
colonials, their second thought was that French revolutionaries were
at the bottom of it. And in this there was some split among the
whites: some inclining to the view that royalists had done the deed
in order to give the revolution a stab in the back, others sustaining
the view that the most republican elements were the guilty ones.

"It is those brutes who are keeping the King in prison who are the
cause of this! They would stop at nothing to injure France!"

"Yes, it is the nigger-lovers of Paris who have done this for us with
their ridiculous idealization of the blacks. And these philosophers of
Paris with their talk of liberty, equality, and fraternity will have to
bear the blame before God, not only for our deaths, but for the
slaughter of these thousands of deluded Africans!"

And the whites guessed again and guessed the Spanish, and each time they guessed they guessed wrong. And even when they guessed themselves, they were wrong, for the table talk they had indulged in, in their attempt to be philosophers, too, and discourse upon the rights of man, that had not caused the revolt, the proof of it being that the ringleaders were for the most part African-born slaves, that is to say, precisely those least exposed to such table conversation or who, if exposed, could least understand anything of the rights of man as elucidated by the Paris philosophers. These Negroes knew only the difference between a life of forced labor dictated by the lash and a life of general idleness with spells of work dictated by personal necessities, and in that they knew all they had to know for them to rise up and slaughter their jailers.

But in the face of this calamity it was necessary to take some measures.

What should one do? Abandon the island as Saint-Vincent had had to be abandoned to the wild Caribs?

Why not a complete massacre of all Negroes? Both loyal and rebel.

"For our Negroes are infected!" the proponents of this idea cried. "Diseased with liberty! And even if forced to return to duty they will never make faithful slaves again.

"Let us, therefore, slaughter them all and restock ourselves afresh from Africa!"

This idea was upheld by certain rich planters and by those who had an interest in shipping, but the poorer planters could not agree to this extreme measure. "Impractical!" they cried. "Ruinous!"

There were wild acclamations in the Colonial Assembly at Le Cap when it was proposed to invite the English to take possession of the island, and, incidentally, extinguish the revolt.

"The English may do a lot of anti-slavery talking in London," the president of the Assembly, de Cadush, pointed out, as he took off his tri-colored cockade and adjusted a black one for England, which he had in readiness in his pocket, "but they never mix business with idealism."

Hurrah for the English, then! They may talk anti-slavery, but their ships do the biggest slave trade of the world. Hurrah for the English, then! They do not mix business and idealism.

Only one important stipulation was made in the island's offer to become part of England: "The slavery of the blacks brought from the coast of Africa and the slavery of their children and children's children shall be maintained forever."

Hurrah for England! All the members of the assembly had black, or else black-and-red, cockades in readiness. Some even had English round hats. New uniforms with England's colors were ordered for the troops.

One planter in his approval of this move to become part of the British colonies, exclaimed: "We are as good Frenchmen as there are in the world. And I know that we are attached to our mother-country by ties of blood, affection, and gratitude. But rather than see our fortunes, honorably acquired, become the prey of black brigands who are egged on by another set of brigands in Paris, we prefer a thousand times to go over to the English!"

And now, to stop this rebellion, no mercy! Torture the Negroes to make them betray their chiefs! Kill loyal and rebel alike on the slightest suspicion! Permit every parish to pass the death sentence! Proceed at once here in Le Cap to the building of five new gallows and two new wheels for racking, on the Negro side of the Place d'Armes.

And remember, judges, you are serving your country by being merciless!

"But what if the Negroes surrender of themselves? Can we permit them to go back to work and mingle again with those who remained faithful and thus be lost to the proper supervision of their masters?"

No! A great R must be branded on their cheeks, where no black can conceal it with clothing, and thereafter any man may know him for his misconduct.

R. A great letter R for rebels!

Halt!

A great letter R for rebellious slaves, but what letter for rebellious masters? Speak! What letter for these men who have just voted to abandon their mother-country and join France's eternal enemy, England?

Ah, but theirs is only a minor treachery compared with the

treachery of slaves. For above such petty treacheries against this or that mapped country rises the greater treachery against that unmapped land, the land of property. What are the puny and intermittent wars between this or that mapped land, between this or that France or England compared with the perpetual war between the unmapped universal countries of those who have not and those who have?

Did not the planters say: "We are as good Frenchmen as any in this world and attached to our mother-country by ties of blood, affection, and gratitude. But rather than see our fortunes, honorably acquired, become the prey of black brigands who are egged on by another set of brigands in Paris, we prefer a thousand times to go over to the English"?

There you have the figures. A thousand times more precious is property, honorably acquired, than all ties of blood, affection, and gratitude. It is only the propertyless who die for their country. The propertied man dies for something a thousand times more precious: his property, honorably acquired.

Honorably acquired, he calls it. Yes, honorably. For did he not pay in cash and credit for his Negroes? Has he not the bill of sale?

Honorable and legal, then, is the fortune he ground out of his slaves!

The slaver, too, acquired his cargo honorably. Has he not the bill of sale?

And the factor on the West Coast of Africa, has he not his bill of sale? Of course he has!

Why, behold, when you trace it back, it is only the Negro in Africa who sold his brother into servitude who has no bill of sale.

There you have the culprit!

Strike the blackguard down! He has no bill of sale.

The rest of us are honorable. Behold, here is our bill of sale!

Here is our bill of sale! Flag of the unmapped land that covers the earth!

Revolt against that if you dare and you will be broken on the wheel!

Revolt against that and you will be branded with a large R on either cheek so that all the world may know you for the traitor that you are!

For the land of the bill of sale is the great mother-country of all. A

thousand times more holy is our country of the bill of sale! Mil-
lionaires! you true internationalists who regiment your workers into
countries, hoist aloft your flag: the bill of sale!

You wretches out in the burning plain before Le Cap, where is
your bill of sale? What! Have you taken your liberty and you have no
bill of sale?

Then beat the general alarm! Go through the streets of Le Cap
and call out all who can bear arms! Down with the rebels against
the bill of sale!

Dum didi dumdum. Dum didi dumdum.

And from the distant wall of smoke and fire came a strange echo:
Tom-tom. Tom-tom. Tom-tom.

Dum didi dumdum. Dum didi dumdum. And the civilized armed
themselves with civilized weapons, with gun and with saber, with
cannon and with grape-shot.

Tom-tom. Tom-tom. And the savage blacks armed themselves
with the savage weapons, with knives and assegais, with pike and
bow and arrow.

And the civilized moved upon the savage and the savage upon the
civilized.

Dum didi dumdum. Dum didi dumdum!

The Negroes on the burnt plantations listen and stop in fear. It is
the white man's drum. The terrible white man's drum.

Dum didi dumdum. Dum didi dumdum!

Hark! They are calling to arms in Cap Français!

Dum didi dumdum! Dum didi dumdum!

Help! The white man is after us!

The Negro shrieks in terror. He falls to the ground, clutches his
amulet, implores the aid of all his spirits and all his ancestors. Oh,
white man, please forgive us: we shall never rebel against you again.

Dum didi dumdum! Dum didi dumdum!

Oh God! stop the white man's drum of war!

Dum didi dumdum! Dum didi dumdum!

Oh, God! it is coming nearer!

Dum didi dumdum! Dum didi dumdum!

Oh God! stop it! Stop it!

But mercilessly the drum beats on.

For this is the white man's drum of war.

No romance this. No mystery. No magic.

This is not the black man's puerile tomtom that a naked man beats in fear against the silence of the forest night.

No. This is the white man's drum. Bold and brave! Backed by lash and chain! Backed by gun and cannon! This is the white man's drum that has girdled and conquered the globe.

Dum didi dumdum. Dum didi dumdum.

This is the white man's call to order of the globe!

Halt! Halt all and one!

Listen, India! Listen, China! Listen, Africa! Listen, all you whose skins are dark!

This is the white man's proclamation to the world:

Master of the world is the white man!

Obey him. Sweat for him!

Kneel before him! Bend to his lust!

Worship his god!

Dum didi dumdum. Dum didi dumdum.

This is the white man's drum!

No romance this. No mystery. No magic.

No idle tale to frighten children or while away the spare time of tired folk!

Who has not read a hundred stories, seen a dozen plays, of the dreadful tomtom of the savages. A thousand authors have blathered of the dreadful tomtom of the blacks, the terror of the jungle. How one's spine shivers in a cosy room to read of dark jungle sorcery, of the black man's cruel witchcraft.

Would you not suppose that before this powerful magic the warships of our nations would quail and the shells of our cannons would not dare to poke their noses out of the bore?

Would you not suppose that the lustful, raping blacks, under the protection of their tomtoms, would people Europe with mulattoes?

Would you not suppose that the blacks would fit out expeditions of sportsmen and scientists to hunt down Europe's game? And negro business men would raid Europe for slaves? And force Europeans to labor in gold and diamond mines to make necklaces for black queens and whores?

Yes, dreadful indeed is the powerful magic of the blacks. Dreadful indeed is the beating of the black man's tomtom.

But it is the white man's drum, backed by lash and chain, by gun and cannon, that has girdled the globe.

And that is why the Negro jumps with mortal fright when he hears it.

But beware, whites! Beware!

Some day the Negro's tomtom will truly be dreadful to hear. It will come out of the forest and beat down the streets of our cities.

TOM-TOM! TOM-TOM! TOM-TOM!

And it will hunt us out among the girders of our dying skyscrapers as once we hunted them through their forests.

TOM-TOM! TOM-TOM! TOM-TOM!

And white blood will flow, and it will flow for days. It will flow for years. And yet were it to flow for a thousand years, never would it erase the white path of Negro bones that lines the bottom of the ocean from Africa to America.

But the black man's time must come. Some day it will be his turn to march up and down the world and beat his tomtom and cry out:

Arise, you black cowards! Arise, you universal boot-blacks! Arise!

Beat out this new proclamation to the world.

TOM-TOM! TOM-TOM! TOM-TOM!

This is the world of men. Black and yellow and red and white.

Halt! Halt, you English who murder the multitudes of your own race in mine and factory to enrich the few!

Halt! Halt, you Germans who poison your own superior race in chemical factories and gas wars in order to stuff gold in your coffers!

Halt, you Americans who poison and murder each other in order to catch up with and outdistance your rivals!

Halt all! Halt, French and Polish and Italian.

This is the world of men and of women and of children.

This is THE world. The ONLY world. The WORLD of ALL.

You weary folk, go home and sleep in peace. Is not the bed of the world large enough for all? And are there not blankets enough to go around?

Go home then and rest. And kind dreams to you.

Oh, black man, when your turn comes, will you be so generous to us who do not deserve it?

AFTERWORD

History, Fiction, and the Slave Experience
David Barry Gaspar and Michel-Rolph Trouillot

How can we in the twentieth century begin to comprehend the full meaning of Afro-American slavery and of the African slave trade? The chain of events is so complex, its chronological and geographical span so extensive, its sociocultural impact so intricate that aspects of it seem bound to escape any single analysis.

Africans were first transported to work in the mines and tropical plantations of the Americas in the sixteenth century as substitutes for coerced "Indian" labor. Early on, a majority of the African slaves were brought to the Caribbean islands where the native populations, much smaller than those of the continental mass, had been almost completely decimated. From that early period through the late nineteenth century, African slave labor became the sinews of the various plantation colonies that were established by aggressive expansionary European states, including Spain, Portugal, England, France, and the Netherlands. At first Spain had claimed the entire Americas except Brazil as its reserved domain, but by the end of the seventeenth century it was forced to concede territories that the equally acquisitive British and French had effectively conquered earlier in the century. By this time too, the Dutch were forced to yield their commercial ties with colonies occupied by British and French subjects to the respective metropolitan crowns of the settlers.

By the beginning of the eighteenth century both Britain and France possessed Caribbean colonies that had been transformed from producers of several crops—the most important export being

183

tobacco—to nearly exclusive producers of sugar for expanding European markets. Britain's main Caribbean sugar colonies were Barbados, the Leeward Islands, and Jamaica; France's sugar colonies were Martinique, Guadeloupe, and Saint-Domingue (the western portion of the large island of Hispaniola). The eastern part of Hispaniola, and neighboring Cuba and Puerto Rico, remained Spanish possessions where both slavery and the plantation system had not yet gained the importance bestowed on them by the French and British colonists.

The main difference between the Spanish territories and those controlled by the French and British in the eighteenth century was sugarcane: sugar and slavery were the twin supports of British and French colonialism in the Caribbean. By the 1750s Saint-Domingue, where sugar had displaced previous exports since the first decade of the century, was the most important French sugar island. Large numbers of slaves were imported from Africa to work on the sugar plantations, degraded labor at the very bottom of the social ladder in a society ruled by whites who kept the system of racial slavery in place with the support of French metropolitan interests. In the words of Trinidadian historian Eric Williams, by 1789 Saint-Domingue had been for enslaved Africans and African-Americans "the worst hell on earth."[1]

That much we learn from history books. But how does one describe hell if one has not been there? Can we tabulate the human cost of that degradation? Can we trust historians to tell us what it felt like to be a slave?

Guy Endore did not think so. S. Guy Endore (1901–1970) was a Brooklynite who graduated from Columbia College in 1924, majoring in Romance languages. He went to Hollywood in the mid-1930s and wrote film scripts for many of the major studios. In the 1950s, he was blacklisted because of his close association with the Communist Party. He also wrote more than twenty novels, translations, and essays. He read French fluently, translating such authors as Pierre Loti and Théophile Gautier. Endore was fascinated by the life stories of individuals he perceived to be exceptional, ranging from Casanova and Voltaire to Joan of Arc and Alexandre Dumas. Although he dealt with some of these characters through realist essays, his most favorite form was the biographical novel.

Endore's use of the biographical novel stemmed from his sense of the limitations of the historical profession. For him, history was inherently prejudiced: it favors some classes and some races. It describes events in "heartless" tones and, contrary to the inquisitive mind, it does not hold up important business for trifling questions of values. It underlines the human experience only when the rich and powerful are concerned, "for it is not history until the rich man suffers" (p. 96). Thus history books preserve for us the tears shed by a European queen on the few whites who died at the beginning of the revolution that destroyed colonial Saint-Domingue (p. 167), but the suffering of millions of slaves are lost among complex tabulations of profit. "Who records them? Who preserves them? No one! Not even the Negroes themselves" (p. 167). The slave's voice is lost in the past (p. 97).

The critique of the many silences of the historical guild on Afro-American slavery that Endore launched repeatedly in *Babouk* was more than accurate when this novel was first published in 1934. *Babouk* is a novel about slavery, set in part in Saint-Domingue in the early days of the Haitian Revolution. As such, it contrasted with three overlapping silences within the guild and the rest of academia: an overarching silence over the Afro-Americans, which included slavery and slave resistance; a silence on past and present Caribbean realities; a silence on the slave revolution that transformed the French colony of Saint-Domingue into independent Haiti in 1804.

By the 1930s, autobiographies of former slaves, such as that of Frederick Douglass, which had reached a considerable audience in the United States in the middle of the nineteenth century, were considered *passé*. As early as 1896, even Douglass's posthumous books were commercial disappointments for his publishers. In the first quarter of this century, while anti-black repression grew in the South, U.S. scholars studying Afro-American slavery were scant. The most influential book on the subject was *American Negro Slavery*, first published in 1918. Its author, Ulrich Bonnell Phillips, was a racist Georgian who wrote with apologetic nostalgia of the Old South and the benefits of enslavement. Phillips died the very year that Endore published *Babouk,* but his earlier work was still the staple reading of history graduate students and remained so until the early 1950s.

If in 1934 few college students in the United States had learned

anything worthwhile about Afro-American slavery and slave resistance, even fewer had ever read anything at all about the Caribbean. Not that the Caribbean did not matter to U.S. interests. The
very year *Babouk* came out, U.S. Marines were withdrawing from
Haiti, ending nineteen years of military occupation but leaving an
ongoing legacy of North American inteference in Haitian political
life. At about the same time, U.S. forces also occupied the neighboring Dominican Republic. Puerto Rico, in turn, was in name and in
fact a U.S. colony, and the U.S. government had just helped depose a
populist leader in Cuba (in 1933). Still, North American scholars did
not study the Caribbean. Anthropologist Melville Herskovits had
published a few articles on "the Negro in the New World," but his
books on Haiti and Trinidad had not yet been written.

The Caribbean and slavery received little more notice elsewhere.
A few European specialists, mostly French and British, viewed the
history of both slavery and the islands as sub-branches—if not
footnotes—of the colonial history of their respective states. Seminal
works by scholars from the British colonies, such as Eric Williams'
Capitalism and Slavery, which would later familiarize some North
Americans with the Caribbean past, had not seen the light of day.
Thus *Babouk* also came out amidst a near total silence on slavery in
the Caribbean and a complete blackout on the impact of that institution on Afro-Americans south of the U.S. border.

Babouk's first publication must also be set against the background
of the silence of Western historians on the Haitian Revolution. In the
early 1930s, the deeds of Saint-Dominigue's slaves had no place in
the annals of Western history. To be sure, the revolution had attracted considerable attention when it occurred, and in the nineteenth century a few Western visitors had published sensationalist
works describing—and often denigrating—the new country. But the
later U.S. writers who took advantage of the 1914-1934 occupation
to produce their own versions of sensationalist fiction or travel accounts were only poor imitators whose books were quickly forgotten.
While sensationalists titles came and went, few historical works on
the rise of Haiti were written in English in the first quarter of the
twentieth century. The year 1914 saw the publication of two accounts of the revolution. One, T.G. Steward's *Haitian Revolution,
1791–1804*, which was quite sympathetic to the blacks and es-

pecially to Toussaint Louverture, quickly fell into oblivion.[2] T. Lothrop Stoddard's *The French Revolution in Santo Domingo*, whose title already reveals a Eurocentric perspective, fared slightly better.[3] But for Stoddard (who is sometimes revived by more recent writers), slave resistance is often an unfortunate accident and the main drama of the Haitian saga was "the tragedy of the annihilation of the white population."[4]

Thus by 1934, except for Haitian scholars—on whom the revolution continues to exert a deep fascination—not much was being written on Saint-Domingue by professional historians. As the epitome of slave resistance, the Haitian Revolution was of no interest to U.S. scholars like Phillips, fascinated by the virtues of the Old South, or to European colonial historians concerned with the past glories of empire. They barely accorded it a few pages in their most important works, emphasizing France's "loss," the destruction of the plantations, or the massacre of the whites in tones reminiscent of the laments of the early nineteenth century. To paraphrase Endore, only with the tears of whites did the revolution become history.

It took the first edition of *The Black Jacobins*, the seminal work by Trinidad-born C.L.R. James, published four years after *Babouk*, to alert some professional historians to the internal dynamics of the revolution. And even then, the impact was at first limited.[5] Yet the Haitian Revolution was important at the time of its occurrence if only because it transformed what was then the most profitable slave colony of Europe into the first independent country of the Americas with a predominantly black population and, for years to come, the only American state where freedom was not a white privilege.

The French colony of Saint-Domingue reached its highest point of importance between 1763 and 1791. After the Peace of Paris, the larger planters and their metropolitan backers took full advantage of the gradual and relative economic decline of the British sugar islands, while others with more modest means invested in coffee, for which demand was growing fast in Europe. That prosperity contributed much to the treasury of France, to the wealth of the plantocracy, and to the miseries of the slave population who lived and worked on the sugar, coffee, cotton, and indigo plantations, and in other rural or urban ventures. Estimates of that wealth vary, with accounts reaching sometimes as high as 800 sugar plantations, more than

2,000 enterprises producing coffee, and close to 1,000 others producing cotton or indigo. The colony produced an estimated 131
million pounds of sugar and 70,000 pounds of indigo in 1787. In
the late 1780s, it held world records for the production of both sugar
and coffee, though returns from the latter remained far behind those
of sugar.

Prosperity for the planters did not necessarily trickle down to the
slaves, who were merely driven harder. To replace the dead and
maintain high production levels, more and more enchained Africans
were poured into the colony, at rates sometimes exceeding 400,000
a year, further intensifying social tensions and resentment from
below. In 1791, in the midst of the turmoil created in both France
and the colonies by the first two years of the French Revolution, the
slaves launched an uprising that eventually led to the destruction of
both slavery and French metropolitan power.

The initial revolt started on August 1791 in the northern parishes
that provide the setting for most of Babouk's story. Some of the
leaders were captured almost immediately, but armed resistance
continued long enough for a mature revolutionary vanguard to
emerge in 1793 under the leadership of Toussaint Louverture. By the
end of the 1790s, Louverture was the commander-in-chief of Saint-
Domingue, although he ruled ostensibly in the name of France,
which then seemed to accept—albeit reluctantly—the end of slavery
in the colony as a *fait accompli*.

In 1802, however, Napoleonic France reacted militarily to Louverture's growing power. Napoleon sent some 86 warships and 22,000
soldiers to recapture Saint-Domingue and restore slavery. The former
slaves suffered a number of defeats and most of the chiefs surrendered. Louverture himself was exiled to France where he soon died.
But armed resistance had not died, and a few months after Louverture's capture a new revolutionary vanguard emerged under the
leadership of one of his early followers, Jean-Jacques Dessalines.

Unlike Toussaint Louverture, from whose mistakes he had
learned, Dessalines thought that freedom was incompatible with a
white presence in Saint-Domingue. Complete political independence was an indispensable guarantee of freedom. In that sense,
the new vanguard had merged in a unique way the goals of the
French and the U.S. revolutions: theirs was a fight for freedom from

masters at home and abroad, for the rights of all men. Like the U.S. revolution, it was anticolonial. Like the French revolution, it aimed at terminating inherited social differences. But in the context of the times, it went far beyond both, for it was led by blacks, and former slaves at that. More important, perhaps, it was successful: with the support of mulatto generals converted to the cause of the former slaves, Dessalines led his army to a series of victories, and in January 1804 he proclaimed the country independent under its old Indian name of Haiti.

We cannot go into all the reasons why this spectacular chain of events remained barely a footnote for the historical guild at the time of *Babouk*'s first edition, and why it continues to be treated as a mere episode of the French Revolution by scholars who by now should know better. Suffice it to say that some things have changed since 1934 and others have not. Colonial Saint-Domingue and early Haiti remain understudied, but there are now well-respected specialists of both. More importantly, scholars like Eugene Genovese and Robin Blackburn, albeit a minority, now underscore the centrality of the Haitian Revolution in the long downfall of African slavery in the Americas. Today, slave resistance is not only acknowledged; it has become a legitimate object of study, indeed the focus of intricate—and sometimes arcane—debates among academics. All in all, scholarly books and articles, drawing upon documentary sources, continue to mutliply encouragingly. What slaves thought, did, and felt is now taken into account to the extent that the record allows.

And the record itself keeps expanding. Scholars have been able to make good use of eye-witness accounts of slavery and the slave trade left by whites and also by Africans (who were slaves themselves) in order to explore several dimensions of the African experience of enslavement in the Americas. Among the best-known works in English is the autobiography of Olaudah Equiano, an Ibo from the interior of present-day Eastern Nigeria. Published in London in 1789, this now famous book describes Equiano's experiences from freedom to slavery and back to freedom again: it allows scholars to approach a deeper appreciation of the human experiences of an African who became a victim of European forces of commercial and political conquest of other parts of the world.

In spite of such advances, however, the issues investigated, and the approaches adopted by professional historians, especially in regard to the slave trade or the issue of slave resistance, are often couched within narrow ideological boundaries. Further, even if historical methodology is cleansed of its ideological biases, it remains worth asking whether or not a discourse with scientific pretensions can encapsulate the human experience of the slave or, more precisely, of one or many *individual* slaves. Readers of Equiano's autobiography will have noticed that Equiano's experiences were not those of the typical plantation fieldhand. Such atypicality does not diminish the historical significance of the work because it forces readers to confront the realities of the more typical situation while appreciating the fact that the individual experiences of the enslaved were many and varied in relation to a wide range of contexts, situational and personal. But how much can one extrapolate from the experiences of say, Equiano or, for that matter, a "typical" house slave from South Carolina, to those of a fieldhand in Jamaica or Saint-Domingue?

From Melville Herskovits and Franklin Frazier to contemporary scholars such as Lawrence Levine, Sidney W. Mintz, Richard Price, or Sterling Stuckey, researchers have pondered on the long-term impact of slavery on the Afro-American. But since previous history preserved mainly the tears of the queens, since very few slaves inscribed their voice in script, since the few who did tended to be atypical, how much of the earlier experience can scholarly discourse reconstruct? Isn't the voice of the slave lost forever for that form of writing? Isn't the suffering or the revolt subsumed under the weight of the historical evidence? Suffering and revolt are, after all, experiences of the human subject. They require someone who feels the pain or the anger. Can this kind of experience be more amenable to another kind of writing, namely what we sometimes refer to as "literature"?

Guy Endore thought so. For him, history is not only limited by the sociopolitical preferences of the historians, their choice of queens over commoners, of rich over destitute, of whites over blacks. It is also limited by the supposed relationship between history and reality. Long before it became fashionable for some historians to say so, Endore questioned the immediate relationship between historical documents and past reality in a postscript to *The Sword of God*:

Jeanne d'Arc, the historical novel about Joan of Arc that he published in 1931, before *Babouk*.[6] In the afterword to *The King of Paris*, a novel based on the life of Alexandre Dumas and published in 1956, Endore wrote: "What shall we call this book anyhow? Novel? Biography?" He answers that the book is "exceedingly true" because "it is a work of fiction not only solidly based on research, but going beyond research."[7]

For Endore, the purpose of the historical novel was to go where the recorded story stops and to fill in the vacuum. This always requires a careful reading of the sources, but at times it also requires deliberate invention, the making of events we know did *not* happen but would have happened in the manner described if indeed they *had* happened. Anticipating arguments made by more recent writers of biographical fiction, Endore sees these "lies" as more revealing than the heartless facts, whenever the subject matter, the particular individual who is at the center of his narrative, is too big for history. He writes of his book on Dumas: "You see, the more one studies the Dumas material, the more one is forced to the conclusion that research alone will never do justice to the man."[8]

Babouk was also too big for history, an individual to whom research alone could not do justice, especially since, in this case, the historical record was—and indeed remains—much more scant than the rich sources from which Endore drew to cast his Jeanne d'Arc or his Dumas. Thus here Endore plays more freely with the historical material, even though he makes substantial use of the sources then available.

Endore derived the climax of Babouk's life—his participation in the revolt and his death—from the story of a Saint-Domingue slave known as Boukman, Boukmann, or Boukman Dutty. Babouk is thus half-Boukman and half-invented, as his name already suggests. Historians and contemporaries do not fully agree on the details of Boukman's life, but all give him a crucial role in the insurrection of the slaves of northern Saint-Domingue in August 1791.[9] He emerges in the leading Haitian textbook as the most famous rebel leader before the rise of Toussaint Louverture.[10]

In fact, we know little of the prerevolutionary life of Boukman, who is said to have come to Saint-Domingue as a slave from Jamaica.[11] A privileged slave, he was either a coachman or a *commandeur* on the Turpin plantation, in northern Saint-Domingue. He was also perhaps an early dissident, as were many other slaves transferred to Saint-Domingue by British planters.[12] Some writers make him both physically and mentally exceptional, an unusually tall man who exerted considerable influence over other slaves. More importantly, Boukman was also a priest of the native Afro-Haitian religion, better known now—and often denigrated—under the label "voodoo." Indeed, many historians name Boukman as one of the two masters of ceremony at a major religious ritual that occurred on the night of August 14, 1791, and gave the signal for the first uprising of the revolution.

According to the most popular version of the story, Boukman assembled a number of slave conspirators, most of whom were drivers or domestic slaves on neighboring plantations, in Bois-Caïman, a forest on the edges of Lenormand de Mezy's plantation. There an old slave priestess performed a sacrifice on a black pig and the conspirators drank the blood swearing to execute Boukman's order to kill the whites. A few days later, during the night of August 22, some of the most important plantations of Saint-Domingue were in flames, including the Turpin plantation where Boukman worked.[13] Within four days, one-third of the northern province was in ashes.

Even though the revolt he started eventually led to the defeat of the French and the rise of an independent Haiti, Boukman himself was captured in a few days, as the French quickly moved to crush various pockets of armed resistance. Boukman was decapitated and the French exposed his bloody head, stuck on a pike, in the Place d'Armes in the town of Cap, with the inscription: "Head of Boukman, chief of the rebels," so that other slaves who thought the man invincible recognized, at last, the greater power of the whites.

Stories of Boukman, of the Bois-Caïman ceremony, and of the first few days of the revolution vary considerably, different in almost each historical account.[14] One can understand Endore's frustration at the record, especially in 1934, and his decision to fictionalize this hero more than such characters as Joan of Arc or Dumas, about whom he had a greater pool of historical details. Endore turned Boukman into Babouk, a Mandingo who is captured as a child in West Africa in mid-century and sold to French slave traders who transport him, along with a large human cargo of other captives, to Saint-Domingue. The narrative thread is quite simple. The adolescent Babouk reaches adulthood on the Gallifet sugar plantation, increasingly dissatisfied with his condition but well-liked by the other slaves, who acknowledge him as great storyteller. Sometime after the first tremors of the French Revolution, Babouk organizes a slave revolt that fails.

Endore uses this story line to trace several important phases in the life of a slave. Three of the most important and thought-provoking in Babouk's development from African captive to rebel leader are his experience of the Atlantic crossing (or Middle Passage) to Saint-Domingue, his adjustment to the new environment of the French colony and of the sugar plantation, and his rapid maturation into a rebel through his daily exposure to the oppressiveness and brutality of slavery.

Endore first explores different dimensions of the traffic in Africans that fed the plantations of the Americas to illustrate that the slave trade and Caribbean slavery were mutually reinforcing. In so doing, he amplifies moments of the slave experience not always appreciated by historians. In evaluating slave life and the slave's responses to slavery in the various slave societies of the Americas, scholars have tended to focus on the plantation setting and have not given sufficient attention to the earlier traumatic phases of enslavement, including captivity in Africa, sale to the European slave trader, and transportation to the plantation colony across the Atlantic. Even before the enslaved Africans arrived in the Americas they had been through a great deal, both physically and psychologically, as the first two chapters of *Babouk* illustrate. While embarked on a forced Atlantic crossing that was a physical trial in itself, the captive Africans experienced many more deeply traumatic journeys of the spirit as they struggled to make sense of their predicament.

Endore also spends some time on the acclimatization period encountered by the newly arrived slave. For those who survived the crossing, the process of adjustment to the new environment of slavery in the colonies was conditioned both by the new situations they encountered and by the trials already endured. Suffering from diseases and physical complaints contracted after embarkation in Africa, a large number of slaves died within a year of arriving in the colonies, while many more never fully recovered, even though slaveowners in various parts of the Americas allowed recently arrived Africans a seasoning period of light work to become used to their new way of life.

The central chapters of the novel paint a multidimensional portrait of slavery in Saint-Domingue. Endore also places the fate of the slaves within the wider context of the Atlantic world(s) of production, profit, power, trade, and warfare, forcing the reader to reflect often upon the current situation of blacks in different parts of the world. The author's frequent digressions on these larger issues notwithstanding, a recurring theme is the development and operation of slavery on a daily basis, with a strong emphasis on the slaves' varied responses to their condition of subordination and social death. For Endore, resistance, which can also include armed rebellion, is one of these many responses.

That Endore explores these responses through the case of one half-fictionalized individual does not necessarily imply that he dismisses history. Reading the novel carefully, one realizes that Endore made extensive use of his knowledge of the French language. There are many signs of his familiarity with both the history of colonial Saint-Domingue and that of independent Haiti. One suspects Endore made copious use of the works of early Haitian historians and even, perhaps, of the first volume of Sannon's *Vie de Toussaint Louverture* to plot Babouk's last few days.[15] There are also hints that he read the monumental work of Moreau de Saint-Méry, that of Malouet, and a number of less known and then out-of-print books that were nevertheless accessible in research libraries in the New York area. For instance, Endore cites a passage from *Soirées bermudiennes*, published in Bordeaux in 1802, by a former Saint-Domingue planter. Most of the plantation names, as well as the names of the French masters, are drawn from the historical record. The Gallifet plantation was located about eight miles from the town of Cap, and the saying "happy as a Gallifet negro" was indeed widespread in northern Saint-Domingue. Gallifet's attorney, Odelucq, a member of the local assembly, was indeed killed in the first few days of the revolt, sawn between two planks by the former slaves.[16] Peculiar incidents such as the launching of the balloons did indeed occur.

In short, this is a novel filled with history, both in the larger picture it presents and in some of its details. But with his Joan of Arc and his Dumas, Endore also invents. He invents, most often, on grounds of verisimilitude, according to what the probable truth was at the time of writing. Still, in crude terms there is as much fact as fiction here, even though the facts are often reordered or modified to fit the narrative of Babouk's life. Endore makes a particularly subtle use of famous court cases, dropping them in as the story goes along to flesh out the larger social context of his narrative.

There are some weaknesses in his use of the background record: the complex role of the free people of color, for instance, is barely explored. Endore's sketch of the work regimen is crude, while his views on sexuality in the slave society are sensationalist. But there are also nuances and details in the story that students of Carribean slavery will recognize and appreciate, especially given the time at which the novel was written: the importance of ties binding Africans who came on the same boat, the *batiments;* the cupidity of the European men of religion, the almoners and priests willing to make money by selling Christian magic to the Africans; the maneuvers that planters and merchants devised to bypass the rarity of cash; the difficulties of an old slave trying to remember an African song from her youth; the conflicts between African-born and Creole slaves and the sometimes successful imposition of a European-dominated cultural hierarchy; the planters' daily need to rationalize their cruelty vis-à-vis the blacks who "looked so damnably like human beings" (p. 169).

However competent he is at handling historical material, Endore's ultimate target, however, is not just history as "past" but history as a source of reflection—thus the high number of "anachronistic slips" for which he ironically begs forgiveness (e.g., p. 53). Indeed, Endore seems to have been very much interested in linking the black past to the present of his time, to lynchings in the U.S. South, to the exploitation of the black working class, to worldwide discrimination, to the West's cultural hegemony. Perhaps if we understand Babouk's life, we might come to a better realization about how far blacks today have not come since the days of plantation slavery.

Babouk is a meditation upon the lingering plight of the black people in a world that continues to be hostile to them, but also, by extension, a reflection on domination and exploitation in general.

For instance, Endore uses Babouk's escape and his meeting with Hatuey to remind us that native Americans were the first victims of trans-Atlantic colonization. To make these and similar points Endore punctuates the narrative with personal comments, and repeatedly uses irony to ask what he calls "trifling questions" (pp. 0, 00). He is often quite blunt and *Babouk* sometimes reads like a political pamphlet. At other times, the mode is less personal, but the message no less direct. Correlating the economic success of a plantation with the unusually high death rate, Endore asks whether or not high death rates made sugar sweeter (p. 00). We now know that in Cuba the planters used to say, "Sugar is made with blood."

Endore thus sometimes anticipates professional historians quite nicely, or with his "trifling questions" fills in voids in the record and issues of values. But he is at his best when he pushes the irony to its limits, withdrawing his authorial voice to force the readers to discover for themselves the obscenity of slavery. After describing the agony of a slave being burned alive in Saint-Domingue, Endore adds: "The enticing smell of roasted meat that spread over the Place d'Armes was ruined by the sharp odor of singed hair and nails" (p. 00).

Since Endore wrote *Babouk*, the Haitian Revolution has occasionally provided the background of other works of fiction. The best is Alejo Carpentier's masterful *Kingdom of This World*, first published in Spanish in 1949 and by now one of the most popular novels in any language set in Saint-Domingue/Haiti. Slave novels enjoyed a new boom in the 1960s and 1970s, but the most facile tokens of this subvariety are now luckily out of mode. The larger genre—the historical novel—has had its ups and downs in the last twenty years but enjoys a steady core of loyal readers. Today the biographical novel has become fashionable once more, enticing such writers as Gore Vidal and Gabriel García Márquez.

One would be hard pressed to find a recent title that did for a real life slave what Vidal accomplished with Lincoln or what Márquez did with Bolívar. Yet there remain a number of commendable works that have drawn upon a combination of historical evidence and fictional heroes to probe into areas of the black experience that the canons of historical scholarship do not allow historians to attempt in quite the same way. Using the work of historians, several novelists have explored territories that are now clearly charted in documentary sources, and which are all the more challenging for that. Such deeply probing reflective works offer historians new ways of seeing that can sharpen their evaluation and understanding of the complex past, and force them to more carefully reconsider the evidence upon which the practice of their craft requires them to rely.

In the creative process of rethinking the record with a sharpened sense of human possibilities, historians must also face the troubling and challenging question of what constitutes evidence and, ultimately, how history *creates* its object. In that sense, writers of fiction, less constrained vis-à-vis the official record, can keep historians on their toes and open them to new worlds. But as Endore's work suggests, in spite of his own repeated attacks against historians the historical novel is not possible without the record that historians help establish. Writers of both genres are engaged in irreconcilable and yet complementary endeavors.

NOTES

1. Eric Williams, *From Columbus to Castro: The History of the Caribbean, 1492–1969* (New York: Harper & Row, 1970), p. 254.
2. T. G. Steward, *The Haitian Revolution, 1791–1804* (New York: T. Crowell, 1914).
3. T. Lothrop Stoddard, *The French Revolution in San Domingo* (1914; Westport: Negro University Press, 1970).
4. Ibid., p. viii.
5. Neither *Capitalism and Slavery* nor *The Black Jacobins* made much impact on U.S. scholarship when first published. They reached a substantial audience only in the 1960s, on the heels of the civil rights movement.
6. S. Guy Endore, *The Sword of God: Jeanne d'Arc* (Garden City: New York, 1931), pp. 371ff.
7. S. Guy Endore, *King of Paris* (New York: Simon and Schuster, 1956), p. 496.
8. Ibid., p. 497.
9. Francois Joseph Pamphile Lacroix, *Mémoires pour servir à l'histoire de la révolution de Saint-Dominque*, 2 vols. (Paris: Pillet Ainé, 1819), p. 90; Thomas Madiou, *Histoire d'Haïti*, vol. 1, 1492–1799 (1847; Port-au-Prince: Editions Henri Deschamps, 1989), pp. 93–97; A. Beaubrun Ardouin, *Etudes sur l'histoire d'Haïti* (1853–60; Port-au-Prince: François Dalencourt, 1958), I, pp. 50–54; Roger Dorsinville, *Toussaint Louverture ou la vocation de la liberté* (1965; Montreal: Editions du CIDIHCA, 1987), pp. 59–60; Horace Pauleus Sannon, *Histoire de Toussaint Louverture*, 3 vols. (Port-au-Prince: Imprimerie A. Héraux, 1920–33), I, p. 89.
10. J. C. Dorsainville, *Histoire d'Haïti* (1942; Port-au-Prince, 1976), p. 63. For passing—and sometimes contradictory—remarks on Boukman, see also C.L.R. James, *The Black Jacobins: Toussaint Louverture and the San Domingo Revolution*, 2 vols. (1938; New York: Viking, 1962), pp. 86–87, 96; Thomas Ott, *The Haitian Revolution: 1789–1804* (Knoxville: University of Tennessee Press, 1973), pp. 47, 49. Michel-Rolph Trouillot is currently pursuing research on the life of Boukman.
11. Thomas Ott makes him "a fugitive from Jamaica" without apparent reason. See Ott, *The Haitian Revolution*, p. 47.

12. David Geggus, *Slavery, War and Revolution: The British Occupation of Saint-Domingue, 1793–1798* (Oxford: Clarendon Press, 1982), pp. 40–41.

13. C.L.R. James places both the ritual and the uprising on the night of August 22, contrary to many other writers, and claims that the Gallifet plantation was burned that very night. But James, who quotes Boukman's prayer at the ritual, seems also to embellish on the story as derived from different sources. See James, *Black Jacobins,* pp. 86–88.

14. There are, for instance, major differences in various historians' accounts of Boukman's connections with two other rebel chiefs, Jean-François and Jeannot, both of whom survived him.

15. Sannon, *Histoire de Toussaint Louverture.*

16. Madiou, *Histoire,* p. 94.